BURIED at Bears Ears

PAT PARTRIDGE

Buried at Bears Ears

Copyright ©2025 *Pat Partridge*

All Rights Reserved

DISCLAIMER

The following is a work of fiction. While specific locations mentioned and the Bears Ears National Monument exist, the people, events, and story depicted are fictitious. Any resemblance to actual individuals, if any, is entirely coincidental.

San Juan County Register (Utah): April 17, 2015

Utah's Five Native American Tribes Rally to Protect Bears Ears

At an inter-tribal meeting held in Bluff yesterday, five Native American tribes—Navajo, Hopi, Ute Mountain Utes, Ute Indian, and Zuni—officially formed the Coalition to Protect Bears Ears for the purpose of creating a 1.4-million-acre national monument in southeastern Utah. It is the first time a coalition of sovereign tribes have petitioned the federal government to protect their historical and cultural resources through an official monument designation.

The announcement was immediately met with criticism from the San Juan County Commission and Utah congressional leaders. "For two years, we've tried to work with the tribes to develop a comprehensive plan that recognizes multiple resource use as the goal," the County Commission replied when asked for a statement. "The land has tremendous value for grazing and mineral extraction, not just conservation. A national monument could destroy the livelihoods of families who have loved this land for generations."

Navajo Nation president Jacob Benally differed. "We knew we needed to take a bold approach," he said. "For hundreds of years, Native voices have been ignored when making land-use decisions. Instead, our historic lands have been looted and desecrated. That is no longer acceptable."

Given historical abuses and broken treaties, the tribes have not typically trusted the federal government on land-use issues. The coalition among the tribes is also a first. Disputes among the tribes have a long history, and one anonymous source indicated that "holding the coalition together will be its own challenge." Some Natives openly opposed the monument designation.

San Juan County Register (Utah): May 14, 2015

County Director of Land Use Dies Under Suspicious Circumstances

The body of Connor Smith, San Juan County Director of Land Use, reported missing three days ago, has been found by hikers at the base of an escarpment in Mule Canyon. The San Juan County Sheriff's Department is investigating. Foul play has not been ruled out.

"We believe he may have tried to climb up, slipped and fell," Sheriff Martin Cooper told the Register. "There were bruises consistent with a fall. We will autopsy the body to determine a more precise cause of death."

Although Smith was an experienced hiker and climber, his wife, Nancy, told police her husband had not indicated he planned to hike that day. "He loved the outdoors and hiked often, but he was a safety freak and always let me know where he was going."

In his role as Director of Land Use, Smith was working on a proposed master plan for county lands to identify and recommend specific parcels for recreation, preservation, conservation, grazing, and mineral rights. "We won't let the work linger," County Commissioner Sam Begay said. "We've already assigned someone to continue his important work. It will be our tribute to his memory."

Chapter 1

Darkness crept in from the east. To the west, listless clouds hovered in the unbounded desert sky that glowed in deepening shades of orange and magenta. A lone coyote howled close-by, and Joe Cutler, Professor of Archaeology at the University of Chicago, put down his heavy duffel to listen.

The coyote howled again. Joe guessed the wily animal must be within a hundred yards.

That brings back memories. Difficult ones.

Only three years earlier, his wife, Helen, and daughter, Megan, had joined him on an excavation in the majestic Bears Ears area of southeastern Utah. They'd made camp tucked away in the upper reaches of Butler Canyon and planned to explore ancient Ancestral Puebloan cliff dwellings the next day. Ben Hatathli, a Navajo elder and Joe's good friend, had joined them to serve as their guide.

They'd hunkered closely around the campfire to hold off the chill that settled into the canyon during that moonless summer night. The blaze from the dead juniper branches, snapping and popping, gave the illusion of safety, hiding the world beyond its illumination, a world of wide-awake creatures who, with sharper eyesight, roamed and killed for survival, some walking, some slithering.

A pack of coyotes started to sing. Their loud, high-pitched yips and yowls startled and unsettled his wife. But their otherworldly singing enthralled Megan, just twelve at the time.

Ben smiled. "Coyote created those stars you see up there," he said to Megan.

She looked up, but the glare from the campfire obscured most of the stars. "What do you mean?"

"Coyote is a god of the Navajo people, the Diné. When Coyote thought the Black God was taking too long placing each star in the sky, he took the sack of stars and threw it over his head, and that is how they landed where you see them now. The white man gave it a different name, the Milky Way."

"No way!" Megan said.

The Navajo elder smiled. "Yes, our way."

"That is so cool!"

"True, young Megan, but beware Coyote. He is a trickster."

"What kind of tricks?" she asked through a yawn.

Her mom, shivering, intervened. "Mr. Hatathli can finish the story tomorrow, sweetie. It's getting late."

Ben Hatathli nodded his assent. He put out the fire, and the Milky Way emerged clearer, a school of iridescent fish in the deep, dark ocean of sky. The following day brought new adventures, and the story of Coyote's mischief went untold.

That was three years ago, a different life.

Now fifteen, Megan was no longer the cheerful twelve-year-old enthusiast who begged to join his summer digs. Her interests had broadened—degenerated, Joe thought—to include raggedy teen clothing that buried her femininity and screeching music he was spared hearing because earbuds had taken up permanent residence in her auditory canals. Then there were boys. Fortunately, the one boy she took an interest in had a few redeeming qualities; after all Megan had been through, he'd made sure to meet the boy and his parents.

Joe had been surprised Megan succumbed to what seemed like stereotypical and trite concerns of adolescent girls. He hadn't been ready for the change. Still wasn't. She meant the world to him, more now than ever, but little in their relationship was easy anymore. She was smart and inquisitive and had excelled in school the past year, a good sign. Most days, she appeared to be moving past her troubles from two years earlier, but their bond had weakened, tattered around the edges like a favorite shirt past its prime. The gap between them was no longer a small breach they closed with smiles, hugs, and "I love yous."

Megan had a natural curiosity, a warm heart, and a beautiful smile—when she shared it. What she didn't have was a mother.

When Megan and his wife, Helen, joined him on the trip to Bears Ears three years earlier, the Unwelcome Guest, his wife's name for the cancer growing inside her body, had been an inescapable part of their lives for almost a year. Her chemo had sapped her otherwise indomitable energy but not her spirit, and she'd wanted to make one more trip as a family during one of Joe's digs. The two, mother and daughter, had helped with the excavation for a week. Sweaty but happy, they carefully removed loose dirt from around the stone masonry that had been the foundation of a small dwelling, as if each brick held the lost history of the family that lived there hundreds of years earlier.

The dwelling Megan and her mom excavated was part of a larger Ancestral Puebloan settlement. Joe and his team of graduate students were painstakingly studying it, trying to piece together answers to seemingly unanswerable questions—How did they eat, hunt, pray? What was family life like? Who were their enemies? Like forensic cops, the team worked with little more than shreds of baskets, dried and preserved food remains in ancient trash heaps, and, sometimes, bones. But answers remained elusive, mysteries that even the best archaeologists struggled to understand.

Megan herself found multiple potsherds and arrow points. Although discovered items were not to be disturbed unless needed for study, she snuck an obsidian arrow point into her pocket. Back home, she hid it in the stuffing of an old teddy bear that still held a place of prominence on her bed. She eventually told her dad about it. She said it was to ward off other unwelcome guests—the last one had taken her mom away. Joe told her to keep it.

On the trip three years earlier, Joe made sure they took time to wander the rugged backroads of Cedar Mesa, Comb Ridge, and the Valley of the Gods, and to hike to ancient ruins, some over a thousand years old, tucked under overhanging red sandstone cliffs...at least those reachable without exhausting his wife. It was a special trip—one he and Megan looked back on with a fondness that approached reverence. But neither talked about it. Reminiscing came with too much pain.

The coyote finished howling, and other coyotes didn't respond with their coded high-pitched calls to begin hunting as a pack. *He's a loner. I get it.*

The year after Helen died, loneliness settled into Joe's life like a fog made of cement, pressing down on his chest, clouding his thoughts with "what if" regrets and fantasies. Only over the last year had he begun to escape the omnipresent sadness of waking up each day alone.

Joe lifted his duffel and inserted the key to unlock the modest motel room in Bluff, Utah. It would be his home during the weekends over the next two months when he and his team took a break from living in tents at the excavation. The dig site would be hot, dirty, windy, and no-see-um flies would be a constant nuisance, yet he looked forward to the freedom from distractions the remote site offered. The desert always awakened his city-deadened senses. Its harshness instilled humility. Its vastness offered solace.

Maybe, it will be a balm for Megan and me.

As he entered the room, an odd, unpleasant smell greeted him, not readily identifiable. He sniffed deeper. Perhaps a mouse or lizard had died inside a wall, although the odor wasn't nauseating like something putrefying.

Must have been a while since someone was last here. I'll ask the motel to clean it better.

He tossed his well-worn duffel onto the floor next to the small pine bureau, slid open the window to let in fresh air, and turned up the rackety air conditioner tucked under the window. He wanted to cleanse the air in the room before he tried to sleep.

Tomorrow would be busy. Megan was flying down from Chicago with two female grad students from his class who would be part of the excavation team, along with one other special member of the dig team: Felicity. Megan had stormed out of the room when he told her that Felicity would be coming. For weeks she pleaded to stay in Hyde Park with a friend while he was away, in her words, "having fun in the sun." His firm "you're coming" ended the discussion, but not her quiet coldness toward him since.

Joe had lost count of the visits he'd made to Utah's red rock country. This one, he was sure, would be special. The discovery of an ancient site Joe had made the previous excavation season could change the direction of Indigenous archaeology. He tried not to be smug about its importance—his reputation established long ago—but this summer's dig could rewrite the textbooks, forever. He was looking forward to getting started.

Maybe I'm really moving on now.

Joe stripped off his travel clothes, hung them in the tiny closet, and headed to the small, sparse bathroom for a much-needed shower. Soon, he would spend his days covered in red dust, but now he wanted to rinse away the lingering, mothball-like odors of air travel. He emerged fifteen minutes later in boxers, shirtless. He was tired but relaxed. And feeling content.

The bed invited him. It was covered in a hand-stitched patchwork quilt made popular by the area's Mormon settlers over a hundred years earlier, and its simple, repetitive pattern looked comforting, reassuring. He pulled back the quilt and sheet quickly, ready to be embraced by their warmth.

Then he froze.

A fat prairie rattlesnake, coiled as if to strike, lay in the middle of the bed. But its threatening rattle was silent.

Its head had been chopped off.

A chill cascaded through Joe's body from his scalp to his toes, and he could feel the blood drain from his head. He was faint, speechless, thoughtless. He needed to get away. Wearing only his boxers, he rushed from the room into the night air. He took a deep breath, then another, then another. He felt his heart rate begin to slow, sensed his blood returning to his head. Involuntarily, a fierce scowl furrowed his face.

What's going on? Is this someone's idea of a joke? A really sick joke?

That's when he heard the coyote's piercing call again, still close-by. It howled and yipped and yapped for half a minute, its elusive, hypnotic cries seeming to reach toward the stars. Then it went silent. Which was when Joe realized something peculiar about its call.

That coyote voice might not be coming from a four-legged animal.

Chapter 2

Joe reached over and turned off his travel alarm moments before it was scheduled to buzz. It was 6:30 a.m. The cloudless early morning sky was already a light, bright turquoise blue, and the robins and magpies were making their presence known even through the window, now closed for safety. He lay back in bed, rubbed his face hard with one hand, then threw off the bed covers. He had not slept soundly, but he needed to start his day.

Too much at stake to lie here worrying about last night. Which didn't stop him from worrying.

He flipped on the light on the side table, then exited the bed slowly, alert for other unpleasant guests that might be waiting where he placed his feet. He scanned every inch of his room, watchful for any movement, as he got out of bed, as he checked the door to make sure it was still locked, as he walked cautiously into the bathroom. He checked for scorpions in his boots, something he did every morning when in the field but not something he expected to need in his room.

The previous night, Joe immediately switched rooms after his encounter with the dead rattler. The owner of the Red Rock Inn, Elijah Smith, who lived above the office, had been mortified about Joe's headless snake greeting.

"Joe, I don't know what to say. I don't know how someone even got in the room. It should have been locked."

"It *was* locked. At least it was when I got there."

"I'll move you to a different room immediately. How about the presidential suite?" He was trying to make a joke. Joe didn't crack a smile.

The owner frowned with worry. "You're going to stay, aren't you?"

"Yes. For now."

Joe knew his team was Elijah's VIP customer of the season—seven rooms rented over a long stretch, over eighty customer nights total, the difference between a summer just squeaking by and the down payment on a new Ford F350 pickup the motel owner had been eyeing. Plus, he knew Elijah from previous stays. He didn't consider Elijah a friend, exactly, but they shared common interests. Elijah, a fourth-generation local, had explored the nearby canyons his entire life and visited dozens of ancient sites. Years earlier, he had taken Joe down a side slot canyon off Dark Canyon and showed him a Puebloan II period dwelling that until then hadn't been recorded by anyone in the archaeological community. As far as Joe knew, Elijah had never succumbed to the temptation to pilfer artifacts for the black market.

"Please don't mention the snake to anyone, Joe," Elijah had pleaded. "Especially don't let Robert Hightower hear about it. He would love to smear the motel again."

Bad blood between Elijah and the publisher of the *San Juan Register* had simmered for years, going back to coverage of a gruesome murder at the motel five years earlier that had scared away guests. Elijah, furious, had sued Hightower and the paper for harm, but lost the case. The publisher defended his right to report the news—the murder of Henry Long Arrow, a Navajo leader, was big news—but the legal fees had dented each business's bank account noticeably.

Robert Hightower *was* a friend of Joe's. He was one of the few Anglo community leaders in Blanding who boldly valued the archaeological importance of the red rock country of southeastern Utah. At some risk to his paper's survival, years earlier, Robert had taken a stance for a balanced land use policy and argued that the Ancestral Puebloan sites needed permanent protection, even at the expense of traditional commercial uses. That was *not* a belief shared by most of the local Anglo population. Most descendants of Mormon pioneers who had settled the area generations earlier saw the land as more valuable for cattle grazing and what it yielded through extraction—oil, coal, and uranium—as well as purloined Native American artifacts, including those dug up from ancient graves.

Joe expected a busy day, starting with breakfast to meet with his local team before his student team arrived in the afternoon. He'd hired four local workers—all with experience on archaeological digs—two local Navajos, Robert Hightower's son, and one person he'd never met.

Joe pulled up to the Rainbow Bridge Café in the pickup he'd purchased the previous season for a few thousand dollars, a faded-white Ford F150 with 120,000 miles, seating for four, and enough dents to keep a body shop busy for a month. He stored it offseason in the back parking lot of the *San Juan Register*, courtesy of Robert Hightower. Payback for hiring his son, he figured, although neither man had bothered to acknowledge the exchange.

Ben Hatathli was waiting patiently outside the entrance. His age a mystery to Joe but likely in his early seventies, Ben's eyes were gentle and knowing, the creases at the corners of his eyes hinting at the fullness of his life. He wore blue jeans and a Navajo patterned shirt, and a wide turquoise and silver bracelet rested solidly on his right wrist. Ben had been part of every dig Joe had undertaken in Utah and northern Arizona for over fifteen years. He moved slower than others, less because of physical limitations than his decision to approach each moment with an attentiveness bordering on reverence. If the heat bothered him, he never let on. His quiet work without complaining was an inspiration to the grad students, making their grumblings about the working conditions seem trivial. His Navajo heritage and calmative presence added authenticity to the experience they sought. Plus, Megan idolized Ben. A recognition a dad doesn't naturally get.

Ben smiled as Joe approached. "Greetings, Kemosabe."

Joe nodded, and a slight grin spread across his face. "Greetings."

The "Kemosabe" nickname was an inside joke between the two men, one that would *not* be repeated among the other team members. "Kemosabe" was a long way from being a Navajo word. Made famous by the Lone Ranger's Native sidekick, Tonto, in the tv series of the early 50s, the word had been concocted by the original radio show's creators from the name of a youth camp, Kamp Kee-Mo-Sah-Bee—in Minnesota. While many Native Americans considered Tonto's deference to the Lone Ranger disreputable at best, Ben treated it lightheartedly. The story reflected cooperation and mutual loyalty between a white man and a Native, a far cry from the typical depiction of untrustworthy, dangerous Indians in John Wayne westerns of the same era. It was also a far cry from the many perfidies, ignored promises, and broken treaties that had created layers of distrust for over two hundred years.

Ben opened the door. "The others are inside."

In a large booth toward the back of the café, three younger men, silent as Joe and Ben entered, looked up from their cell phones. All three stood to greet Joe.

Russell Begay shook Joe's hand. "It's good to see you again, Joe."

"I'm glad you could join me again."

"My honor," Russell said. In his early 20s, muscular, trim, and composed, Russell hailed from one of the more prominent Navajo families in Utah and Arizona. He had limited excavation experience, having helped Joe for several weeks the previous year, but having the influential Begay family in his camp, both literally and figuratively, was also an immeasurable plus to Joe. Unlike most younger Navajos, Russell spoke and read Diné, the Native language that had been at risk of disappearing within a generation, but which was being resuscitated by some younger Navajos.

"How's your family?" Joe asked.

"Fine. Thank you for asking."

Joe knew "fine" was overstating it. Russell's parents had fallen on hard times in recent years, and Russell needed the money from the dig to reduce his college debts. He'd earned his bachelor's at Diné College on the Navajo reservation and had recently enrolled in a master's in anthropology program at the University of Utah.

"Hello, Professor Cutler," said a young Robby Hightower.

Joe smiled. "I told you last year, it's just Joe. Okay?"

Robby blushed and nodded. At just eighteen and a recent high school graduate, he was self-conscious about being the youngest on the team. But Joe was glad to have him. Robby had been with Joe the previous year when he made his important discovery. He was lean and strong, handled the heat and hard work without complaint, knew the backcountry intimately, and treated the artifacts they discovered with gentle hands. He also was good with a rifle, having hunted with his dad in the Henry Mountains since getting his first 22-caliber at age eight.

Doug Edwards was the last to greet Joe. They'd never met in person. His broad smile was disarming, and his handshake was firm and friendly. "So, you're the infamous professor Joe Cutler."

"I suppose so," Joe said.

Joe didn't know if his new hire was referring to his important archaeological discovery of the previous season, or his close encounter with the Chicago Police Department and a woman who wanted him dead. Probably the latter, Joe thought, but he wasn't going to ask.

Doug, in his late twenties, had been recommended by other archaeologists. They said Doug was an experienced excavator, could spot a potsherd or arrow point from twenty feet away, and was naturally outgoing. He made people laugh. He could also cook a decent meal in the field, could conjure up hard-to-find supplies, and drove a one-ton, four-wheel-drive Dodge Ram 3500 pickup they would need. There was one caveat the referrals mentioned—his tanned, muscled body, a chiseled Matt Damon chin, and a twinkle in his eyes were often a distraction for dislocated female grad students who missed the creature comforts enjoyed back home, including those from male creatures.

Over hearty breakfasts of eggs, bacon, and biscuits and gravy that would have pleased a diehard Southerner, the men discussed the logistics for the dig, including when they would stay in the field and when in Bluff. Joe reviewed a final to-do checklist and assigned responsibilities. Doug's larger pickup would be needed to tow the 200-gallon water buffalo tank, as well as the generator and fuel and a backup solar-powered generator. Russell was assigned to retrieve the digging gear stored in a rental storage unit in Blanding, the medical supplies, and the cooking gear and food.

The young waitress, a high schooler at her summer job, stopped by for the sixth time to refill coffee cups and, she hoped, to exchange smiles with young Robby Hightower, whom she knew from school. Robby, like Doug, attracted female attention effortlessly, with his easy smile and deep-set, soft brown eyes beneath a head of wavy brown hair. Unlike Doug, he did it unconsciously without realizing the impact he had. But the waitress got no coffee takers. The men were sufficiently buzzed and ready to work, in fact, itching to get going.

Joe proceeded to go into more detail about the discovery his team had made the previous year, what he hoped to find this season, and his plans for submitting an article about the discovery to *The Journal of American Archaeology* before the end of the year.

"Our work may rewrite the textbooks." A twinge of cockiness snuck into his voice despite his best efforts.

The men were silent and nodded politely. The world of a University of Chicago archaeologist was difficult for them to grasp.

Then Doug smiled. "One last question, boss. Who's bringing the pole?"

"What pole?" Joe said.

"The dance pole for when one of your hot, bored grad students wants to put on a show under a moonlit sky."

The others were speechless. A hushed moment passed.

"You bring it," Joe said. "If none of them volunteer, you get to do it."

The others laughed, including Doug. "Deal!" he said.

Joe was pleased with their enthusiasm and the beginnings of camaraderie, even if on the crude side, that would make everything easier. Camaraderie isn't always there, he thought. Even stupid jokes help. He felt lucky. He never relished the "boss" role.

They had covered the agenda and had begun to ramble on about mundane stuff, including wagering on how many 100-plus degree days they'd have during the dig, when Joe's cell phone rang. It was a local number but not one he recognized.

"This is Joe Cutler."

"Hello, Professor Cutler," a pleasant female voice said, a hint of a Navajo accent. "This is Marie in county commissioner Begay's office in Monticello. The commissioner was hoping you could come down to his office today. The sooner, the better."

Joe raised his eyebrows. It was an odd request. "Can I ask what it's about?"

"I'm sorry. I don't know. But he does consider it urgent."

"I can be there at eleven, maybe a little later. Will that work?"

"I'll clear his calendar and let him know."

The call ended, and Joe stared out the window, not noticing the curious looks from the other men at the table.

"Everything okay?" Russell Begay finally asked.

Joe looked at him. "Your uncle wants to see me. Now."

Less than two hours later, Joe sat restlessly in the waiting room of Samuel Begay, the first Native elected commissioner from the southeastern part of massive San Juan County. College-educated and the owner of two successful car dealerships, Begay was a powerful leader among Utah's Navajo population and begrudgingly respected by the Anglo population for his business skills and political instincts. Joe didn't know him well, but they'd met a few times.

At 11:15, Begay opened his office door and greeted Joe.

"Professor Cutler!" The commissioner smiled, held out his hand. The two men shook.

"Just Joe, commissioner."

"Certainly. And call me Sam. I apologize for the short notice. I'm honored you could come so quickly."

He put a hand on Joe's shoulder and ushered Joe into his office, closing the door behind them. Like many Navajo men, he was of modest height but possessed broad, strong shoulders. His hair was pulled back in a short ponytail, bound with a colorful beaded band. A bolo tie with a turquoise stone clasp hung in the front of a crisp white shirt. He exuded confidence and intelligence.

The commissioner's spacious office included a large desk that held both a computer and a bronze bust Joe recognized: Chief Manuelito, a key Navajo fighter and leader, who earned the name *Hashkeh Naabaah*, Angry Warrior. The wall behind his desk held an abundance of snapshots, many with other tribal leaders, but also a recent one of him and the governor of Utah with the Bears Ears buttes rising in the background behind them. An oak table with four comfortable chairs was tucked in a corner underneath an old double-horse blanket in the Two Grey Hills style that Joe knew was worth thousands. On the adjoining wall hung a compelling painting of the backs of a Navajo family walking alongside a bony horse pulling a small, overloaded wagon. It was titled "The Long Walk" and commemorated the forced relocation of over 10,000 Navajos from their Native lands to Fort Sumner in New Mexico between 1863 and 1866. It remained a traumatic tribal memory kept fresh a hundred-and-fifty years later through Navajo storytelling.

The two men sat at the table. "How long has it been since we last met?" the commissioner asked.

"Last summer at the end of the digging season. I was with Russell. We were attending the powwow in Bluff."

"I remember. You were alone then, right?"

Joe figured he was politely referring to the absence of his wife and daughter.

"Yes."

"I'm glad Russell was able to help last summer. It meant a lot to his family."

"He's a good worker," Joe said. "I'm looking forward to his help this season. The local team and I just met over breakfast. My students and my daughter arrive later this afternoon."

"I see," the commissioner said. He paused and looked down at his hands. A frown reflexively creased his lips. He looked up at Joe with a weak, forced smile.

Joe instantly had a bad feeling, but he was unprepared for the commissioner's next words.

"I need you to call off the dig, Joe. In fact, I insist upon it."

Joe didn't even ask why. He sat up straighter and looked the commissioner in the eye. He thought about all that had brought him to this point. This was no time to be passive.

"No, commissioner. I won't do that."

Commissioner Sam Begay stopped smiling.

"Oh, I think you will, professor."

They kept talking. It didn't go well.

Chapter 3

Commissioner Begay stood a few inches back from the window, partially hidden by heavy, dark green curtains. He watched as Joe Cutler exited the county administration building and strode toward the parking lot, his quick pace hinting at anger.

It was bound to happen, he thought.

He walked over to his office door, opened it, and spoke to his assistant, Marie. "Hold any calls for the next ten minutes."

He quietly locked the door, then returned to his desk. Knowing every call from his office phone was logged in the system's database, he picked up his cell, which, by design, he paid for himself and dialed a number he'd recently memorized. He would delete the record of the call as soon as it ended.

"Good morning, commissioner," a male voice answered.

"Maybe not so good."

"I take it the professor refused to stop the dig. No surprise there." A touch of I-told-you-so arrogance slipped into the speaker's voice. "He's not the kind of man who will be scared by a county commissioner when his excavation permit is from the Bureau of Land Management, not the county."

Begay didn't appreciate his importance being summarily dismissed. He'd built his political reputation and won two terms as county commissioner by finding a way to build an-always-fragile support base among his Navajo brethren and among more prosperous and reasonable Anglos. He was contemplating a third term, but he might just return to the private sector. It was time to build his retirement nest egg, something harder to do when under public scrutiny.

The person on the other line knew all this. And more. Not a good time to show anger, the commissioner figured. He tamped it down. "Can't the BLM just pull his permit? You've got friends there. See what you can do."

"I will. But we've got to be careful. Neither one of us can afford to have the BLM babbling about 'outside pressure.' That would blow up fast. Probably worse for me than for you."

"I've already asked him not to dig. I can't take that back," the commissioner said.

"That's true." A brief silence followed. "What reasons did you give him?"

"I told him the dig needed to be delayed until the federal government decided whether Bears Ears would become a national monument and, if so, what its boundaries would be. His excavation now, I said, would just confuse the situation and might derail the monument designation."

"Good. An appeal to his better angels. What did he say?"

"He said, 'That's bullshit.'"

The bullhorn burst of laughter that ensued forced the commissioner to back the cell phone away from his ear.

"Yeah, that sounds like Joe."

The commissioner found nothing amusing in it. "What now?"

There was no more laughter. "I think it's going to take more powerful persuasion."

"What do you mean?" Begay didn't like what he was hearing. Discreet, behind-the-scenes *negotiations*—his preferred term—were his stock in trade.

"The less you know, the better for both of us."

"No one will be hurt," the commissioner said. "You agreed to that."

"Actually, I said no one *needs* to get hurt. But I can't predict the future if someone does something stupid."

"What do you mean by 'something stupid?'"

The other caller chuckled. "I wouldn't worry. No one should get hurt. We'll just make it so they *want* to quit. Like I said, the less you know, the better."

"I pray your game plan works."

That got a laugh. "Tell me, commissioner, do you pray to the Navajo gods or your Mormon ones?"

"That's not funny." The commissioner respected both his Navajo traditions and the Mormon faith his parents had converted to.

"You're right. Our situation is definitely not funny," the caller said.

Then the call went dead.

Commissioner Begay looked out the window. It was now midday. The sky had become hazy, as if a layer of gauze covered the blue sky. The temperature had risen quickly into the uncomfortable zone, chasing anyone with any sense into the nearest air-conditioned haven.

The commissioner kept his office at a pleasant 74 degrees, but he was decidedly *not* comfortable.

Chapter 4

Felicity made sure she had a window seat for the last leg of the trip from Salt Lake City to Moab and stared out the window at the evolving landscape—the vast marshes surrounding the Great Salt Lake as they took off; the Wasatch Mountains that rose like a protective wall alongside the Salt Lake Valley as the plane turned south; expanses of forests interspersed with farming country; and, finally, the dry, rugged landscape of southern Utah she had come to visit.

She'd been warned to expect "a lot of red rocks," but, instead, she gazed upon a desert landscape awash in a palette of colors—deep rusty red and burnt orange, earthy tans and browns, sandy grey almost white in places, and layers of rock a dullish purple. From high above, she marveled at canyons and ravines and dry creek beds that radiated from higher-elevation plateaus. Like looking at the root system of massive trees, she thought.

The Chicago detective in her smiled. She imagined dropping some Chicagoland inner-city thug into one of the remote ravines. Some idiot who roamed the tangled web of streets and buildings in a tough Chicago neighborhood, believing himself lord of the land, master of the universe, because he had a .38-caliber pistol tucked in his pants and his face hidden under a hoodie. He'd quickly realize how small he really was. And he probably wouldn't make it out on his own. Neither, she realized, would most cops she knew. Or herself, for that matter.

"Just follow the water," Joe had said, and Felicity could see that even the driest creek beds eventually led to someplace better—less deadly—like a river. And to water.

Felicity knew the difference between fearlessness and stupidity. In the line of duty, she'd put herself into danger knowingly, but it was never fun. Adrenaline kicked in to give a cop a dose of energy, of determination even, but adrenaline didn't stop a bullet. Back in Chicago, she'd taken a bullet to save Joe. Without her Kevlar vest, she knew, she would be feeding the weeds now.

They flew over the Green River, which snaked through the desert in deep rocky trenches carved over millions of years. Then, as they went into the descent to the Moab airport, the plane swung near the Colorado River, muddy from recent runoff, with ribbons of green vegetation outlining its shorelines. She thought she spotted a few sandstone arches in Arches National Park, and she hoped to get an opportunity to see them up close. Off in the distance, dark green forests covered the sides of the La Sal Mountains, and their snow-capped white tops seemed an impossibility, a mirage.

Not in my wildest dreams.

She glanced over at Megan in the seat beside her, who quickly turned back to her phone. Megan had also been craning her neck to take in the landscape below, but she didn't want to let on she cared. During the flight, Megan, earbuds embedded in her ears, had displayed every imaginable body language signal she was *not* in the mood to be chatty; she had, however, surreptitiously glanced Felicity's way from time to time. *Sizing me up? Or trying to figure out how to take me down?*

Felicity tapped Megan on the arm. When she turned to face Felicity, Megan's face displayed the combination of disdain and disinterest that only a teenager can manage.

"What?" Megan had taken one of her earbuds out.

"Amazing landscape, isn't it?" Felicity wanted to find some common ground.

"Yeah, it's cool," Megan said icily. "I've seen it a bunch of times."

Felicity tried a smile. "First time for me. I think it's spectacular."

"Sure. I guess." Megan put her earbud back in and turned away.

Conversation over, Felicity figured. Short and not sweet.

When Felicity stepped off the plane onto the patched-up asphalt tarmac of the pint-sized Moab airport, she paused to take in the panoramic view—a sandy, treeless landscape that extended beyond her vision. Redrock mesas, some near, some far, topped the horizon in almost every direction, bulbous clouds loomed to the west, and the sun bathed everything in warm, dry air. The scale of the seemingly unending openness made her lightheaded. In a good way.

As they entered the airport terminal, Felicity walked behind Megan. She knew Joe's daughter should take precedence, but her heart rate ticked up at the thought of seeing Joe. Which surprised her. She was a detective who stayed calm even when dealing with horrible murder scenes. This was different.

Chapter 5

He was almost there. The drive from Bluff to Canyonlands Airport in Moab had taken about an hour and a half. Robby Hightower drove with his elbow protruding casually out his truck window. He wanted to feel the sun on his well-tanned arm, let the truck's speed create its own cooling wind. He scanned the horizon. A smattering of cumulus clouds had formed to the west like white cotton balls sprouting from the horizon. On hot days like today, they could grow into massive cumulonimbus clouds soaring thousands of feet high. But whether they would deliver the much-needed rain for the thirsty land or simply dissolve like a mirage was something not he nor anyone would bet on, not even the local meteorologist.

They'd taken two vehicles to accommodate the four arriving members of the dig team and their gear. Joe drove his larger pickup, which seated four, and Robby drove his own pickup, which had long since eclipsed the 100,000-mile mark on the odometer. Nicknamed the Beast, he had repainted it a dull green himself—less visible in the woods—and covered the seats with knockoffs of Navajo rugs to hide tears in the upholstery. The dashboard was faded to a dull, muddy grey. The Beast had the sex appeal of a buzzard, but he was smart enough to borrow his mother's nicer-if-boring Subaru for any dates, unless his date wanted to hike the canyons, a rare occurrence. He loved the Beast nonetheless and maintained the engine like it was a spoiled child.

Robby knew Joe asked him to help chauffer the arriving team because Doug and Russell, both older and more experienced, had headed out to the excavation site with the water tank and other gear. He didn't mind. There would be abundant opportunities to fill his pores with sweat and red dust and prove himself. He hadn't been hired because of his deep experience on digs; he was on the crew because of Joe's friendship with his dad and because he was good at spotting interesting items others missed.

I see things others don't see.

He was looking forward to seeing Megan again. It had been three years, and he knew from his parents' conversations she'd been through a lot during that time. She'd run away from home, disappearing for a week, the year after her mother died. Then, just last year, when her dad was the prime suspect in the disappearance of a grad student, she'd been kidnapped and barely escaped. Now, her dad, his boss for the next two months, was dating the police detective who had pursued him as the prime suspect in the girl's disappearance.

Wow, that's crazy shit!

Robby felt like he'd led a sheltered life compared to hers. He'd never even been to a city the size of Chicago. And definitely nothing like being kidnapped! He'd never been threatened by anything more dangerous than a rattlesnake or an angry elk cow protecting her calf. He looked forward to seeing Megan and hearing her stories.

But he wasn't prepared for the Megan who entered the terminal from the tarmac.

Is that really her?

She walked in slowly, wearing torn jeans and a loose-fitting plaid shirt, with a black and tan backpack slung casually over her shoulder. She tried to look nonchalant as she took her earbuds out, but she was clearly scanning the room for her father.

Oh wow! She's...different now.

The Megan he had last seen was a cute twelve-year-old. Now she was a girl possessing...what? Presence, he thought. She was tall like her dad, her long legs accentuating her statuesque posture, and her pleasant curves were unmistakable despite her loose-fitting clothes. She seemed self-confident and, in an instant, cooler than the local girls. He hadn't expected her entrance to stir him up, but it had. She was also only fifteen.

Joe, who had been standing next to Robby, rushed forward, bent down, and wrapped Megan in a bear hug. At first, she reacted with a moment of embarrassment, stiffening slightly. But soon, her beautiful smile broke through her mask of indifference, and she hugged him back. Unfortunately, Joe, facing the other way, couldn't see her smile, a moment of mutual connection lost without eye contact.

While hugging her dad, Megan noticed Robby. She extracted one hand from her dad's back and waved. He smiled and waved back.

Joe stood to greet the other arrivals, and he motioned Robby over.

"Everyone, this is Robby Hightower, a local man who helped me on the excavation last year. His father and I go back a long way."

Robby smiled, pleased Joe had called him a man. Not just *young* man.

"This is Ruth Ann Robinson," Joe said as he introduced a dark-haired woman wearing a navy knit V-neck. "She went on an excavation in New Mexico over near Chaco Canyon as an undergrad."

She smiled and nodded as she shook Robby's hand. "Nice to meet you, Robby."

"My pleasure." Robby could tell she'd spent time in the gym or rock climbing. Her arms displayed tanned, wiry muscles, and the hand she offered was firm, with a weathered palm a bath in lotion wouldn't soften.

"And this is Angela Young," Joe said.

A blonde in new field clothes who'd been scanning the airport waiting area swiveled to greet Robby. She instantly turned on a stunning smile as if turning on a faucet, and Robby was struck by her classically strong features—large eyes set below manicured eyebrows, high cheekbones, and full lips covered in a rusty red lipstick. Plus, there was something oddly familiar about her.

She took Robby's hand with a firm, confident handshake, the skin noticeably smoother than Ruth Ann's. Her voice was confident. "Just call me Angie."

Joe added more details for everyone's sake. "Angie actually grew up in Monticello, just 50 miles from here, until her family moved to Salt Lake City. But this is her first real dig."

Angie laughed. "At least it's the first dig I'll admit to."

Robby chuckled at Angie's joke, but it didn't surprise him when Joe greeted the comment with a subtle frown. For over a hundred years, the locals, especially the white populations of Blanding and Monticello, treated the ancient artifacts found among the Ancestral Puebloan ruins like vacationers treat seashells at the shore—there for the taking. Robby didn't know the full, sordid history, but he knew thousands of ceramic bowls, ancient baskets, woven sandals, innumerable potsherds, even skeletons had been removed from hundreds of ancient sites that dotted the canyons and mesas. Items in superb condition were often worth thousands, and the looting had never really stopped.

A somewhat older, attractive woman stood beside Angie. Late thirties, Robby guessed. She was also dressed for field work in new tan pants and a well-pressed tan field shirt. She looked directly into Robby's eyes and smiled warmly. Robby could tell from the wrinkles at the side of her eyes that she'd seen more of life than the other two women combined. Robby instantly knew who she was.

"This is Felicity Daniels," Joe said. "A personal friend. This is her first excavation. But let's just say she has an eye for detail. Her regular job is as a detective for the Chicago Police Department."

"It's good to meet you," Robby said. "My dad has spoken about you."

Felicity smiled. "Hmm. I haven't even met your dad yet. I wonder who his source is." She looked at Joe. "I don't think I'll even ask if it was good or bad."

"All good." Robby smiled. He was always at ease with women.

He glanced over at Megan who had remained silent, the introduction of Felicity dampening her smile as if she'd been stung by an angry yellow jacket.

"Hi Megan. It's really great to see you." He wanted to say something about how beautiful she'd become, but he stopped himself. *Even I'm not that dumb.*

"Hi Robby." Her smile peeked through. "I think you must be four inches taller than the last time I saw you. But I recognized you immediately."

"Yeah, probably. You're, umm, taller, too."

Megan laughed gently, and Robby was, to his amazement, thrilled.

"There they are!" Angie shouted. She started to wave, and a couple in their late 50s headed her way. As they approached, she gave each of them a hug.

"Everyone, this is my uncle Harris Young and my Aunt Rosalie. Uncle Harris is my dad's brother."

"I believe we've met before, haven't we?" Joe asked as they shook hands. "At an event last year, I believe."

"Perhaps," Harris Young replied. He smiled broadly. "Did you give a lecture or something I might have attended?" He was dressed in khakis and a checked dress shirt, a solidly built man with muscled arms and shoulders, the kind of man who would be comfortable in the outdoors or at a conference table.

Angie interrupted. "Uncle Harris and Aunt Rosalie live in Monticello and promised to meet me at the airport because I haven't seen them in a while."

"Actually, sweetie," her aunt said. "We're here to drive you down to Bluff ourselves if that's okay. We'll get dinner first. That'll give us a chance to catch up on all the family gossip." Her smile, bright and effortless, was remarkably similar to Angie's.

"Gee, Aunt Rosalie, I don't know. We're sort of a team and just getting started." She turned to Joe, beamed her thousand-watt smile.

"I don't see any problem," Joe said. "If I were in their shoes, I'd want to do the same thing. We'll have lots of time together as a team soon enough. Just get to your motel room by 10:30 tonight, okay? Breakfast is at 7:30. Then we head to the site."

With Angie having different transportation, Robby realized he wasn't even needed. Joe's truck could handle the other three women. He was about to mention it when Megan settled the matter.

"I'll ride with Robby." It wasn't a suggestion.

"Okay, sure," Joe said.

Robby suspected Joe had been looking forward to the ride with Megan but figured this wasn't a good time to pull the dad card. Out of the corner of his eye, he noticed Felicity nodding approval to Joe, which seemed to seal the deal.

Robby smiled. "When's curfew?"

Megan rolled her eyes.

Joe's face relaxed. "Well, we're having dinner in Blanding at your parents at 7 p.m. I think you're on the invitation list."

The group's backpacks, sleeping bags, and duffels appeared on the luggage carousel. Megan grabbed her sleeping bag and pointed out her duffel, which Robby snatched up with one hand. Its heft made him wonder what she could possibly need that made it so heavy. Boots? Makeup? Four pairs of jeans? What?

"Ready?" he asked.

"Lead the way."

Megan paused, looked over at her dad, maybe ten feet away. He was talking quietly to Felicity as they gathered her gear. She called over to him.

"Don't forget. Curfew is early tonight." She tried to imitate her dad's in-charge tone, directing her comment to both her dad and Felicity, then waved and turned. "Let's go," she said to Robby.

Robby led the way to the Beast, which suddenly seemed like an inappropriate carriage for transporting Megan.

"Is this your truck?" There was excitement in her voice.

"Yeah, it's, umm, functional."

"It's cool!"

"Thanks." Robby couldn't think of anything else to say.

"You probably couldn't pay my supposedly cool friends in Hyde Park to ride in it, but I think it's awesome!"

She got into the cab. He was about to toss her duffel and sleeping bag into the back when he caught sight of a three-foot-long gopher snake in the back corner of the otherwise empty truck bed. It was also clearly dead.

How long has that been there? He didn't remember seeing it when he left Bluff. *And why is it dead? The heat in the truck wouldn't kill a desert snake like that.*

He turned to see Megan smiling at him through the back window. Although only eighteen, he'd managed to ruin several promising moments with girls. He made a quick decision--

Now's not the time to mention the snake. Maybe never.

Chapter 6

Since Megan was riding with Robby, Felicity sat beside Joe as they drove south. Ruth Ann had taken the back seat. Soon, they entered bustling Moab, which was far busier than Felicity expected. Off-road vehicles noisily rumbled down Main Street along with an armada of 4-wheel drive pickups, jeeps, SUVs, and campers.

"This is the testosterone capital of the U.S.," Joe said. Disdain dripped from every word. "It's become the world headquarters for arrogant idiocy. Vast areas of the surrounding slick rock and mesas are open to off-roading by lunkheads who believe they're invulnerable because their vehicles have rollbars to protect them from their stupid selves when their vehicles tumble down an embankment end over end."

From the backseat, Ruth Ann laughed. "Tell us how you really feel, Joe. As a rock climber, I love the Moab area, although I agree with you about the noisy off-road vehicles. But a lot of the people who come here are climbers, mountain bikers, and whitewater rafters who love this amazing area."

"Yeah," he said, "loving it to death."

"Maybe some do," Ruth Anne said. "But most climbers follow 'leave no trace' practices. We even use rock-colored chalk when we climb so our handprints aren't noticeable. I've climbed a dozen amazing rock faces here. Castleton Tower. The Rectory. Stolen Chimney. Men in Tights. Adventures in Babysitting. And lots more."

Felicity laughed. "Who names these places?"

"No clue," Ruth Ann said.

Felicity looked at the sheer cliff in the distance. She imagined climbing it with her bare hands, where one slip-up could end exceptionally badly hundreds of feet below. She shivered.

Joe made a few stops along the way to let Felicity snap pictures, but they still arrived a half hour early at the Blanding home of Robert and Susan Hightower. Robby and Megan were already there.

Felicity had worried the Hightower home would be tricky terrain, a place where Joe's wife, Helen, had been a regular guest. She'd feared a cold formality. Instead, she was welcomed warmly from the moment she entered. While Joe and Ruth Ann helped Susan Hightower with the final dinner preparations, Robert gave her an enthusiastic tour of their spacious log cabin home on the western edge of Blanding.

Felicity was enthralled. Warmth emanated from its knotty-pine paneling, and whiffs of juniper burning in the fireplace softened the edges of the day's tensions. A large bull elk head, it's antlers an elegant swirl of bony points, stared glassy-eyed from over the mantel. Hand-woven Navajo rugs hung from the wooden beams that traversed the great room's high ceiling.

Robert pointed to a modest-sized rug hanging on a wall that had a simple diamond pattern.

"That one's almost two-hundred-years old and a little worn for wear. It's also worth more than my pickup."

A glass side table, its base made of gnarled juniper, held intricately carved and painted kachina dolls representing Navajo and Hopi spirit figures, which Robert identified.

"That one's Bear, who helps the sick get well. That one's Crow Mother, who watches over children. This one is Hoop Dancer, who represents the circle of life. This one is Eagle Dancer, the symbol of strength and power." He picked it up gently and handed it to Felicity. "It's the pride of my collection."

Robert pointed to a gray, clearly ancient pot, chipped along its rim, its exterior a corrugated style that mimicked weaving.

"Is that a pot from the Basketmaker Two period?" Felicity asked excitedly.

Robert chuckled. "You sure you're a cop and not an archaeologist?"

She smiled. "I've had a good instructor."

"Yeah, that was probably Joe's idea of a date. I hope he takes you out to a decent dinner occasionally."

"It works out. I like to cook."

Robert laughed again. "Good. That means he won't starve. Susan and I worried about him simply forgetting to eat." He looked out the window. "Come on outside. Let's take in the view."

Robby and Megan had wandered down to the small corral at the bottom of the two-acre plot. The sun was getting lower, and Felicity had to shade her eyes to take in the sweeping view from the spacious redwood deck.

"Those are the Bears Ears buttes off in the distance." Robert pointed to two mostly flattened peaks that rose above the surrounding mesas. "At 8,700 feet elevation, they're puny compared to some of the mountains around here, like the La Sal Mountains you passed up near Moab."

"So why are they so controversial?"

Joe had explained the battle over Bears Ears, but now, seeing them herself as they poked their rounded, ear-like shapes above the desert landscape, she couldn't understand what the fuss was about. *They look a little like Mickey Mouse ears.*

"It's not only those peaks people are fighting over. The name 'Bears Ears' is now associated with a vast land mass the Native tribes, led by the Navajo, want to turn into a national monument."

"How vast?"

"They want to protect over two thousand square miles. You could drop all of Chicago in just a corner of it."

The view reminded her of Lake Michigan. From one of Chicago's high-rises, the lake seemed endless. At least this was solid ground. As someone whose inner balance, both physical and mental, became unsettled on the water, she preferred terra firma.

"It's a lot to take in."

"Yeah. That's the reaction a lot of folks have at first. Scale and distance are different here. Folks will drive two hours for a good pizza. A hundred years ago, distances in the deserts of the southwest weren't measured in miles. They were measured in days or weeks or months of travel time."

Robert lifted his arms wide as if trying to embrace the entire horizon. "The proposed Bears Ears Monument would extend northward almost to Moab, a hundred-plus miles to the west, and go all the way down to the San Juan River and Bluff. It's a huge area."

"What makes it so special?"

"It's not obvious. Around here, what's often hardest to see is what matters most. Ancient ruins might be tucked underneath overhanging rockfaces. While some are out in the open and breathtaking, others are almost invisible. A pile of rocks that looks like just a pile of rocks can turn out to be the remains of a Native dwelling, or part of an entire village a thousand years old. There are also vast swaths of land that have been used for grazing, although, honestly, it's pretty crappy grazing land."

"On our drive from the airport, I didn't see a single cow." In Peoria, where she grew up, fat dairy cattle munched on hay and corn silage delivered to them. Here, Felicity imagined, skin-and-bones cattle must munch on tumbleweed while constantly thirsting for a sip of dirty water.

Robert nodded. "Like I said, not everything is obvious. It's what's underground that folks have lusted over for decades—oil, gas, uranium."

"Are the mineral deposits really that valuable?"

"Oh yeah. What the environmentalists want you to think of as land-destroying 'extractive industries' have been a big part of the local economy for a long time. The ranchers will tell you they built the local schools. Of course, the miners and oil guys think they're the ones who built the schools *and* the town hall."

"So some folk think a monument will screw things up."

"Just about everyone here in Blanding thinks so, at least those who are white. They're convinced it will bring about the end of a lifestyle their ancestors, mostly Mormons, earned for them generations ago."

"What do you think?"

Robert paused before answering. He looked away from Felicity toward the Bears Ears buttes, now shadowed by the setting sun. "A monument will have a huge impact. But, as the saying goes, the devil's in the details. There's an effort to find a compromise, but it won't happen easily. If there's a betting line on it in, most folks would bet on that *not* happening."

Felicity smiled. "I didn't think Mormons gambled."

"Let's just say my church ward doesn't see much of me on Sundays anymore." He took a sip of his beer. "Since the late 19th century, thousands and thousands of artifacts have been taken from this area. You'd be amazed how many were just sitting on the surface. But a lot of rare items, as well as human remains, were dug up by looters at various times. It's a painful history."

"What's going to happen?"

"Well," Robert said, "everyone here thinks this place is special, only they all mean different things." He spoke more slowly. "Change is coming. It always does. Even when we can't see it."

"How about for you?" Felicity asked.

Robert frowned at first, but then his face softened. "When my dad started our newspaper fifty years ago, he struggled. But he made it work. Now, I struggle even worse. Like newspapers everywhere, we have a declining subscription base. We're still alive and kicking because the local businesses don't have many choices for where to advertise. But we've had to branch out and create tour guides, coupon books, and a bunch of things that are so far removed from journalism it's laughable. We even sell t-shirts and hats at the office and online."

He pointed to his white pickup parked beside the house. "My jalopy over there has over a hundred thousand miles, which is really nothing around here, but I couldn't buy a new truck right now if I wanted to. I had to cough up every spare dollar for a printing press overhaul."

Felicity could tell Robert was trying to keep it light, but she could sense his deep frustration. Anger, really. "If you don't mind me asking, any plans to move on?"

"No. This is home. It's weird how this place gets under your skin and gets inside your head."

He gestured down to where Robby and Megan stood side-by-side, watching the western sky, pointing at birds in the distance. "But I sure as hell won't be upset if Robby takes off for greener pastures, the kind that put more green in his pockets. But college will be expensive for us." He chuckled. "Maybe it's a good thing, maybe not, but I think he loves the desert more than I do."

He turned to look at Felicity directly, a gentle smile on his lips. "Now, if you don't mind me asking, why are you here? Digging dirt in this heat will make you think *you're* what's cooking for dinner?"

Felicity didn't see any reason to prevaricate. "Because going on an archaeological dig seemed like a wonderful idea. Normally, in the past, for a vacation I'd just go on a group tour to someplace that interested me. I've been to over ten countries. But I was just a sightseer. This is the real deal."

"Is that all?"

Well..." she smiled, "the archaeologist leading the dig brings me flowers from time to time."

Robert chuckled. "Not just books about old clay pots and arrowheads?"

"Those too."

"In other words, the eminent professor Joe Cutler is smitten!"

Felicity smiled. "Joe? No, he's just distracted, I think."

"If you want to call it that, fine," Robert said. "Even if you and I know better. But I'm glad he found you to distract him. In the past, he got lost in his work. He always took time for Megan and Helen, but when Helen died, we worried he'd really be lost." He paused. "You don't mind me talking about Helen, do you?"

"No, not at all. I wish Joe would open up more. He holds that past close."

"Give him time."

"It's okay. I'm not competing with her, Robert."

"Maybe not from your perspective. What about from Megan's?" Robert looked down toward Megan and Robby as Robby opened the door to their small two-stall barn and the two of them entered.

Felicity smiled. "I've already lost that competition. Lost it before it got started."

"Give her time too," Robert said.

Suddenly, there was a scream, and the door to the barn swung open. Megan bolted out and ran toward the house. Robby emerged moments later and stood at the barn door.

For a second, Felicity had a sinking feeling Robby had tried something inappropriate with Megan, but then Robby called out excitedly.

"Dad, come here! You won't believe this!"

"What is it?" Robert called out. He quickly stepped off the deck.

"A four-foot Western rattler!"

"I'll be right there! Let me get my rifle!"

"No. Don't bother," Robby called. From behind his back, he lifted the fat but clearly listless snake, which he held just below its rattle. "It's already dead. Its head has been cut off."

Chapter 7

When the annoying alarm on the bedside table awakened Joe at 6:30 a.m., he reached over quickly, turned it off, and plopped onto his back. Without thinking he reached over to the other side of the bed hoping to feel the warm, soft skin of Felicity.

She wasn't there. Not anymore.

Following Joe's instructions, when they arrived in Bluff around 10:00 p.m. after dinner in Blanding with the Hightowers, Felicity had settled into her own room three doors down from his. But an hour later, she exited her darkened room noiselessly, the lone parking lot light casting a soft shadow of her body along the wall as she walked briskly, quietly towards Joe's room. He was waiting anxiously and had left his door slightly ajar for her to make a silent entrance without knocking.

But once she closed the door behind her, it was difficult to stay quiet.

"You're beautiful," Joe whispered to her. He rose from the bed, and within moments he engulfed her body in his arms and kissed her deeply. She responded with a soft moan and pressed her body into his.

She laughed. "I feel a little like a thief. A love thief." She shook her head as she looked into his eyes. "I didn't even do this kind of stunt as a teenager. Breaking curfew, sneaking out in the dark, taking the first chance possible to steal a kiss."

"Only a kiss?" Joe said.

"We'll see," she said. "I don't want to disturb the neighbors next door."

"We'll manage." He kissed her again, lifting her off her feet. He put her down on his bed and reached to unbutton her tan field shirt.

"Wait." She grabbed his hand. "Pull the covers down and climb into bed. I'll be back in a minute." She hopped up and headed to the bathroom.

Shortly after, in the dim indirect light cast by the bathroom fixture, Joe watched, mesmerized, as Felicity reentered the room, the soft curves of her body covered only in a dark blue lacy bra and dark blue sheer panties that hugged her hips. Neither stayed on for long.

Their passion exploded with fiery but stifled intensity, hands and lips exploring knowingly, and time seemed to disappear in a symphony of exploring, kissing, touching. When their heat finally subsided into a warm afterglow of smoldering embers, their bodies lethargically intertwined, their breaths fell into a calm sync. In moments, they would have drifted into a deep sleep. Instead, Felicity gave Joe a final kiss on his forehead, extricated herself from his arms, and rose from the bed. She dressed again in the weak light coming from the bathroom, returned, and gave him another kiss.

She quietly opened the door to leave. "I'll see you at 7:30, professor. Ready to go."

"Want to go again, now?" he asked. But he knew the answer. A moment later, Felicity closed the door behind her. Within minutes, Joe fell asleep.

Joe had instructed his team to meet at the Rainbow Bridge Café at 7:30 a.m. He intentionally made it an early start to test their readiness for the challenge ahead. He planned to start early every morning they were at the dig site. He didn't approach an excavation in a militaristic fashion, but he valued commitment.

The motel was only a short walk to the café, and at 7:15, he started walking over from his room. He stopped at Megan's room and knocked on her door. No answer. He knocked again, much louder. After another minute, the door opened as far as the chain latch allowed, and a groggy-looking Megan, her hair disheveled, squinched up her face at the early-morning light.

"What?" she said.

"You're supposed to be ready by now," Joe said. It didn't surprise him she wasn't ready, but it still irked him.

"Oh. I must have gone back to sleep after the alarm went off." She still didn't open the door wider.

"How late were you up?" Joe asked.

"Not real late. How about you?"

The question was intentionally vague. Joe knew she was trying to bait him.

"I expect you over at the Rainbow Bridge Café by 7:45."

"I'll try." She gave him a weak smile.

"Please do," he said. "You're part of the team."

"Are you alone?" Megan asked.

"Yes," is all he said. "Can I expect you by 7:45? It will be a long day today in the field, and I want everyone properly fed. Including you. Otherwise, you'll have to stay here."

Joe was quiet as Megan processed his comment.

"I'll be there."

His voice softer. "Good. Now open the door and give me a hug."

She opened the door wide, and they hugged, longer than Joe expected, her head tucked below his chin. The sun crested over the nearby sandstone bluff and bathed their faces in its warmth. She's special, he thought.

He reluctantly let go, looked at her, and shook his head gently. "And brush your hair. I wouldn't want you to scare your teammates."

"You sound like mom."

Joe considered it a compliment. "Maybe, but she would have awakened you at six."

Her smile peeked through. "You're right. Now, where's my coffee?"

"When you get over to the café, your coffee will be waiting at your place next to me."

"Okay. I better get going." She gave her dad another quick hug and closed the door.

Coffee had been a bond between Joe and his daughter since she was eight, when she'd sneak sips of his coffee when her mother wasn't watching. When they were on digs or camping trips, he and Megan rose early, fixed a pot of coffee, and sipped from their favorite camp mugs while the others slept. She nicknamed her dad "Java Joe," and by the time she was eleven, her mom gave up trying to put a stop to her "joe" habit. In the years since his wife had died, coffee continued to be a shared connection—more accurately, a shared addiction neither wanted to be cured of.

When Joe entered the Rainbow Bridge Café at 7:35, everyone was there except Angie and Megan. At first, no one saw him enter. Doug, his strong voice easily distinguishable, was holding their attention with some story, and a burst of laughter from the table followed. A good sign.

Even Ben and Felicity laughed out loud. Ruth Ann laughed without taking her eyes off Doug. As Joe approached, the others turned to greet him.

"Guten morgen, Herr Professor Cutler," Doug said. He extended his arms outward in greeting. "We've been waiting for you."

"Not too long, I hope," he said. "I stopped to check in on Megan. Let's just say she wasn't ready."

"She is coming, right?" Robby asked.

"Oh yes. She needs her coffee. She'll be here soon."

"I look forward to seeing young Megan again after too many years," Ben said. "She must be all grown and as beautiful as her mom."

"She'll be glad to see you, Ben. She wants to ask you more about Coyote."

The old Navajo smiled softly. "She remembers. That is good. I have much to tell her."

Joe loaded a plate of eggs, bacon, and toast from the café's buffet and took his seat at the head of a table set for nine. He wanted to briefly cover the plan for the day, but not until everyone was in attendance.

"Anyone know where Angie is?"

"She's staying next door to me," Ruth Ann said. "I heard her going into her room around midnight."

Joe frowned. She had clearly *not* followed his request to get to her room by 10:30. Not a good sign. He would talk to her later, privately. He wanted his grad students to both enjoy the experience and get a sense of the rigors of professional archaeological field work. The fine balance between discipline, hard work, and camaraderie was, he'd learned, like sitting on a three-legged stool; just one leg out of whack and the person—or team—was likely to falter. Even fail.

That's not an option. There's too much at stake.

He sat, started in on his breakfast, and mostly listened as Doug continued to regale his tablemates with a story about flipping his ATV on the slick rock near Moab a few weeks earlier. Felicity looked over at Joe, who shook his head. But he smiled too.

Ten minutes later, both Megan and Angie entered the café at the same time. Megan exchanged eye contact with Robby, then took her seat next to her dad. As promised, her coffee was waiting for her, plus a small carafe for refills.

"Sorry I'm late," Angie said with a big smile. "A little hard to get started this morning." But it was clear she hadn't just rolled out of bed. Her hair was perfect down to the strand that fell gracefully across her forehead, tasteful stud earrings adorned her ears, and the subtle touches of makeup around her eyes showed great care in application. Her clothes were crisply pressed. In short, she looked more ready for a photo shoot than a day digging in the dirt.

"Well, well, well," Doug said. "Look who's here. I never connected the dots that the 'Angie' on our team would be none other than the one-and-only Angie Young."

"It's mutual," Angie said. "Doug is such a... such a *common* name. I never suspected it was you." She turned to Joe, beaming a smile that could, in fact, had won beauty contests. "You must have been hard-pressed to find good help."

Doug roared. "I came to the same conclusion! But I needed the work. Plus, you never know who will turn up on these digs in the dirt. It can be a pleasant surprise." He turned and looked at Ruth Ann, then at Angie. "Or not."

Although Joe was often clueless when it came to the subtle dynamics of male-female interactions, he could tell, as did everyone else at the table, Cupid had missed his targets in their case. This felt more like the reunion of rival barracudas.

"I take it you know each other," he said.

"Since high school," Angie said. She took a sip of coffee. "Nice coffee here."

The others clearly wanted to know exactly how well they'd known each other, but no one was going to ask. Not yet, anyway.

Joe introduced Angie to the others at the table she hadn't met, finished his breakfast while the others chatted, and prepared his thoughts on what he was going to say. Keep it short and simple, he told himself.

Megan and Robby, at opposite ends of the table, were unusually quiet and limited themselves to occasional eye contact and smiles.

The team continued to eat, but after a short while, Joe lightly tapped on his glass. All eyes turned toward him.

"Keep eating, everyone, but I want to talk a little about our planned excavation over the next six weeks. It has the potential for being quite special."

"Air-conditioned tents?" Doug asked. A few at the table chuckled. Others kept silent.

"Maybe next season," Joe said, "but I wouldn't count on it."

He continued. "I believe all of you here are familiar with the better-known periods of Native American settlements in the broader Mesa Verde area. The area is big, from modern-day Moab in the north to a hundred miles into Arizona and as far east as the ancient ruins of Mesa Verde National Park in Colorado. I'm talking about the early Archaic period from around 6,000 BCE to 1,000 BCE, and the subsequent Basketmaker and Pueblo periods, all the way up to around 1,300 CE. That's when the entire area was largely depopulated, most likely due to a drought over the preceding years."

Doug interrupted. "Will there be a quiz on this later, professor?"

"Not exactly," Joe said with a smile. "But if you screw up bad, it will be your final paycheck." He wanted his team to appreciate how important the excavation would be.

"Ouch," Doug said. He stayed quiet.

"Our excavation is, instead, going to be about the Paleoindians who roamed through this era long before 6,000 BCE. They're often known as the Clovis because of this."

He reached into his pants pocket and took out a small case, one that might contain a gold bracelet, then extracted a three-inch, dark, sharpened stone. He held it high for the others to see.

"This is a Clovis point, in other words, a spearhead. It's made of obsidian. They're quite rare in this area. It hasn't been precisely dated yet, but it's probably from before 11,000 BCE. You could roam through the canyons of the Bears Ears and Mesa Verde areas and find hundreds of arrowheads in a year, but you could search your entire life and never come across a Clovis point." He paused, for effect. "We found this one four years ago, along with another one last year."

"That's wonderful!" Angie said. "Near here?"

"Yes. They weren't the first Clovis points found in Utah. But..." He paused and smiled. "We didn't just find Clovis points. We found more. We discovered a midden that contained bones of mammals and other foodstuff."

Felicity interrupted. "Sorry, Joe, but what's a midden?"

Joe smiled. "It's a waste pile. The dump. You learn a lot about people by looking at their trash."

"Define trash," Doug said. He looked over at Angie.

"Anything and everything. But more important than finding a Clovis-era midden, which is rare in itself, I believe the site includes the foundations of actual structures they used."

He was clearly excited. He knew Ruth Ann and Angie, as archaeology grad students, understood, at least partly, the significance of the find. As did Felicity. Months earlier, he'd told her of his discovery and let her hold the ancient Clovis point. Its simplicity—and beauty—as a weapon stood in stark contrast to the finely engineered Ruger handgun she carried every day for work.

"The Paleoindians were primarily nomadic, moving regularly to hunt both small mammals and large ones like the mammoth. Archaeologists have never found a Clovis habitation in this area. Only a few indications of a Clovis camp have been identified anywhere in the U.S." His eyes brightened. "I think what we found last summer are the foundations of at least one Clovis structure. And there may be several."

He stopped to observe the others. Everyone, including Megan, was paying close attention. *Good.* But he knew he needed to set expectations correctly.

"Look, if, as I think, our excavation turns up the first Clovis settlement in the southwest, it's going to be big news among the community of academic archaeologists. It will be the lead story for Archaeology magazine, the American Journal of Archaeology, and a bunch of other publications read by millions." He smiled. "Okay, maybe read by thousands." He paused. "But I could be wrong. What I think are Clovis structures might turn out to be from a later era, just structures built on top of a temporary Clovis encampment. In other words, no big deal."

"How will we know?" Ruth Ann asked.

"We'll need to proceed carefully, documenting everything we see and anything we uncover. We'll also carefully study the sediment layers, and, I hope, find objects, things as simple as seeds or dung, that can be carbon-dated. Everything found in each stratigraphic layer will likely be from the same time period."

He looked at the group. "I think this is the perfect team to pull it off. My goal is to get all the essential work done this season, so there's less risk of it being disturbed after our season ends."

"Is the site remote?" Felicity asked.

"Yes and no," Joe said. "It's tucked in close to an alcove that's normally not visited because there aren't any petroglyphs or ancient structures there, but it's fairly close to a dirt road."

"I can vouch for that," Doug said. "It's hardly a hundred yards off Butler Wash Road. When we took gear out there yesterday, I could see where some local yahoos had used the alcove for target practice. Holes in the red rocks, bullet casings on the ground, that sort of thing."

"Yes," Joe said. "I saw the same things last year. But the mischief didn't look recent."

"Yeah, maybe." It appeared Doug didn't agree with Joe's assessment of how recently the area had been vandalized.

"We're going to stay at the site for the first four nights," Joe said, "then we'll be back in Bluff for the weekend. That will be our routine for the next six weeks. Whenever the team is in town, someone will stay at the site overnight."

He took the signs of vandalism seriously, and he didn't want anything to go wrong.

"Any questions?"

There were several. Some were about the Clovis people. Others were about the expectations for staying at the excavation site. All of them indicated enthusiasm for the project. Joe answered each question with clarity and enthusiasm. *This could be fun.*

Finally, it was young Robby who asked the most important question, "Why are we still sitting here? Let's get going!"

Chapter 8

The team that exited the Rainbow Bridge Café a little before nine, ready to dig for ancient seeds and dung ten-thousand-years old, was an eclectic assortment of personalities and backgrounds. As the group exited the café, they instantly encountered another unusual personality.

At the base of the stairs to the parking lot stood an old Navajo woman, her hair pulled back, three rows of colored beads surrounding her neck, the fringe on her tan leather dress tattered from daily wear, her wrinkled face alert but frowning. She appeared to be waiting for them.

"*Yá'át'ééh abíní,*" she said. "*Jóhonaa'éí dóó shí ádii'ní.*"

"*Yá'át'ééh, asdzáán,*" Ben replied. "*Nighan biláájdę́ę́' dóó nízaad dę́ę́ naniná.*"

She replied. "*Éíyee' shich'i' hane' ályaa, diyin dine'é binítch'ih doo' bił ákodaat'éeda áko. Ma'ii éí doo bił hózhǫǫ da.*"

Ruth Ann turned to Russell. "What did she say?" she asked quietly. The others nearby listened in.

"She said good morning," Russell answered softly. "Ben returned the greeting, said she is a long way from home." He paused. "Then she said she came to warn us, that the ancient spirits are restless, and the spirit Coyote is unhappy."

Ben did not reply immediately. But it was clear he knew the old woman.

"Speak English, my old friend Johona," Ben said calmly. "You speak it well enough."

"Yes," she replied, "but the spirits talk to me in Diné."

"What do they say?"

"The spirits know why you have gathered here. You have come to dig the bones of the ancient ones. They demand you stop now."

"We are not here to excavate graves," Joe said. He was not in the mood to be questioned. He had the needed permits. "We're looking for artifacts and the remains of structures of the most ancient people who lived in this area. They were not the ancestors of the Diné."

She wagged a crooked finger toward Joe. "It is sacred ground you disturb."

"All land is sacred," Ben said, his voice as soothing as warm milk. "We will respect it as we work."

She was not satisfied. "Coyote has spoken to me. He is unhappy. He has the power to stop you." She paused as if deciding what to say. "Coyote says you dig your own graves."

Silence fell across the group. Megan's eyes widened noticeably at the mention of Coyote.

Ben, his face stern but calm, approached the old woman, and spoke to her privately in Diné, almost a whisper. She nodded, a wisp of a smile appearing at the corners of her mouth. She opened her beaded wool purse that hung from her shoulder, retrieved a small pouch, and opened it for Ben to inspect. He nodded, and the two of them walked away a short distance, their backs to the group.

"Is this normal?" Felicity asked.

"No," Joe said.

"She claims to be a great medicine woman, but she's a well-known crank around here," Doug said. "She couldn't cure fleas on a dog."

Russell spoke up. "She helped save my uncle when he was bitten by a rattler. She applied an ointment and chanted, and he started to recover the same day."

"What was in the ointment?" Ruth Ann asked.

"I don't really know for certain," Russell said. "Shamanistic healers, the hatááłii, don't share their secrets, except among themselves. They gather herbs, flowers, and other plant materials across a vast area for their medicines. Some of their sources are well-known, like sagebrush, cedar bark, juniper, and sage. But they use hundreds. Usually, the cures are given as a tea, but ointments and powders are also used."

Joe kept quiet. Ben was the grandson of a famous Navajo medicine man, his surname Hatathli a modification of hatáálii. He might have become a medicine man himself, but when only a boy, he was sent to one of the boarding schools that the white power structure in Utah and other states created to indoctrinate young Navajo in American ways of living and learning. Students were not allowed to speak their Native language, though, of course, they did so privately. Ben left the school when he was in high school—more accurately, he ran away—and returned to Navajo Nation and started working. By then, his grandfather had died, taking his traditional healing knowledge with him.

After a few more minutes, Ben nodded and bowed slightly to the old woman. She proceeded to walk away slowly without looking back, the leather belt around her substantial girth clacking as a dangle of shells rattled against her hip. Ben turned and returned to the group. He was holding the small pouch.

"What's that?" Joe said.

"A solution to our problem," Ben said. "Jonnie—that's what most people know her as—says it will keep the dead spirits away if we sprinkle it around our work area."

"Right," Doug said sarcastically. "How much did that handful of dirt cost?"

Ben nodded. "A fair amount."

"Should we expect to see her again?" Joe asked.

Ben considered the question. "I don't think so. But we may. She has her ways. Her name is derived from a Navajo word that means *sunny*, but she is seldom sunny." He took the small pouch and slipped it into his own leather shoulder bag.

"Let me know later what you paid," Joe said. He turned to the group. "Any questions?" It was clear to everyone he didn't want any. No one spoke up. "Good. Let's get going."

Unfortunately, another interruption came from someone *not* in their group. The day was clearly not destined to go smoothly.

Chapter 9

Joe's team had no sooner finished their unsettling exchange with the medicine woman Johona and were about to pile into their vehicles for the twenty-five-mile drive to the excavation site when a pickup skidded into an open parking spot, scattering dirt, dust, and debris. At one time white but now dusted a muddy red, it bore the signage of Archer Drilling Company—Blanding, Utah.

Two men, both in their twenties, emerged quickly from the cab, their worn but clean blue jeans suggesting they hadn't yet started their day's work. Breakfast first, Joe figured. One was tall and muscular, no doubt a former high school football player but now carrying a football-sized paunch; the other was short and stocky but with a swagger suggesting no lack of self-regard. Both sported bushy mustaches and cowboy hats they would no doubt later exchange for hardhats at the drilling site.

"Well, look who's here!" the taller one said. His denim shirt barely held in his powerful biceps as he tipped his hat. "If it isn't Princess Angie *and* her former prince charming, Douglas! You two kiss and make-up." He smirked. "Or maybe something better than a kiss?"

"I would tell you to screw yourself, turd face," Angie said, "but my parents taught me to save my insults for people who are worth the breath."

Ruth Anne's mouth gaped open, not expecting Angie's outburst. The others were speechless, too, except for Doug.

"You really shouldn't get the lady riled up, Riley," Doug said. "She shoots to kill. I know."

The one called Riley scanned the rest of the group, pausing to note the two Navajos, Ben and Russell. "What kind of tour group is this? Or are you planning some kind of peace powwow to save Bears Ears from hard-working men like us?"

"Something like that," Joe said. He'd stayed quiet long enough. The morning had been sidetracked, time was being wasted, and he wasn't in the mood for chatting with local oil field roustabouts. "We're here on an archaeological dig that probably doesn't have much interest to you."

"Hell, I know all about archaeological digs," the one called Riley said. "If you want to see some really spectacular old pottery shit, give me a shout." He laughed. "But bring cash. I don't take credit cards."

"Me too," said the shorter man. "We got Indian pottery shit out the wazoo! Helped pay for my college education."

Riley howled in laughter. "College? Frankie, you flunked out of plumbing school!"

"It shows," Doug said. "Because Frankie's always been full of shit and no place to put it."

It was clear Doug knew both men, likely old high school acquaintances he ran into from time to time in the confining spaces of San Juan County's small towns. It was also clear Doug didn't consider either of them friends.

"How about you, Riley Smith?" Angie said. "Your family ever get around to installing indoor plumbing?"

Riley's smile ended instantly.

Ben spoke up, his voice calm. "I would be interested in seeing your pottery. And I will bring cash. What are your addresses?"

"Mine is..." Frankie started to speak, but he was cut off by Riley.

"Shut up, Frankie," he said. "The damn Injun just wants to know where to send the feds to come bust you."

"That never occurred to me." Ben smiled softly. "Is it illegal to pilfer artifacts and sacred objects of Ancestral Puebloans?"

"Only if you get caught," Riley responded.

"We're not interested in small-time law breakers." Russell looked directly at Riley as he spoke, but his voice was steady, almost flat. "Maybe some other day."

"Who the hell are you, Indian?" Riley said. He sized up Russell.

"Someone who doesn't plan to answer your question." Russell started to walk past Riley toward his truck. Ruth Ann followed.

Riley Smith's face tightened. It clearly didn't sit well with him to let a Navajo have the last word. Or to see a good-looking white woman about to ride in a red man's pickup.

"Hey sweetheart," he said. He reached out and grabbed Ruth Ann's forearm as she walked past. She twisted it away instantly. "Touch me again, and you'll be missing some more teeth."

"Whoa, little lady." He put his hands up in the air. "I just wanted to say, if you need a ride, I'd be happy to oblige." He smirked.

"Touch her again," Doug said coldly, his eyes narrowed, "and you'll need more than denture work."

"Big talk, Dougey," Riley said. He grinned. "Better bring an army that's better than this sorry lot."

Joe had heard enough. It was time to de-escalate the situation. "Let's get going, team. I'm sure we're keeping these men from their breakfast and their hard work at some drilling site."

He looked at Doug, who got the message. Joe took his daughter's hand and started to walk toward Doug's big truck, deciding a short ride back to the motel was a better option than walking. The others followed suit.

"You're damn right, it's hard work," Riley shouted as a noisy truck passed by on the nearby highway.

"Hey Injun!" he called out to Russell, who was getting in his pickup. "You ever had a real job?"

Russell smiled, unperturbed. "Naanish niłnilínigíísh íinilaa?"

"What did you say, Injun?" Riley hollered. His face was scrunched in frustration about not getting in the last word. Or the last hit.

Ruth Ann, beside him in the truck, asked, "What did you say?"

"I asked him if he'd ever read a book?" Russell said as he turned the key.

***

Felicity had remained silent throughout the exchange with the local rednecks, but her cop instincts kicked in the moment the one called Riley opened his mouth. During her years on the force, she'd encountered enough self-regarding smartasses for a lifetime, mouthy ones who were all bloated blather, but some, the dangerous ones, who would back up their words with knives and guns. She'd quickly sized up the two men as most likely harmless. And, she figured, they hadn't been drinking. They were headed to work, and she guessed, showing up late would be a bigger problem than a prolonged *tete-a-tete* with their group.

But as she rode the short distance back to the motel, she couldn't get the interaction with the medicine woman Johona out of her mind. She'd noted the woman's intensity, her directness, her boldness. Her seeming belief that Joe's excavation was evil. And she'd noticed Megan's startled reaction at the mention of Coyote.

I need to learn more about Coyote from Ben.

She'd always thought of coyotes as clever, marauding animals that might snatch someone's pet cat for dinner. Coyotes were regularly spotted around Chicago. But she'd never thought of them as somehow truly dangerous. Or godlike.

She had a lot to learn.

Chapter 10

The blistering sun slid below the top edge of Comb Ridge, and the cooling shade instantly lifted Felicity's spirit. A primitive reaction, she realized, much like the unbridled delight she'd gotten moments earlier from a mere sip of water for her parched throat.

Two ravens cawed loudly from a nook in the crevice of the rock face, seemingly wasting time. Smart scavengers, they were hanging around to see what they could pilfer from the nearby humans. A sagebrush lizard scooted off the rock where it had been sunning itself and disappeared underneath it.

The sun wouldn't completely disappear over the horizon for another two hours, but the lengthening afternoon shadows brought some relief. Soon, the team would wrap up their digging for the day, clean up, start dinner preparations, and, Joe had promised, relax around a campfire. Over the past two days, dirt, mostly fine dust, had worked its way into every stitch of Felicity's clothing and every pore of her body including, she suspected, places that should have been protected by her once tan but now rust-colored pants. Only a few hours ago, the wind had picked up briskly, coloring the air a hazy shade of dull orange. Dust seemed to replace oxygen, and even when she pulled her bandana, wet from sweat, over her mouth and nose, dust and sand invaded where they could. The wind settled down after a half hour, leaving a new coating of dust. On everything.

Even though it was only the second day on the dig, Felicity had developed a deep appreciation of the hard, often tedious work of an excavation, and why not many people were cut out for it. By the end of their four nights at the site, the team's return to the modest motel in Bluff for two nights would seem like a vacation in Eden.

Staying onsite wasn't essential, Joe had told her, but he wanted his grad students to experience the challenges of a remote excavation, where the team provided for their own basic living needs. It would also maximize their excavation time. Archaeology isn't for sissies of either gender, he'd told the group. Doug, smiling, had raised his hand and volunteered to be a sissy and stay back in Bluff; he'd bring fresh donuts every day.

Getting to the excavation site had been its own experience. They'd driven their vehicles down a weary-looking, red-clay road that wound its way northward up Butler Wash on the east side of Comb Ridge. Only high-clearance vehicles with four-wheel drive could intelligently traverse it, but they'd passed a few sedans and RVs, likely holding tourists, slowly trying to dodge the road's hungry potholes and rocky ridges. A thirty-minute drive from Bluff, the dig site itself sat at the base of Comb Ridge, roughly two hundred yards down a sandy two-track that diverged from the main dirt road. Their camp was mostly out of sight, partially hidden by some large boulders and scrubby pinion pines. They didn't expect random visitors.

Sleeping quarters consisted of five tents for the nine of them. Joe had his own small tent, and the others were paired up in reasonably comfortable tents with almost enough head room to stand. He'd made the assignments without asking for input, except from Megan, who had chosen Ruth Ann. The other pairings were Ben and Robby, Doug and Russell, Angie and Felicity. He planned to rotate the pairings over the weeks. Doug had asked if they were going coed.

A day before the others arrived, Doug and Russell had set up two large, blue plastic tarps eight feet tall, anchored deep into the earth to resist gusting winds, but, following the recent sandstorm, Felicity was sure they'd eventually end up chasing them down the canyon like runaway kites. One served as a cover for two pop-up metal tables for food prep; the other covered two longer tables for meals, note-taking, and social interaction.

They'd set up the water tank called a water buffalo, a small generator to run lights at night, and, tucked amid some tall sagebrush, a portable river toilet for eventual disposal of waste back in town. An outdoor shower was added about fifty yards away on the other side of camp, hidden behind a large boulder. Two large, thick, black poly bags were placed atop the boulder; supposedly, each could provide enough hot water and water pressure to create the semblance of a shower. The first day it was never used, and Doug announced at breakfast he was taking bets on who would be the first to wimp out and take the first shower. Maybe me, Felicity had volunteered.

The scale of the Comb had stunned Felicity. Their excavation site was on the east side of the Comb, where it sloped down into Butler Wash, and the first day, she'd asked Joe to walk with her to the top. In the early evening they climbed up the steep sandstone slickrock, pockmarked here and there but mostly smooth from eons of erosion. They'd only gone about halfway to the top when Felicity stopped, her heart rate elevated.

"It's massive!" She tried to slow her breath. "It's much higher than it looks from below."

Joe smiled, unsurprised by her experience. "It's called a monocline." He pointed to his right, northward, then to the south. "It extends, virtually unbroken, for a hundred and twenty miles."

She looked. The massive rock formation stretched beyond the limits of her vision. But from their elevated perch, she could see a good distance down Butler Wash and spotted a few campsites and RVs.

"Want to turn around?" Joe asked.

"Hell, no."

Detouring where needed to dodge crevices, they were only a few steps from the top, when Joe stopped. Both were sweaty and breathing hard.

"You don't have vertigo, do you?" Joe asked, quite serious.

"No. At least I don't think so."

"Okay. But be careful when you get to the edge."

Felicity, eyes widened, approached the edge with caution, and looked down. On the west side, the Comb dropped straight down hundreds of feet. To the west, Felicity could see fascinating rock formations in the distance. To the north, the monocline was a single massive uninterrupted wall of rock, with irregularly spaced ridges and dips.

"I see now how it got the name Comb Ridge."

Joe stepped closer and put his arm around her. Which instantly felt reassuring.

"The Navajo believe it's the spine of the world," he said. "It's a formidable barrier. When the Mormons sent a party from the west to settle this part of Utah in the 1840s, they spent months finding a way around it. Ancient tribes lived on both sides."

The walk back down the slope to their camp took less than half the time, but Felicity's legs were wobbly by the time she reached camp. She didn't ask again to scale the Comb.

The wind and dust having settled down, Felicity took a break and headed over to where Joe was walking slowly, oblivious to the heat, scanning the ground for signs of...what?

"What's got your rapt attention?" she asked as she walked up.

Her presence startled him, and, for a moment, his concentration broken, he didn't answer. Then he bent down and picked up a small object. "Things like this," he said. He held a small, curved piece of red clay pottery, easily mistaken for a small stone among the thousands of small rocks that surrounded him.

"Something special?" Felicity asked.

"No, not really. It's a piece of Bluff black-on-red pottery, likely a thousand years old, but potsherds like this are scattered all along Comb Ridge by the thousands."

He put it back where he found it.

"What it means," Joe said, "is that ancestral Puebloans lived in this area a long time ago. It's a good sign, but we sort of figured that out last summer. This would have been a natural place to live."

He pointed to a section of the Comb where the sloping rock for two hundred feet rolled inward in a wedge shape that went all the way to the ground. As it reached the floor of the wash, water had carved out a substantial alcove. "That sloping formation concentrates the rainfall into one area, which makes the ground below it a happier place for plants. That was true a thousand years ago. Even ten thousand years ago."

He pointed to two large cottonwoods that were forty yards from the base of the alcove at the bottom of the rock wedge. Robby and Megan were taking a break, sitting in the shade of the trees, talking, but Joe didn't notice or didn't care to comment about their presence. "Those cottonwoods have deep roots and continue to draw moisture long after rains have passed. Even the sagebrush in that area grow taller because they have more water."

Felicity hadn't noticed, but it was true. The sagebrush along that section of the rock face were taller.

"Then why aren't you searching over there?"

"Because the water was mostly helpful for plants, both the wild kinds and, perhaps, crops planted as the populations shifted to farming." He smiled. "But you wouldn't want your living abode right there when the skies really open up and that part of the ridge becomes a temporary raging waterfall."

"Right now, that sounds blissful." Felicity was sopping grimy sweat off her forehead with her bandana.

"You'll change your mind quickly when we get a downpour that turns Butler Wash into a giant mud bowl. The red clay becomes a gluey gel. It glomps onto your boots inches thick, and it's hell on driving. Tires can't get traction. The dry washes, those dips in the road we crossed, become impassable. Even four-wheel-drive trucks like ours can end up taking an unplanned siesta trying to drive across."

"We're not in any danger of a flash flood," Joe continued, "but slot canyons near here can turn into deadly rivers of muddy water from a thunderstorm, even from a storm miles away."

"Without warning?" Felicity asked.

"Sometimes," Joe said. "If the storm is upstream and, let's say, not seen or heard, the rushing water is both startling and dangerous, like coming upon a momma bear and her cubs."

Felicity didn't say anything. *Oh great, I'll add flash floods and bears to my list of worries.*

Joe continued. "A downpour can turn a dry creek bed in a slot canyon into a raging surge of dirt-red water. It rises quickly, sometimes several feet, as the rush of water tries to escape the narrow canyons."

"I'm guessing trying to outrun the water doesn't work."

"You got it. The only way to save your butt is to find somewhere to climb higher than the rushing water. But adrenaline and our instinct to flee makes people try to outrun it."

"It's sure not Peoria." Felicity laughed. "Or Chicago." She thought about the flat terrain of Illinois and pictured the Chicago River that ran through the city, which was made to run backwards. Most of the time it didn't seem to have a current. For her, that was fine. She had zero affinity for water, avoiding even sailboat rides on Lake Michigan.

Joe was aware of her nervousness about water. "Don't worry. Even being a good swimmer doesn't help in a slot canyon flood."

"You do realize—don't you?—that's not exactly reassuring."

Joe laughed. "But you have an advantage over most of us. You're smart."

Felicity was, by nature, a learner. And an observer. Both had helped her survive—even thrive—when she was a rookie cop and as a seasoned detective. She'd read and studied the archaeology books

Joe had given her, but they were *about* the ancient tribes who had lived in southern Utah. This was different. She now walked where they'd walked, felt the scorching sun that had scorched them. She tried to picture their simple lives—hunting, gathering, and eventually planting crops in such a challenging environment. Those thoughts made her appreciate, not just their survival, but the survival of *homo sapiens.*

She was about to ask Joe if he'd had any close calls in the desert when there was a sudden shriek from a female's voice. Megan's. No longer with Robby under the cottonwood, she'd wandered over near the base of the sloping sandstone of the Comb.

"Dad, come quick! Now!"

Joe, instantly worried, started running toward her. Everyone else who'd heard her call out, including Felicity, headed toward her quickly. But Felicity hadn't detected fear in Megan's voice, just excitement, and Megan was still standing in the same spot, looking down, not moving, not running.

"Hurry!" She waved, practically dancing on her toes. She pointed excitedly toward the ground.

Chapter 11

Just wow! Megan said to herself. *Wow!* The grin on her face was unstoppable, and she realized she hadn't smiled so hard in a long time. She started tapping her foot, practically jumping, waiting to show her dad and the others what she'd found.

They all arrived quickly. One by one they nodded. She could feel their excitement, their approval. Her dad especially.

"Go ahead and pick it up," he said.

"Really? That's okay?"

"Sure. This isn't something we'll be leaving where we found it. We'll map the location with GPS, take pictures, and scour the area nearby. But you can pick it up."

Megan bent down, then gently but firmly enough to make sure she didn't drop it, lifted the ancient artifact, and held it out in her palm for everyone to see.

"It's a Clovis point, isn't it?" she said.

"You bet." He gave her shoulders a gentle hug. "It's likely ten thousand years old—give or take a thousand years. Only a few have ever been found in the Bears Ears area, including the one I showed you all at the diner."

The point had distinctive curved edges with an almost rocket-like shape that was far different from later sharply pointed arrowheads. It was about three inches long.

"What's it made of?" Ruth Ann asked.

"Hard to tell for sure," Joe said. "It looks like gray Honaker chert to me. Let the others examine it."

"No way, it's mine!" she said. Then she laughed. She handed it to Robby.

"I've found lots of arrowheads, but nothing like this." He handed it to Ruth Ann. Soon, everyone had held it briefly, and it ended up with Joe. He chuckled.

"I ran over here expecting something dreadful. Instead, you found something almost no archaeologist has ever found." He looked at Megan. "Do you mind if I hold on to this for safe keeping?"

"Sure, but it will cost you." She was enjoying the moment.

"Oh?"

"Yes. I get to take the first shower before supper. Agreed?" She looked at the others; no one dared disagree.

While dinner was cooking, Felicity taking the KP lead, Megan grabbed her towel and clean clothes and headed over to the makeshift shower.

"None of you go peeking, got it?" In truth, she imagined one person peeking that would be a thrill, but she knew her dad would throw him off the team if he did. Or off a cliff. *I hope the water is warm.*

It wasn't. It was hot, almost scolding hot from a day of capturing the sunshine. But the water pressure was wimpy. It didn't last long enough, but it was enough of a shower for her to shampoo the dirt from her stringy, sweaty hair and to wash off the red dust from everywhere else. Drying off, she felt exulted, her spirits soaring as she looked up to the few thin clouds in the sky turned a soft pink as the sun set. She liked that she would be the cleanest, tidiest woman in camp. *Robby sure better notice.*

A coyote began yipping and yowling, and Megan instinctively knew it was close by. How close, she couldn't tell. She wasn't suddenly afraid for her life—she knew a coyote wouldn't attack her—but goosebumps rose on her skin everywhere, uncontrollably. She remembered Ben's words three years earlier on her last trip, the one when her mom was still alive—*Beware the Coyote. He is a trickster.* She was just a kid then and had wanted to know more, but they had gone to bed instead. She never got the rest of the story. And life never returned to normal after that trip.

I will ask Ben tomorrow.

The coyote stopped its calling as suddenly as it began. She finished dressing and walked briskly back to the safety of the group. She didn't know her dad had also stopped what he was doing to listen closely to the yipping of the coyote. Nor did she know he got goosebumps too.

Chapter 12

As day three of the excavation came to an end, Joe was pleased. As expected, progress was slow. Which was fine. He needed his team, his students in particular, to appreciate the importance of careful work, especially at an excavation that could yield a stunning find. Screw up the details and what might be a major discovery could be discounted by petty sniping among the archaeological community.

The first day, using excavation string and wood stakes, they laid out grids across the dig site in one-meter squares, plus a fixed point, the datum point, as the reference for all other measurements. And they created a contour map of the undisturbed surface before the first trowel was allowed to break ground. A smaller grid covered the area where Joe's team were excavating the midden, the trash heap, he uncovered the prior year. The larger grid covered the area where Joe hoped to find the remains of Clovis-era dwellings. They would use sophisticated total station survey equipment to provide detailed location data on everything uncovered.

The team from the prior season had backfilled the trial trenches to protect them during the long gap between excavations. By the second day they'd removed the backfilled dirt and begun to dig further. Joe had demonstrated to everyone the preferred techniques for using shovels, trowels, scoops, brushes, and screens although Ben, Doug, and even Robby had prior experience. He wasn't taking any chances. Every bucket of sediment would be carefully screened for artifacts, and every artifact found would be bagged, labeled, and logged according to where it was found in the stratigraphic layer.

He checked on the progress at the midden site where Ruth Ann and Russell were working. They had excavated down to the depth Joe's team had dug the previous year and had begun to expand it.

"When we got down to the final layer from where the team dug last year," Ruth said, "we found what appears to be seeds." She picked up a carefully-labeled plastic bag that contained what seemed to be ancient grains. She handed it to Joe as he stooped down.

"Looks promising," he said. Accurate identification of the tiny objects and meaningful dating of their age would need to take place later, back in the university's labs. He'd found similar-looking seeds the previous year, and they'd been carbon-dated to approximately 10,000 years old. As they widened the dig, he expected they would continue to make discoveries.

"Are they maize seeds?" Ruth Ann asked.

"I hope not. Maize wasn't introduced around here until 4,000 years ago." He looked at the plastic bag again. "Let's check them against our reference books later at the camp."

If they were indeed maize, Joe knew, it didn't mean the site wasn't from the Clovis era. Later indigenous tribes may have left the seeds. But it wouldn't help his case.

"We found something else, Joe," Russell said.

"What else did you find?"

"This." Russell handed Joe a larger, heavier plastic bag. He was trying without much success to look calm.

Joe's eyes widened. It contained a bone, or part of a bone, that looked like it fit into the socket of a joint, most likely a segment of a leg bone. And it was big. Clearly not the bone of a human. He held the bag and examined the bone remnant from multiple angles, then took the bone out and studied it even more intently. He was an expert on man-made objects like pottery, clothing, tools, and weapons, and knowledgeable about ancient food remains, but he was no expert when it came to animal bones seldom recovered in the American Southwest.

"Is it what we think it is?" Ruth Ann asked, unable to wait for Joe to speak.

"What do you think it is?" Joe understood their hesitation but wanted them to voice their thoughts.

"Some kind of mammoth bone," she said.

"I wish I could give you a definite answer," Joe said. "We'll need an expert to confirm it."

"Well, what do *you* think it is?" Russell asked.

Joe liked they weren't going to let him off the hook. "A mammoth bone. Most likely from a juvenile mammoth, not a full-grown one."

Ruth Ann's brows went up. "You mean the adults' bones are bigger than this one?"

"Oh yeah," Joe said. "A mature adult could be up to thirteen feet from the ground to the top of its head. Larger than today's African elephants."

He handed back the bone to Russell. "Juvenile mammoths were much easier to kill than an adult using something as primitive as a spear for a weapon. An atlatl might have helped."

"I was thinking that," Russell said.

"What's an atlatl?" Ruth Ann asked.

Russell smiled. "It's sort of a hand-held launcher a hunter or warrior used to throw a dart-like projectile with greater force." Russell's voice showed his Native pride. "I've used an atlatl but only with targets. Taking down a mammoth would be an amazing feat. It must have been a juvenile." He was excited. "I bet we find more bones."

Joe nodded. "Let's hope so." He was actually counting on it. He knew they might uncover enough bones to prove they'd found the remains of at least one mammoth. During the latter parts of the Pleistocene age, mammoths, saber-tooth tigers, and giant bisons roamed throughout much of what is now the American Southwest. The climate was far different then, lush even. Around 12,000 years ago, those animals were prey for roaming bands of Paleoindians that depended on large mammals as a food source. Which meant that if a Clovis trash heap contained mammoth bones, a Clovis dwelling might be found too. Up to that point, only Clovis temporary camps had been found, and those were few and far between.

Joe considered the discovery made by Russell and Ruth Ann. "This will be exciting to discuss over dinner," he said. "You're off to an amazing start."

When he suggested they call it quits for the day, Ruth Ann and Russell looked at each other but no words were exchanged. "Maybe in a little while," Ruth Ann said. "We want to keep going."

"Keep your discovery to yourself for now," Joe said. "You can reveal it at dinner." He wanted them to have their moment.

Soon it would be dinner time. Or at least cooking time.

Four years earlier, he and Ben were taking a lunch break at an excavation in Mosaic Canyon, thirty miles north of their current site. Joe mentioned that he'd never discovered a Clovis point in his career. Ben then reached into the leather satchel that hung from his side.

"You mean something like this?" he asked. He unwrapped a small piece of leather bound with cord. A Clovis point lay in his outstretched hand. He passed it over to Joe.

Joe held it gently. "Where'd you get it?" He knew it could've been purchased from a disreputable dealer, but he knew Ben wouldn't have been suckered into buying a bogus point. It definitely looked real.

"Joe," Ben said seriously, "If I tell you it was on federal BLM land, will you report me?" Ben knew the law and respected it. But when he discovered the Clovis point, he'd felt compelled to remove it for safe keeping. A hiker or camper could stumble upon it and simply take it home as a souvenir, clueless to its archaeological significance. He'd waited to present it to Joe.

"I'll take responsibility," Joe said.

The next day, the two of them took a break from the Bull Canyon dig, and Ben took Joe to the location in Butler Wash where he'd come across the Clovis point. Immediately, Joe could see why the site was promising. An alcove in Comb Ridge offered protection from the elements or other dangers, the water supply would have been more reliable than most places, and a climb to the top of the Comb Ridge would offer a vantage point from which to spot potential prey in the distance, especially if the prey were large mammoths that roamed the area during the Pleistocene era.

Joe noticed one other thing. He suspected Ben did too.

"Did you notice that rockslide?"

"I did," Ben said. "It is an old one."

At the base of the ridge, there were signs of a major rockslide that might have occurred within the past several hundred years or, perhaps, tens of thousands of years ago. A sudden, massive slide could create what's known as a "high-energy deposition" of debris capable of quickly burying dwellings. If that was the case, what had been buried might not have rotted away over the ensuing millennia the way most non-stone items simply disintegrated. Subsequent eras undoubtedly experienced further shifting of the earth as wind and water and more slides and flash floods carved, reshaped, and covered the history buried in the ground. But geological changes sometimes uncovered history too, the reason a Clovis point had been found on the surface after emerging from its burial location ten millennia earlier.

"I want to dig around here." Joe swept his arm in an arc that covered a hundred-foot stretch of the ancient slide. "And not just for old arrow points."

"I will join you," Ben said.

That was four years ago. Joe hadn't been able to return until just the prior season. He and his team the previous summer had dug test trenches across a wide swath, looking for tantalizing signs of Clovis life. They found them. They found another Clovis point, located the midden, and just as their field school was ending, reached stones about four feet down in one of the test trenches that appeared to be the foundation of a primitive structure. They also found a small, partially disintegrated piece of thick hide that later, back in Chicago, was identified and carbon dated as a fragment of mammoth hide.

Joe wasn't surprised Russell and Ruth Ann—Team One—had hit archaeological pay dirt first. A midden could contain many things—food waste, the bones of prey, and a host of things only suitable for the trash pile. Fewer items were found in ancient shelters—clothing fragments, tools, and, sometimes, weapons. But such items weren't found often. Unlike trash, they were usually taken when the inhabitants moved on. Besides, what Joe wanted most to find was the dwelling itself. No definitive Clovis era dwelling, not even the foundation or remnants of one, had been discovered in the American southwest. Archaeologists speculated the Clovis never built abodes that survived from one season to the next, but instead remained nomadic. But the fact that no Clovis habitats had been found didn't mean they didn't exist in the archaeological strata. It simply meant one hadn't been discovered. Yet.

He started to walk over to the other trenches where the other teams appeared to be wrapping up for the day. As Joe approached Team Two—Felicity, Robby, and Doug—Felicity spotted him coming. She'd rolled up the sleeves of what had been a crisp tan field shirt now the color of the reddish dirt she was digging in. She stood up in the trench, her hair matted and sweat showing under her arms and across her stomach. She wiped her forehead with the back of her grimy hand, raised her hand, and waved to Joe.

He waved back cautiously, his hand rising only to mid-chest. He was trying to maintain some semblance of indifference. Of not showing favoritism. Yet everyone on the team, he figured, could feel the frisson, the sparks of electricity, that hung in the air when they were together. Including Megan.

Joe had expected having Felicity on the excavation team would be a pleasant distraction. It wasn't. It was a disturbing distraction. The heat, the sun, the rugged terrain only intensified his desire for her, but it went beyond raw sexual attraction. It had from the beginning, a year earlier. She was smart, inquisitive, and instinctively attentive to the minute details of her environment, people, him. She was, Joe had realized months ago, a lot like his deceased wife, Helen. Only different. Bolder. She was, after all, a decorated detective who worked the homicide beat in Chicago. They'd met when he was the suspect in the disappearance of his favorite grad student, but that now seemed like an unreal memory.

They hadn't been together intimately since the first night at the motel in Bluff, but he'd fantasized about her every night, tossing and turning in his sleeping bag. The last three days they hadn't even exchanged a kiss. Far too long.

Joe didn't notice Megan noticing him and Felicity. Megan was twenty yards away, working at the other trench, and Joe hadn't looked her way. He missed seeing the furrowed brow and tightening of the eyes on his daughter's face when Felicity waved and when he smiled and waved back. He missed her throwing her trowel into the soil hard enough for it to imbed itself like a throwing knife. He missed her wiping her mouth with her sleeve and spitting in the dirt as if she'd swallowed a bitter pill. Ben, however, had noticed Megan's quiet outburst and allowed himself a slight, knowing frown.

Team Two was making good progress. After the backfill from the previous season had been removed, the team started to extend the excavation. It was slow going. With Joe's guidance, Doug had carefully strung string that paralleled each layer of exposed soil inside the trench. Because each layer was from a known geologic period, any artifacts found during careful excavation could be dated with some degree of accuracy. The lowest level they'd dug, about five feet deep, dated back some 8,000 to 12,000 years.

Joe looked down into the trench as all three diggers paused. "Impressive," he said. He knew they'd been taking copious photos as they dug, but he wanted one of the team. "I want to take a photo of y'all standing in the hole."

"Good idea," Doug said. "But first let me take my shirt off to really give the photo some pizzazz!"

Joe frowned but Felicity laughed. "Please do. I'm sure it will be just right for the wall calendar I'm planning."

Doug roared. "In that case, maybe you should take yours off too! That could go in my wall calendar."

"I'll pass for now," she said. "I still have a job back in Chicago I want to keep."

"A loss for mankind." But Doug didn't press on.

Joe shook his head. "I can see the heat is starting to get to you two. How about you, Robby? Need your shirt off too?"

"Yes," he said. "But I just want a shower."

He called out loudly enough for everyone to hear. "Time to call it quits everyone. Robby wants a shower."

Joe took a picture of Team Two standing in the trench—with their shirts on. Once they'd climbed out, he took another picture of the trench with Felicity holding a tape measure to show the precise depth of each stratum. He wanted to memorialize the day's efforts for himself. Tomorrow they would begin digging deeper and extending the length of the trench in search of more evidence of structural foundations and any remains that could be from the Paleoindian era. After dinner, he would encourage everyone to discuss their work, their finds, and their initial impressions.

Joe turned to visit Team Three's newer excavation. That's when he saw Megan, her hands on her hips, looking his way. He waved to her. She didn't respond, at least not with a wave.

Chapter 13

Megan didn't mind KP duty. She knew her way around a kitchen and how to prepare meals, but cooking for nine over a camp stove was a challenge. Normally, she cooked for just her dad and herself. She'd developed a repertoire of meals that, while hardly gourmet, spanned enough of the food groups to keep them healthy—with help from the frozen food section of the grocery store.

Megan had enjoyed cooking alongside her mom when she was little—mostly treats like cookies and cakes—but at twelve, she'd taken on more serious kitchen duties when her mom became too weak to stand and cook. Her mom would sit at the kitchen table, smiling, coaxing, and coaching her how to prepare roasts and chops, how to steam vegetables, how to wash lettuce and make a decent salad. She even learned how to make Hollandaise sauce. Sometimes her mom sat at the table and snapped the beans and diced tomatoes. Sometimes her dad would help. But Megan especially treasured the time alone with her mom in the warm kitchen when sunshine coursed through the window and lit up her mom's pale face like golden aspen leaves in autumn.

Megan didn't get to pick the menu at camp, but she wanted to show off her cooking. With Russell's help, she chopped four pounds of Idaho potatoes and three pounds of carrots. She simmered five pounds of ground beef in a large pot, added three cans of tomato sauce, the vegetables, salt and pepper, and, she decided on her own, a fistful of garlic powder and a handful of dried chile pods. *This stew is not going to be bland.*

It definitely wasn't. It was delicious. At least, that's what everyone said. They asked for seconds and drank a lot of water. While her dad wouldn't allow for any serious drinking during the dig, he offered a beer to anyone who wanted one. Just one.

Megan watched her dad sitting by himself at the end of one of the two dining tables. His plate was empty, which made her smile. *Must have liked dinner.* She watched his face surreptitiously, something she did often. She could tell his mind was churning but didn't know why. Why didn't he look happier now that he was at his special dig? Now that Felicity was with him.

For the past three years, she and her dad had lived in the large house in Hyde Park alone. It was such a quiet existence Megan figured even ghosts would find it eerie. Both preferred books to TV, and both liked long stretches of time alone or sitting together quietly in the well-worn, overstuffed high-back chairs in the den off the kitchen, each reading or doing homework. *Homework* seemed the only word to describe the mounds of papers and books her dad brought home from the university.

They seldom talked about her mom's death. The cancer had progressed slowly—so terribly slowly—like a distant storm cloud that never arrives. Each week her mom lost weight, lost more appetite, lost more hours she could stay awake. The only thing she gained was pain.

Then she was gone.

Time slowed even more. Her sadness needed a place to go. For over a year, it found a home in anger. Anger at her dad. At the world. At her mom. She ran away—not looking for answers—but because her dad couldn't provide what she needed, even though she couldn't say what that was. For five days she fled her past, struggled with her present, and had no sense of her future. Scared, desperate, she returned home, knowing her dad was likely overwhelmed with fear. Afterwards, with help from counselors, they worked to make things better. Her life began to feel normal, she reconnected with her friends, did well in school again. And then one of her dad's grad students went missing. He became the prime suspect, and she was abducted. That had brought Felicity—highly-regarded Detective Felicity Daniels—into their lives.

As she finished her own meal, she noticed Felicity talking to Doug and Ruth Ann at the next table. She winced at the ease with which Felicity connected with them. *Am I just jealous?* Megan had wanted someone to be part of her dad's life, someone who could restore his amazing optimism, but somehow the change came too soon. She didn't dislike Felicity—not in the way she could easily dislike some turdface guy or snotty girl at school—but she wasn't ready to befriend her. Felicity was smart, funny at times, attractive, and made her dad smile. She was even a good cook. Without thinking it through, Megan instinctively knew the source of her dislike—Felicity was a lot like her mom. Only different. Embracing Felicity as some kind of substitute felt like a betrayal of the worst kind.

Her dad stood up, cleared his dishes, and looked down Butler Wash as the last light faded behind Comb Ridge. He walked over to Felicity, bent down, and talked with her privately, and Megan watched her face brighten. He said something to Ruth Ann, who beamed and patted a small satchel that hung at her side.

"Hey everyone," her dad announced loudly. "Ruth Ann and Russell have something to show you. I think you will be impressed." His smile almost turned into a grin. "I sure am."

Ruth Ann stood, described their day digging in the midden, mentioned the ancient seeds they'd found, and then reached into her satchel. "And we found this."

Eyes widened as she extracted the plastic bag containing the large bone fragment.

"Take it out and pass it around."

Ruth Ann handed the bare bone to Doug, who sat to her right.

"Damn! It looks like someone had one helluva barbecue. You can even see where there are knife marks or gnawings on the bone."

"I wouldn't jump so fast to that conclusion, Doug," her dad said, "but yes, I noticed them too."

The bone was passed around. Each held it gently, fascinated, turning it around in their hands, noticing its heft, trying to grasp that it could be 10,000 years old.

"What is it?" Felicity asked.

Ruth Ann answered. "We think it's part of a mammoth bone. But that's just our less-than-perfectly-educated guess." She smiled.

The bone was passed to Megan. "It's big."

"It is," her dad said, "but it's probably from a juvenile mammoth, or it would be much bigger. I think it's part of a leg bone—see the bulging ball at one end that would fit into a hip or knee socket—but we'll need an expert to make a final determination."

The bone created a buzz around the table. Megan noticed everyone seemed to perk up, like they'd all gulped a shot of some intellectual Red Bull energy drink.

"No telling what we'll find tomorrow," Ruth Ann said.

Her dad spoke up again. "Felicity and I are going for a ride back down Butler Wash. We might climb up to the rim of the Comb along a trail I know. Anyone want to join us?"

No one said yes. Clearly, they sensed he wanted some private time with Felicity. And nobody, Megan figured, wanted to climb to the top of the Comb after the workday they'd had. Even Megan remained silent.

Ten minutes later, her dad and Felicity headed down the road, and, even from a distance, it was easy to tell when he downshifted to dodge a pothole, the grumpy sounds of the old pickup's engine echoing off the hard sandstone flank of Comb Ridge.

As her dad headed off, Megan began the supper cleanup, making her own racket cleaning the large pots and utensils. The camp lanterns provided the only light as darkness descended. Her mind was elsewhere. As she was finishing, she was startled when she turned and Ben was standing beside her.

"Would the *chi'iké í* Megan like to learn more about Coyote?" he asked calmly.

"Chee-ee-kee?" Megan asked.

"It means young woman," Ben said. "I thought you might like to learn a few Navajo words."

Megan smiled. "Yes, the chee-ee-kee would like to learn some *Diné*. And yes, I would like to learn more about Coyote." Maybe she could learn a few tricks she could use.

"Let us take a walk," Ben said.

Russell told her he would finish the cleanup. Megan hurried to her tent to grab her down jacket; the night air would chill quickly. Ben was waiting outside.

"Follow me closely," he said. Without saying more, he headed toward the massive grey sandstone slope of Comb Ridge itself.

I hope he doesn't want to climb to the top. I'm drained.

The waning quarter moon provided only faint moonlight, but Ben had chosen not to bring a flashlight. Instead, he moved carefully, each step placed carefully, and Megan followed in his footsteps as best she could. When they reached the point where the sandy floor of the gulch intersected the incline of the Comb rock face, Ben paused. "We are headed there." He pointed to a flattened area in the ridge about forty feet up that Megan could barely make out.

"Lead on," she said. She began to relax, her edginess fading.

Ten minutes later, they reached the spot, settled onto a flat area, and sat close together. A light breeze nudged Megan, and she zipped her jacket snugly up to her chin. Directly below them the campsite glowed from the firepit and the two propane lamps hanging under the blue tarpaulins. To Megan they looked like small islands of safety amidst the vast night.

"Look to your left, to the darkness," Ben said.

Megan did. "I don't see anything."

"Keep looking. And don't look back toward the bright camp lights."

Soon, she could see a faint outline of the Comb's massive grey stone against the dark sky, but in the distance, even the massive sandstone wall faded into the darkness too. Down on the floor of Butler Wash she could make out shadowy intimations of large boulders, tall cottonwoods, and the dry creek bed that flowed only after rainstorms. As her eyes adjusted more, she began to see stars and planets—yes, I'm sure that's Venus—although some disappeared behind wispy clouds that glowed softly in the gentle moonlight.

"Do you like the darkness?" Ben asked.

"I don't know," Megan said. The darkness of the desert was all encompassing compared to the night in Hyde Park. She knew and had experienced the dark side of nights in the city, where streetlights cast deep shadows and provided little protection against whatever dangers lurked in blackened alleys.

Ben nodded, at least Megan thought she saw him nod. "We are all afraid of the dark sometimes, *chi'ikéí*. Those who prey on others use the darkness to cloak their ways."

Megan tried to laugh. "You're trying to scare me, Ben. And you're doing a good job at it."

"Young Megan, I don't want to frighten you." Ben's voice as calming as a warm bath. "There is a great difference between the beauty of the night and the darkness in men's souls." He paused. "See those stars up there?" He pointed to the stars that made up the Big Dipper. "Whether you are white or black or *Diné* like me, those stars do not care. They do not change. Whether here or in your Hyde Park, they help locate the great star in the north. With it, you and I can find our way, even in the dark."

"Maybe you can," Megan said. "I don't know about me."

Ben turned so they could see into each other's eyes. "Finding one's way is never easy. But you will find it, young Megan, if you look with open eyes."

Megan nodded. "You're trying to tell me something special, aren't you, Ben? But maybe I'm just too stupid to get it."

He laughed gently. "No, you are maybe too smart. Don't let being smart get in the way of learning."

"I think I get what you're telling me, or at least trying to tell me."

Ben reached over and placed his palm on her hand that rested on the rockface—his hand is so warm, Megan thought. He paused before speaking, his breathing itself gentle.

"When you lost your most beautiful mother, Helen, darkness descended all around you. And inside you." He squeezed her hand gently. "It is hard to see the stars when all around you is dark. And you can't see the stars if you keep your eyes shut."

Megan answered quietly. "It was a terribly dark time for me, Ben. You can't imagine." The loss of her mother still haunted her, and, even with Ben beside her, the night seemed to darken instantly.

"Your pains are your own. Mine are mine. We all experience grief, young Megan, and few pains are worse than the kind you felt. But grief can turn to anger that wounds us even more." He took a breath. "I, too, felt a light went out when your mother passed to the other side."

"It was so hard, Ben. She was the best mom."

Ben nodded. "She is still there for you, in the stars. And others are there for you too." He raised his eyes to the heavens. "The stars will continue to shine for you, *chi'iké̄i*, but you must want to see them."

"I do," she said. Tears welled up in her eyes. "I do." She wanted to not just feel the squeeze of his hand but to hug him and not let go.

"Turn back and look at the camp now," he said. She did.

"Our camp is a light in the dark too. It is a place that offers you safety and strength. A place where you can shine. *Chi'ikéí,* there are many stars, many lights you can follow if you are open to seeing them." He paused. "Do you understand?"

She took a deep breath, nodded. She wanted to hug Ben for comfort. And she wanted to hug her dad.

Off in the distance, a lone coyote let out a yip, yip, yip, followed by a long howl. Neither spoke as it made its beautiful but eerie calls. Megan looked at Ben's face. His demeanor had shifted.

"Don't other coyotes usually call back?" Megan asked.

"That is a lone coyote," Ben said. His eyes had narrowed, his brow furrowed in seriousness and intensity, as if he was ready for a hunt. Or to defend his family.

"Will you tell me more about the god Coyote?" Megan asked.

"Not tonight, *chi'ikéí.* I don't think that would be wise." Then, stunning Megan, Ben howled back in the loud voice of a coyote, sounding very real, his own yips announcing his presence.

Chapter 14

Joe brought his pickup to a stop at a pullout and cut the engine. Instantly the rumbling of its unruly motor was replaced by an unworldly quiet, a breeze rustling through the sagebrush the only sound. From their camp in Butler Wash, they had driven back to the main road, gone up the sloping east side to the pass that cut through the ridge, descended quickly, and turned onto the dirt road that paralleled the Comb on its western side.

A faint bluish-green glow on the horizon was all that remained of daylight, but it was enough to reveal the massiveness of the ridge that rose almost straight up four hundred feet. Viewed from the west, the Comb was an uninterrupted wall of dark sandstone, its edge notched in intervals much like a comb. It looked impenetrable.

"Now I really understand why it's called Comb Ridge." Felicity had to tilt her head up to scan the wall of stone that rose less than fifty feet from where they parked.

Joe rolled down his window and took in a deep breath of cool desert air.

"The Mormon pioneers who approached from the west in their wagons first saw the Comb many miles north of here. None of them had ever seen anything like it. They were crestfallen but, of course, still bursting with prayers. It slowed their advance by months. There was no way through. They went around it south of here, probably traveling through where we are now. The pass we drove through was cut many decades later."

"It's an unforgiving land," Felicity said.

"Yeah. Maybe. But I'll take the harshness of the desert versus the hardness of Chicago any day. Let's go sit on the hood for a while. It's probably still hot enough to warm our fannies."

Felicity reached into her tote bag. "I snuck a bottle of wine." She smiled as she lifted the bottle by its neck. "And two camp cups."

A huge grin emerged across Joe's face. Every minute alone with Felicity lifted his spirits, and he could feel the tightness in his chest loosen. "Nice surprise. Mine is this." He reached behind his seat and grabbed a thick wool blanket. "Bring your jacket."

"Okay, but won't you keep me warm?"

"Count on it."

They settled in on the hood facing west and pulled the blanket over their laps. Soon it would be dark except for whatever moonlight penetrated through the low, wispy clouds. The stars overhead began to appear. Felicity poured them each a cup of wine.

"Cheers." Joe raised his cup.

"To chilly nights in the arid desert," Felicity said.

"To nights with you anywhere. But especially here."

He swung his cup slowly in a wide arc across the horizon. He couldn't help himself and launched into an explanation of what he found so amazing about the place. He explained that a vast area of the southwest had been underwater for millions of years. And that later, a massive collision of tectonic plates over 40 million years ago thrust Comb Ridge upward, followed by eons of rain and wind that removed the topsoil from the down-sloping east side, revealing the hard grey sandstone that rose above their excavation site.

"It's humbling," Felicity said. She sipped her wine as the last of the day's light faded over the distant horizon. She edged over closer to Joe's body and placed her hand on his under the blanket. "Would they really drill for oil out here?"

"I don't think so," he said. "But they're battling over it like it was paved in gold. I don't think this area around here has ever been shown to have important mineral deposits. A land use plan was due from the county, but according to a story in Robert's paper, it was delayed because the person in charge died recently."

"Died?" Felicity's cop radar clicked on when she heard the word. Her fingers tensed slightly against Joe's.

"Supposedly, he fell from a ridge in Mule Canyon, not too far from here. But according to the story in Robert's paper, his wife doesn't believe that's what happened."

"What does the sheriff think?"

"I don't know. The paper said he was investigating but believed it was an accident. Robert might know if it's still under investigation."

"Do you suspect his death is related to the battle over the proposal to create the Bears Ears monument?" Felicity asked.

"I doubt it. The battle over Bears Ears is mostly among local and state politicians, the Native tribes, and the federal government."

"Yet, the county commissioner asked you to stop the dig because of the monument issue."

"Good point," he said and went quiet.

Felicity didn't say anything, instead laying her head against his shoulder. Joe realized she didn't want to spoil the moment, but he considered Felicity's words. He recalled the startling meeting with commissioner Begay and the commissioner's veiled threat. His brow furrowed from the memory, but he decided not to repeat to Felicity the warning by the commissioner. Not yet, anyway.

His mind turned to other places where oil, gas, and mining, not to mention grazing, conflicted with archaeological interests. Some sites had been destroyed; others were under constant pressure. He thought about Nine Mile Canyon, two hundred miles to the north, where a dirt road wound among dozens of stunning Fremont era petroglyphs. There the rock art was threatened every day because the road was a short cut for hundreds of tankers coming from the oil fields.

He had never been an activist archaeologist, preferring to stick to science, to his digs, to learning, to making discoveries. He didn't want to think about it now. He wanted to savor this moment with the incredible woman sitting beside him, to smell her hair, unwashed for two days, to hold her hand that had been digging in dirt. He wanted to sit with her quietly and watch the constellations and Milky Way gradually reveal themselves against a backdrop of deepening dark sky—out in the nowhere spaces of the desert where civilization didn't cast its omnipresent harsh lights.

He laced his fingers with hers. Her hand was warm and felt...what? Feminine? It wasn't that. She possessed a mystique he found irresistible, intoxicating. Almost scarily so. A year ago, he could not have imagined his life would be intertwined with someone like her. Did she really know how he felt about her? *Do I even know?*

He looked over at Felicity, his yearning palpable, but she didn't notice. She was lost in a reverie about the scenery, not him. It made him smile.

"This place is amazing!" she said. A grin spread across her face.

"I'm hoping we get a chance to see lots more together." He wanted to share more of this place he loved. He wanted to make it hers.

"I'm ready when you are," Felicity said.

"There are huge red rock monoliths in the Valley of the Gods not far from here. And maybe later we can go south to Monument Valley. I'm hoping we can find time to visit petroglyph sites and ancient pueblo ruins. But there's just no time right now."

"Don't worry, professor," she said, her eyes lighting up. "I'm pretty blown away already. Maybe taking it in slowly is the right way to go." Felicity looked up at the moon, then at the stars. She pointed to the South. "Is that Venus and Jupiter?"

"Yes."

The two planets, appearing close together, shone brighter than they would in Chicago. "This place is beautiful."

"You are too," he said.

Felicity snorted. "You are so corny!" She shook her head. "Is that your best pickup line for girls in the desert? Oh well, it worked." She twisted around and gave him a long kiss. "Do you think the hood of this old truck can handle a bit of a beating?"

Joe looked into her eyes. He wanted her fiercely, but tonight he needed something else. What? Closeness? He smiled. "Too many bugs. Trust me."

"Okay, but I can handle a few bug bites for a good cause."

"We'll be back in Bluff in a few days. With a real bed."

She nuzzled against his shoulder and kissed his neck.

Joe squeezed her but didn't go further. The moment passed in silence. Felicity withdrew gracefully, closed her eyes, and took a deep breath. Her face softened, but her brow furrowed slightly. She looked at him with the knowing look he'd come to love.

"Are you happy, Joe?"

He didn't answer. He always believed he liked direct people who asked direct questions, but in truth, like most people, that wasn't always the case.

"I'm happy you're in my life. And Megan makes me happy in her own way. I enjoy my work. And I think the excavation this summer will be something special." He stopped.

"But..." Felicity said slowly.

"What?"

"This place brings back memories that hurt, doesn't it?"

Joe had promised himself he wouldn't think about Helen when he was on the dig. It wasn't working out that way. Her spirit shadowed him, casting its spell of memories and longing. He had felt it the previous season, too, but it was stronger this time. Megan's presence, and Felicity's, spun webs of conflicting emotions inside him.

Joe didn't want to hurt the woman he was with because of the woman he couldn't be with. "I don't deny missing Helen. But it's complicated in ways I don't understand."

Felicity turned toward him. "What would she want?"

"That's obvious. She said it herself. She wants me to move on."

Felicity reached over and ran her hand through his hair, her fingertips massaging his scalp gently. "There's no hurry."

Chapter 15

"Joe," Doug whispered. "Joe."

"What?" Joe replied, groggy.

A light sleeper, he awoke quickly but reluctantly when he heard Doug's voice. He'd gone to bed late after he and Felicity returned from their private excursion. The first light of day glowed over the butte to the east, but he wasn't ready to get up. Doug, he knew, was on KP duty and had arisen early. Like the rest of the team, Joe wasn't anxious to rise any earlier than needed. Nursing kinks and aches from the prior day's hard work and another night sleeping on the ground, he, like the others, looked forward to two nights sleeping in real beds back in Bluff.

"We have a problem," Doug said. "You better come see."

"What is it?"

"I'd rather show you. I don't want to wake the others talking."

Joe pulled on his dusty jeans and field shirt and grabbed his light jacket as he exited the tent. Doug nodded toward the cooking area, and Joe walked by his side until they came to the water tank they'd set up. Beneath it was a huge puddle of muddy water.

"Shit," Joe said quietly.

"The tank's basically empty."

"Is this how you found it?"

"Yes. The spigot was wide open. It drained out while we slept."

Joe gave it a moment of thought. "Any idea who used it last?"

"No," Doug said. "There's more."

What?" Joe ran his hand over his face, rubbed his eyes.

They walked over to where two large coolers sat in the back of Doug's pickup. Both lids were open. Most of the food looked okay, the cool night helping to keep everything chilled, but some of it had begun to thaw.

"Great," Joe said with disgust. He would need to talk to Megan and Russell. They had KP duty the previous night and *should* have been the last ones to use the coolers.

"Damn!" Joe whispered loudly. "Who's on KP duty with you today?"

"Angie." Doug's lips tightened as he said her name.

Angie and Felicity were bunking together. "Let's go wake them."

Angie was slow to awaken, but Felicity arose quickly, wide awake the moment she saw the look on Joe's face. He showed her the water tank, then the truck, explaining that the lids of the coolers had been left open. She immediately started looking at the ground around the truck, then headed back toward the cooler.

"What's up?" Joe asked.

"Your best evidence of an outsider will be footprints. I'm trying to see how much of a mess we've made of the tracks this morning."

"Oh," Joe said. He hadn't considered they needed to be careful where they walked.

"Keep everyone else away from the water tank and the truck, okay." It was not a question. "I want to study the footprints for a while, then check them against everybody's boots on the team. Maybe we can determine if any prints are from an outsider."

Joe nodded.

"And don't tell anyone I'll be checking their footprints. No one wants to be a suspect."

"Tell me about it." A hint of a smile crossed Joe's face for the first time that morning. Felicity knew why.

For three terrible days the previous May, Joe had been the number one suspect in the case of a missing grad student. Her Hyde Park apartment had gone up in flames, killing a fire captain in an explosion. Joe had been the last person seen with her, and somehow, he'd ended up with her cell phone in his possession. He'd been celebrating with a group of grad students, drank far too much for the first time in over twenty years, and couldn't recall what happened. Felicity and her partner, the key investigators, questioned him, turned his home inside out, and tracked him wherever he went. Then things went from bad to worse.

A spark of a connection between Joe and Felicity had been lit during the investigation, and when Joe was exonerated, he followed up. The spark turned into a much warmer relationship quickly. They liked each other. A lot.

***

All sleepiness vanished for Felicity. She was in detective mode now, but in a vastly different environment from Chicago—a different kind of wild. She wasn't as sure about herself, but she kept her calm and considered her next steps.

"Let's find out if anyone heard anything during the night. I can't imagine we all slept through someone or some animal disturbing the campsite."

"I'm pretty sure only two-legged animals could open the spigot," Doug said.

Angie pleaded complete ignorance, said she didn't hear anything, and Joe instructed her and Doug to continue with breakfast prep. They still had enough water in a large jug.

Felicity quickly retrieved her cell phone. There was no cell coverage in Butler Wash, but she could take pictures of all the footprints in the dusty earth surrounding the truck and the water tank. Both areas were heavily used, and the footprints were jumbled together like a pile of jigsaw puzzle pieces. She clicked away regardless and would analyze the details later. She would also find a way to sneak photos of everyone's boot prints as the day progressed.

As the other team members stirred, Joe awakened Megan and asked her to walk with him over to his tent. Felicity accompanied them but remained silent. "When you cleaned up after dinner and washed the dishes and pans," Joe said, "did you use water from the main tank?"

"Of course." Megan looked at him like he'd lost the last of his marbles.

"Yeah, stupid question." He tried to smile. "Someone left the spigot of the tank open and it emptied out."

"You think I did it?" Her voice was louder. A few of the team noticed.

"No. At least, not on purpose, but..."

"No but, Dad. I didn't do it on purpose or by accident. I didn't do it!" A few other heads turned their way.

"Okay, okay," Joe said quietly. "Do you know if Russell went to the water tank after you?"

Megan became a little more thoughtful. "No, I think I was the last one to fill up two buckets to clean stuff with." She paused. Her brow tightened. "He didn't do it either."

Felicity watched quietly. She didn't see any reason to doubt her.

"Okay, sweetheart." Joe gave her a hug, but Megan tensed. "I need to tell the others. Let's go."

They walked back to where the others had gathered near the tables, waiting for coffee, waiting for breakfast. "I have some unpleasant news for everyone," Joe said.

Felicity stood off to the side, unnoticed, to watch their faces as Joe spoke.

"Last night while we slept, someone...someone seems to have come into the camp and opened the spigot to our water tank. It's basically empty." When he paused, everyone knew more was coming. "And someone opened the lids to our coolers. Most of the food is still fine, but it looks like someone planned to cause us some mischief."

Mischief, Felicity thought, that's a quaint word; more like vandalism. She wanted to take over, ask questions, but she knew that would be out of line. And she didn't want her teammates to begin thinking of her as a detective on a case. Not yet.

Joe continued. "Did any of you get up during the night? Did any of you hear someone moving around?"

Only Ben said yes.

"I heard someone moving around deep into the night, Joe. He was very quiet. I didn't look to see who it was. Figured he was relieving himself and would want privacy."

"Why do you say *he*?" Felicity asked.

Ben nodded. "Good question." He smiled. "Just my hunch, I'm afraid."

"Well, did anyone get up to pee during the night?" Joe asked.

"I did," Russell said. Doug turned to look at him, surprised. Clearly, he had not heard Russell leave their tent.

"Hear or see anyone?" Joe asked.

"No."

"Listen," Joe said. "We still have work to do today before we head back to Bluff this afternoon. We'll eat breakfast, then go back to our projects. Unless some of you are worried and want to head back to town now. That's okay too."

No one spoke up for a moment.

"I'm good," Russell said, nodding slowly.

"Me too," Robby said.

"Gotta keep our eye on the prize," Ruth Ann said.

The others agreed or nodded. No one wanted to head back early. At least, none admitted it.

"Super." Joe tried to put a smile in his voice. "Doug and Ben are already scheduled to stay in camp while the rest of us go back to Bluff and lounge around." He took a deep breath. "We'll pick up where we left off yesterday like nothing happened, okay?" A few nodded and offered weak smiles. A few raised their eyebrows.

Felicity noticed Megan just shook her head. *She's probably thinking, 'Yeah, nothing to worry about. Right.'* She knew what

Megan had been through the previous May back in Chicago. Megan had seen firsthand when awful things happen when nothing bad is expected.

Joe turned to Russell. "Russell, please go back to Bluff after breakfast and bring back about thirty gallons of water. The roundtrip should take you less than two hours. We'll be fine until then."

As breakfast ended, Felicity noticed Ben over by the truck, looking down. She walked over.

"Would you like to see my footprint?" Ben asked. He found a clear spot in the ground and placed his boot firmly down. He looked up at her. "Pretty clear, don't you think?"

She chuckled. "So you're studying them too."

"All animals leave tracks," he said. "Some are easier to identify than others." He squatted, pointed to a particular boot print partially obscured by two others. "I think this is the one you want to study."

"Why do you say that?"

"I don't believe it belongs to anyone in our camp."

"Really?"

"I could be wrong," Ben said, "but I know our team detective will find that out. That is why I want you to see mine as clearly as a raven painted on a white canvas."

She bent down, turned her back to the others in the group, took her phone out, and quickly took a snapshot of Ben's boot print.

"Thank you," she said. "You are very perceptive."

"Perhaps." Ben nodded in recognition. "I am almost old enough to begin seeing things." He looked Felicity in the eyes. "Now, if our own detective will excuse me, I want to search around the edges of our camp to see if this boot print shows itself again. Animals never realize they have left tracks. Even the wily ones do it. Even coyotes. Men are different, men can be more cunning and hide theirs."

"Let me know if you find anything."

***

After breakfast, Robby grew curious too. He had some time before his group would return to their dig, so he headed over to the base of the Comb and began hiking up its steep slope. A hundred feet up, he stopped. He looked south down Butler Wash, shielding his eyes from the intense morning sun. Nothing. He looked north, a mild breeze fluffing his hair. In the distance, maybe a quarter mile away, maybe more, he spotted a single blue tent, an ordinary, small low-slung one like the one he often used, tucked up among a few imposing boulders and sagebrush. Not hidden, exactly, Robby thought, but not in the open either. A white pickup, the kind that were as common as ravens in San Juan County, was parked fifty yards away.

Most likely a couple of ordinary campers, he figured, knowing he'd find lots of campers scattered farther up the wash. He saw no activity at their campsite, even though the sun had been up over an hour. No people, no fire, no smoke.

Maybe they're already out on a hike. Or sleeping in. He planned to sleep in tomorrow, back in his own bed in Blanding. But something didn't feel right, either. *When we come back, I'll bring binoculars. Or just hike down there and check it out. Just a friendly hello.*

He would make it seem natural, expecting a friendly reception from anyone who was camping there. Most campers were friendly, most of the time.

He might have been more wary if he'd known someone at the campsite was watching *him* with binoculars from behind one of the boulders.

Chapter 16

Ben sat quietly. The shimmer of stars against an infinite blackness offered solitude and solace, but Ben ignored the night's invitation to let his mind wander. He was on sentinel duty. His senses were attuned to the surrounding sounds, moonlit shapes and shadows, and the slightest hint of movement.

A meager fire reduced to simmering coals burned in the camp firepit. He had secreted himself in front of scrubby sagebrush in the shadows twenty feet beyond the firelight where he could see anyone moving into the light without himself being seen. He wanted the advantage.

It is simpler to see from darkness into light than from light into darkness. Light can be blinding.

Normal night sounds peppered the stillness as the cooler nocturnal desert awoke. Most creatures, he knew, would be cautious, avoiding the light from the fire. He heard, then spotted, a rodent skittering along. It was a pinyon mouse, its whisker twitching, and it cautiously approached the firepit, found some scrap of food, and hastened away. He listened for the subtler slithering sound of a Western rattlesnake or desert night snake that would want the pinyon mouse for dinner, but none seemed near. At the softest edge of the light, he made out a black-tailed jackrabbit moving on its silent, padded feet. He heard in the distance the loud chirp-like call of a Mexican spotted owl and then, moments later, a coyote off in the distance.

So far, there'd been no sounds or sightings of two-footed mammals.

Doug would relieve him when his watch ended at midnight. They had agreed to stand guard over the camp as the rest of the crew returned to Bluff for a weekend of sleeping in a bed where scorpions and snakes weren't a concern, or at least less likely.

Ben glanced at the position of the stars to estimate the time, smiled, and looked at his watch. He'd guessed about right. Doug would replace him in less than an hour.

Like a good hunter, Ben knew to keep his eyes moving, alert to any movement. From his post away from the fire, he could scan far beyond the illuminated area. He scanned the great sandstone incline of Comb Ridge that tilted away from their campsite, its pockmarked stone barely visible in the light of a half-moon.

Was that something moving up there?

Yes. He glimpsed a slight, silent movement of some kind of animal. At least forty yards away, a shape, mostly only a shadow, moved along the lower part of the Comb and slipped behind the large boulders where the team had set up their makeshift shower. There was no further movement, but a shadow, ambiguous in shape, extended from behind one of the boulders, as if something or someone had stopped to peer out without being seen. With the moon high in the sky, the shadow was shallow, not elongated, and it was hard to determine what cast it. A deer, maybe. A bear, unlikely. A coyote, too small. A person, a definite possibility.

The shadow disappeared. Whatever caused it had retreated behind the boulder.

Ben rose soundlessly, hoping whatever made the shadow could not see him. In silence, he stepped deeper into the darkness beyond the firepit light and began a wide, circuitous route toward the large boulders. He stopped every few steps to search, to listen. Nothing. He held a flashlight next to his leg, turned off. Shining it would only make it harder for him to see anything—any movement—beyond its limited beam.

Soon he was only ten yards from the break in the boulders where he'd seen the shadow. He didn't know what to expect but prepared for the worst.

He was about to take his next step, when a voice, a man's voice, came from deeper in the shadows.

"Stop right there, Indian, unless you want to die."

Ben stopped but said nothing.

The voice sounded familiar but muffled somehow to make it less distinguishable. He suspected it was a white man, but it could be the voice of a Native who had lived among the Anglos.

"What am I going to do with you now?" the man in the shadows said.

"You can go back to where you came from," Ben said calmly. "And I can go back to where I came from."

"That would defeat my purpose."

Over many years, Ben had learned that men with purpose were to be treated with care. He kept his voice calm.

"What *is* your purpose?" he asked.

"I don't suppose it will matter if I tell you," the stranger said. "To stop the dig."

"Why?" Ben asked.

"The land has a better use. A higher purpose."

"And what is that?"

"None of your business," the stranger replied.

"Ahh, it is business then," Ben said. "Business is seldom my business. But always it is with the white man."

"It is with men of all skin colors."

Ben could detect a hint of impatience in the man's voice, and he knew his situation was not good. The stranger was undoubtedly armed, most likely with a rifle. He could bolt suddenly and run, zigzagging like a fleeing buck to make himself a harder target to hit in the dark. But Ben was no longer a fleet-footed young buck, and he had no way of knowing if the stranger was a good shot, a good hunter. He could suddenly beam his flashlight into the stranger's eyes, but he would only get one chance, and he didn't know exactly where the man was standing. How the encounter would go was hard to predict. Ben wished he had brought along the pouch the medicine woman Johona had given him, but it was in his tent. It might have brought him good luck; maybe it still would.

He decided to engage the man first.

"Who decides what you call a higher purpose?" Ben asked.

"Tonight, me. But I'm not the only one."

"I see," Ben said.

"Do you?" The stranger laughed, but it, too, was muffled.

"Do I know you?" Ben asked.

There was no answer. Just stillness as each second evaporated into the dark.

"No, not really," the reply finally came.

Suddenly, the man stepped partially from the depths of the shadows, and Ben could make out a man about his own height, in blue jeans and a dark sweatshirt. He held a rifle at his waist, pointed at him. The stranger wore a baseball cap and a dark blue bandana across his face, bandit style.

He is mostly invisible, unrecognizable, Ben thought. Except for the eyes.

The eyes were Ben's target. With smooth, fast movements, he flicked on the powerful flashlight and raised it quickly to waist height but away from his body so that a shot fired at the light might miss him. The beam hit the stranger in the eyes, and he reflexively raised his hand to deflect the glaring light.

Ben got one brief look at the stranger's mostly hidden face, then bolted toward the darkness. Within moments, one shot rang out.

At the speed of sound, some 760 miles-per-hour, the blast from the gun echoed down the hardened sandstone wall of the Comb and all the way across to the far side of Butler Wash. Every creature—those that slithered and those that walked—instinctively froze, if only for an instant. It was not a sound of nature. Some stayed frozen in place, some went into hiding. The man who'd made the sound took off at a loping run, hidden by the dark.

The bullet he'd fired traveled over twice the speed of sound before finding its target.

Chapter 17

The room was dark and still. Outside, the same. Whatever animals moved about at this late hour did so with stealth to avoid predators or because they were predators. Joe glanced over at the green-lit numbers on the digital clock beside his bed. In five minutes, it would be midnight, the planned time Felicity would leave the warmth of the bed they had vigorously and excitedly shared. They'd fallen blissfully asleep after their pent-up passion had run its course, but now Joe was wide awake.

He liked the calm after sex. His heart pulsed steady and slow. His mind wandered freely as he soaked up the smells and sounds and warmth of the woman beside him that he, what, maybe loved? Yes, loved, he thought, although it was a thought he struggled with.

He pondered the day's events and what the next day might bring.

After the discovery of the water supply vandalism, the team had eaten breakfast and returned to their excavations. A somberness settled among them. Talk was limited to the basics needed to get the work done, and even Doug's boisterous laughter went into hibernation. The heat seemed more oppressive than ever. When a pickup or camper rumbled by on the main dirt road, work stopped and heads popped up to watch and listen. Joe's included. And Felicity's.

Lunch was quiet. Rather than discuss the excavation, Joe addressed the issue that was on everyone's mind. He'd heard of vandalism at archaeological digs before, he told them, but it had never happened on one of his. He told his team he would report the incident to the sheriff's office when they headed back into Bluff, once he was in cell phone range. He'd done so. He'd made one other thing clear—anyone could quit at any time if they felt in danger. No one spoke up, either then, or privately, later.

Joe's thoughts swirled, a dust storm of confusion. He shifted his weight in bed and took a deep breath.

"You awake, too?" Felicity said quietly, her back to Joe.

"Have you been lying there awake?"

She rolled over to face him. "For a while. I thought you were awake but didn't want to disturb you."

Enough light snuck into the room from a parking lot lamp that Joe could see into Felicity's eyes. Eyes he liked looking into.

"You'd be good at hide and seek."

She smiled. "I always won. Comes in handy as a cop." Her tone shifted. "What's on your mind?"

"Today. The vandalism. The sense of violation the whole team felt. And..." he paused.

"The fear?" Felicity asked.

"Yeah, fear seemed to seep under everyone's skin."

"Fear flows from the unknown, Joe. We don't have any answers or clues yet to who or why someone emptied our water tank. Fear fills the void."

"I don't want to stop the dig because of some idiot's vandalism."

"No one wants to quit, Joe. Everyone was a bit jumpy today, but we kept digging. No one complained."

The day's digging had turned up promising discoveries. Ruth Ann and Russell had discovered two more large bones, likely from a mammoth, at the lowest level of their excavation. They had also uncovered dark clay potsherds at about the same depth that were likely from a much more recent archaeological period by thousands of years. Which could mean the bones had been found by indigenous visitors and added to their own trash pile, much later. If so, the midden was only hundreds of years old, not ten thousand-plus. Felicity and Doug's team, proceeding slowly, had uncovered small pieces of wood that could be from the foundation of a Clovis era structure, but they, too, could be from a much more recent period. Carbon dating was needed to accurately determine their age.

So far, the team hadn't uncovered larger pieces of wood nor any stones indicating a structure had existed thousands of years ago. But Joe was optimistic.

Felicity looked at the clock. "I've got to leave soon." She'd insisted on returning to her own room at midnight.

"Did you notice any odd behavior from the team today?" Joe asked. "Do you think anyone on the team sabotaged the water supply?" He knew she'd been observing everyone closely.

"I haven't seen anything suspicious."

"Nothing? I thought maybe your cop instincts picked up some odd vibes."

Felicity smiled. "The longer I work as a cop, the less I trust my instincts. Sometimes my instincts are spot on. But if I'm wrong, bad shit can happen. If it happens on my watch, there's hell to pay. I put more faith in *not* trusting anything, or, for that matter, anybody. Just look for evidence. I question *my own* assumptions. And everyone else's."

"You trusted your instincts when I was a suspect," Joe said.

A sly smile graced her face. "Only to a point, Joe. Only to a point. Mostly I just observe. Sometimes the solution is obvious, fitting a pattern that's been repeated by humans over and over. Like a spouse who murders the other spouse for money. Or because of cheating."

"That's a cheery thought," Joe said.

"No, just predictable a lot of the time." She ran her fingers through his unruly hair. "Sometimes the mystery is only solved by uncovering a jumbled mess of facts and studying them from different angles. Usually, they eventually fall into place."

She sat up, pulling a sheet up to her chest. Joe knew she wasn't suddenly shy; she expected him to keep his attention focused elsewhere. For now.

"Remember when we went bowling with Megan?" she said. "You showed us how to hit a strike, not by hitting the head pin dead on, but by hitting it at an angle from the side, preferably with spin on the ball. The action of the ball at an angle redistributed the power and knocked down all the other pins."

Joe remembered. They'd had fun. Both women had gone on to nail a few strikes.

"Solving a crime is a lot like that. You seldom find the answer head on. And the facts never line up neatly like ten pins. You've got to come at the evidence at an angle and eventually a pattern, a solution, emerges."

"And all the pins fall down?"

"Sometimes."

"Did your study of shoe treads turn up anything?"

"Yes and no. The suspicious boot print didn't seem to match anyone in our group."

"I'm glad everyone in our group is in the clear."

"I didn't say that. Someone could have switched boots," Felicity said. "But I do think it's a male boot print."

"You sure?"

"Of course not!" She shook her head, held up her arms in exasperation. "Haven't you been listening?"

"Right now, I'm just looking." Felicity had let the sheet drop and her body called to him like a beacon, her bareness softly illuminated in the faint light. He reached over and wrapped his arms around her, pulled her to the bed, and clasped her tightly against his own warm skin.

"Men." She kissed his neck, then started to push him away gently.

He got the message. Time for her to go. He kissed her one last time. And then his cell phone rang.

I hope it's not Megan checking up on me.

It wasn't Megan. It was Doug. With news no one wants to deliver or hear.

"Ben's been shot."

Chapter 18

"What happened?" Joe asked, stunned, when Doug delivered the news.

"I'll tell you everything as soon as I can. I called 9-1-1 when I got into cell range. An ambulance is going to meet me at the Bluff fire station. I'm less than ten minutes away. They're taking Ben to the hospital in Blanding."

"Blanding's almost thirty minutes from here," Joe said.

Doug's voice dropped. "Yeah, I know. But they won't be going the speed limit." There was a brief pause. "It's bad, Joe. I don't know if he'll make it." Another painful pause. "He's unconscious. He's lost a lot of blood."

"But he's still breathing, right?"

"Yes. I tried to stanch the bleeding...but I don't know, Joe."

"I'll meet you at the fire station." Joe punched off the call. He was standing. And naked. Blood rushed to his head. He looked at his pile of clothes, then turned to Felicity. He could tell she'd grasped the essence of the call.

"Ben's been shot. The nearest hospital is in Blanding."

He tossed his cell phone onto the bed and raced to pull on his clothes. Felicity followed his lead.

"What about Megan?" Felicity asked.

"Can you stay here with her?"

"No. I'm coming." She walked over to him, looked him in the eyes. "This is my thing, Joe. I want to size up the situation and, if possible, ask Ben what happened."

"He's unconscious. He may not make it."

"I figured that. But if he comes around, even briefly, I want to be there."

Joe stopped his frantic dressing for a moment to study Felicity's face. Yes, he realized, I've seen that detective face of hers before. She's good at her job. And he wanted to know who would shoot Ben. And why. *Why!*

"He's my friend," Joe said, his energy momentarily deflated. "My good friend."

But there was no time to cry.

As Joe pounded on Megan's motel room door for what seemed like an eternity, he dreaded what he had to tell her. She needed to come with him to Blanding. If Ben wasn't going to make it, she would want to say goodbye.

"What is it?" she called from behind the door, although she could see him through the peephole.

"Ben's been hurt," Joe shouted.

"Ben?" Megan cried out as she threw open the door.

"Yes. They're taking him to the hospital in Blanding."

"Oh god! What happened?"

"I don't know yet," Joe said, a partial truth.

He gave her a quick hug, then looked into her eyes. "Put on your clothes as fast as you can. We're going to follow the ambulance."

He wanted to hold her tightly, let her cry, let her sob uncontrollably, she'd been through so much the past few years, but there wasn't time. *Later.*

The EMT crew had already transferred Ben's body from Doug's pickup to the ambulance and were shutting the back door when Joe, Felicity, and Megan arrived at the Bluff fire station.

"Let me see him, please," Joe said as he rushed over.

"He's unconscious," the EMT said, but he opened the door wider.

Joe and Felicity peered inside. Ben's motionless body lay partially upright on a stretcher, an IV giving him much-needed blood. They had already stripped off his shirt and applied a large dressing over the wound, held in place by tape that went around his body. The EMT was carefully applying hand pressure to the bandage, but blood still seeped around its edges.

"No more time," the EMT said.

Joe dodged the door as the EMT shut it quickly.

"I'll follow in my pickup," Doug said as Joe turned from the ambulance. His shirt and pants were splattered with Ben's blood. In the bright glow of the halogen lamps outside the fire station, he looked like the victim of a shooting himself.

"Ride with us," Joe said. "I want to know what happened?"

Doug protested that he would make a mess of Joe's truck, but Joe insisted. The ambulance turned on its siren and started to pull out. "Let's go everyone!"

Soon they were racing up Highway 191 following closely behind the ambulance, with no way of knowing how Ben was holding up.

"Tell us what you know," Joe said to Doug as they sped along.

He'd considered waiting until he could ask without Megan having to hear the details, but he knew his headstrong daughter would eventually find everything out one way or another.

"I don't really know much," Doug began. "It happened a little before eleven-thirty. I was sleeping lightly because my sentry shift started at midnight when I heard a gunshot. I figured it was some yahoo illegally hunting deer at night, but it was close enough to our camp to get my attention. I crawled out of my sleeping bag and looked around. The moonlight was pretty bright, but I didn't see anything. I called out to Ben, but he didn't reply. I hurried over to the campfire, but he wasn't there. That's when I started to worry."

He paused, shook his head. "Joe, I didn't know where to look, so I headed in the direction I thought the gunshot came from. But it was mostly a wild guess. I raced around in the dark for at least five minutes before I heard a low moan that led me to Ben's body." He paused. "That's a long time to bleed."

"That's not your fault," Megan said. She had been sitting quietly, listening, and her comment suspended the conversation for a moment.

Doug continued. "His body was up by the big boulders beyond our showers. He was lying on his side, a puddle of blood under his chest. I could tell he was hurt bad, but he was still alive, breathing shallowly."

"Did you see anyone? Or hear anything?" Felicity asked bluntly.

"No, nothing."

"Did it sound like a rifle or a pistol shot?" she asked.

"I don't know. If I had to guess, I'd say a rifle."

"What'd you do then?" Joe asked. He didn't want Doug to feel like he was being interrogated by Felicity.

"I picked Ben up and carried him as gently and quickly as I could to my truck and laid him on my back bench seat. I propped his head up and grabbed a clean t-shirt that was in my truck and applied some pressure to the wound. But that wasn't going to be enough, I could tell. He needed help fast. I tried to dodge the potholes getting out of Butler Wash, but I needed to drive as fast as I could. He moaned at every bump we hit. It was awful." He paused. "I've never dealt with anything like that before."

His voice became more matter of fact. "I called 9-1-1 about ten miles out of town where I knew cellphone coverage kicked in. Then I called you."

There was a moment of silence, but Doug had one more thing to add, and he seemed to direct his words to Felicity.

"After I hung up, I called Sheriff Cooper. He's sort of a friend of mine. He's going to meet us at the hospital. It's been a long time since there's been a homicide in this county."

At the word *homicide*, Megan started to sob.

Chapter 19

The Blanding Hospital emergency room staff were waiting when the ambulance pulled up. The back door of the ambulance flung open, and Ben was rushed into the emergency room area, with Joe, Felicity, Doug, and Megan following. The medical staff sped Ben to one of the two operating rooms. The EMTs had called in Ben's condition, and a surgeon from the larger hospital in Monticello was on his way.

The handful of anxious people sitting in the waiting room stared at Doug and his bloody clothes. Whispers followed. Soon, one of the staff came over and quietly asked him to leave so he wouldn't disturb the other hospital patrons.

"Why?" Doug protested. "Don't you see blood in here?"

The staffer tried to calm him. "Yes, more than we like. It upsets our visitors."

"Yeah. Well, it upsets me too."

Doug frowned but headed out the revolving doors. Joe, Felicity, and Megan followed. As they exited, Sheriff Martin "Bull" Cooper was waiting for them.

"Hi Bull," Doug said.

***

Sheriff Cooper got a good look at Doug's blood-drenched pants and shirt. "Maybe tonight it should be *Sheriff* Cooper, Doug. You look like either a victim or perpetrator of something I need to know about."

He offered his hand to Doug. They shook, as men do who know each other. But it hadn't been too many years since he'd put handcuffs on Doug when he was a younger and more careless man. Cooper let it go. *Past is past.*

Aroused from sleep, he hadn't bothered to put on a uniform, but he wore his badge on the denim shirt he'd thrown on along with well-worn jeans. The badge usually worked well enough on its own.

It didn't hurt, Cooper knew, that he stood six-feet-two-inches tall. And while his football playing days were in the distant past, he was, as he said to himself, still "sturdily built." As usual, he wore his cowboy hat over his full head of dark hair notched with gray at the temples. He'd been elected sheriff seven years prior, and had, over the ensuing years, found ways to keep most constituents happy, including the business folks who funded his campaigns.

Doug introduced Joe, Megan, and Felicity. When Doug didn't introduce the woman as Joe's wife, Cooper still figured the good-looking woman was more than a casual acquaintance.

"We've met before," Joe said, as he shook the sheriff's hand.

"We have?" Cooper took a moment to look closer at the professor.

"About three years ago. At the tribal rally supporting creation of the Bears Ears Monument."

"You were there?"

"Yes, I was a speaker."

Cooper made the connection and the memory clicked. "Oh, sure. I remember. You're the archaeologist from up North. From Chicago, right?"

"That's me."

The sheriff's reelection platform had included opposition to the national monument designation. He and three deputies had been at the rally for crowd control, but they'd done little to stop hecklers who were determined to interrupt the speeches of those who supported the monument.

When the professor didn't make any further comments about that day, Cooper figured he wanted to stay on his good side under the current circumstances. *That's good, he knows when to keep his trap shut.*

"I appreciate you coming out tonight instead of sending a deputy," Joe said. "I'm sure we got you out of bed."

Cooper nodded. "Comes with the job."

The five of them went over to a covered area, a single light shining down coldly on a steel picnic table. A bevy of noisy moths swirled around the lone light as if drugged. Cooper sat on one of the benches and stretched his back. Doug took the seat opposite him. The professor and the woman named Felicity stood to the side, and the daughter stayed further back, partially in the shadows.

"What happened?" Cooper kept a neutral, steady voice. It was a question he'd asked hundreds of times. He didn't take out a notebook.

Doug told the details of the events at the dig site in Butler Wash—the sound of a gunshot, his search for Ben, finding the body, rushing him to Bluff in his pickup.

"Did you see anyone or hear anything suspicious?" Cooper asked.

"No. Nothing after the gunshot."

"No sound of a car or truck fleeing the scene?"

"No. Nothing, I said."

"Yeah, I heard ya the first time," Cooper said. "Just jogging your memory, that's all."

There was silence for a moment. Cooper considered his options. Should he keep asking questions or wait until tomorrow?

Felicity broke the silence. "Doug, did *you* have a gun?"

Doug turned to look at Felicity. His brow firmed, his voice colder. "It was locked in my truck."

"Pistol or rifle?" Felicity asked.

Cooper interrupted. "Excuse me, pretty lady, but I'm asking the questions here." But "pretty lady" was *not* what he wanted to call the nosy woman.

"She's a cop, Bull," Doug said. "A detective with the Chicago PD."

Sheriff Cooper raised his eyebrows. "Not exactly your beat around here, detective." He made the word *detective* sound like a title a notch below *garbage collector*. He didn't have anyone on his force classified as a detective. Didn't need one. "We don't have a shooting a minute in these parts. And we're not used to pretty cop ladies looking over our shoulders."

Felicity didn't respond immediately. Then she smiled. Her voice was calmer. "My apologies, Sheriff Cooper. Just an old habit kicking in."

The sheriff smiled back. "Understood," he said. He figured the cop lady did, in fact, understand. *My jurisdiction. I'll ask for your input when I want it. Like never.*

The interview continued.

"I'll need you to make an official statement tomorrow, Doug," the sheriff said.

"Sure." It was clear Doug didn't relish making the drive to Monticello, the county seat, to repeat everything all over again.

Joe filled in the details of the previous day that led to Ben's sentry duty. When he described how the water tank had been emptied and the coolers left open, Cooper nodded his head a few times but didn't exhibit much immediate concern. He still didn't take notes.

"I'll need your statement tomorrow too," he said. "But how about first thing in the morning, say eight o'clock, a couple of deputies and I meet you and Doug out at the crime scene to take a good look." It was not a question.

He noticed the cop lady raise her eyebrows, and Bull Cooper figured she was surprised he wasn't going to secure the scene right damn now. He saw her purse her lips, but she didn't say a word. He didn't show outwardly the smile he felt inside. *That's good. She knows who's in charge.*

***

When Joe called Robert Hightower's cell phone, it rolled over to voicemail, and Joe decided to call Susan, Robert's wife, rather than leave a message. She answered on the fourth ring, groggily.

"Joe? Is something wrong? Has something happened to Megan?"

"No, Megan's fine. Is Robert with you? Put me on speaker and I'll tell you both."

"Robert's not here. He went fishing with some guy I don't know up in the Henry Mountains two days ago. He won't be back until tomorrow afternoon. Is everything okay?"

"I'm here in Blanding. At the hospital. Someone shot a member of my group. Ben Hatathli."

"Oh my god! I know Ben. Who did it?"

"We don't know. It happened at the dig site."

"Is everyone else okay?"

"Yes. Most of the team were staying in Bluff for the weekend."

"Joe, this is all so awful. How can I help?"

Joe looked over at his exhausted, frightened daughter. And at Felicity, wide awake and alert.

"I was wondering if Megan, Felicity, and I can stay at your place tonight. I've got to meet the sheriff tomorrow at our Butler Wash camp, then head back to Monticello. I don't want to go back to Bluff tonight." He lowered his voice so the others wouldn't hear. "I'd like to leave Megan with you for a few days, if that's all right."

"Of course, Joe! Come on over. Megan can stay as long as you want. I'll wake Robby and we'll get everything ready."

***

It was almost three a.m. when Robby opened the front door to greet Joe, Felicity, and Megan. He'd been waiting.

"You look tired," he said to Megan softly. She was the last to approach the front porch where he held the door open for her.

"I am. But I can't get Ben out of my head."

He wanted to sound supportive. "Tell me about it in the morning at breakfast. After you get some sleep."

"Okay. But can I at least get a hug?"

Robby's face flushed, and he hoped Megan wouldn't notice it in the soft light of the porch. "Of course." He reached his arms around her, and Megan placed her head on his chest. He gave a nice squeeze but didn't hold it long for fear of upsetting his boss, her dad.

"Thanks," Megan said.

Her smile was genuine, Robby thought, and for a moment her cheeks appeared to flush too.

Her calm didn't last long. She made it abundantly clear she was not pleased with the proposed sleeping arrangements. She and Felicity were supposed to share a bed in the guest room, and Joe would sleep on the leather sofa in the great room, which Susan had already prepared with sheets, pillow, and a quilted blanket.

"I'll sleep on the floor instead," she said.

"That's okay, if you want to," Joe replied. Clearly, he was not in the mood for the rebellious version of his daughter.

"She can have my bed," Robby offered.

Robby's mom put her arm around Megan's shoulder. "Come lie on my bed for a while, sweetheart, and we'll get all this settled shortly." Megan seemed to give in, too tired to put up further resistance. She led Megan down the hallway to the master bedroom. A few minutes later, she returned to the great room.

"Megan took her shoes off, crawled under the blanket on top of the sheets, and fell asleep right away."

Robby smiled reflexively. *Maybe that hug helped.*

He offered to show Felicity to the guest room, but his mom said she'd do that.

"You go on to bed too, Robby," she said, nodding her head calmly. "I'll need your help fixing breakfast in the morning."

"We can all help," Felicity said.

His mom smiled. "Thank you, but no thanks. You've had a hard night. Call me old fashioned, but you're our guests."

Robby chuckled. "The next thing she'll say is 'end of discussion.'"

A smile emerged on his mom's face. "That's right, end of discussion. What time do you want breakfast?"

"About six-thirty," Joe said. It came out part statement, part begging.

"Sounds good," she said. "If you're not awake by six-fifteen, I'll bang a few pots." She fluffed Joe's pillow. "That's in about three hours. Don't waste them staying awake."

She turned to Felicity. "Come on. I'll show you to your room. And since you'll probably pester me anyway, you can make the coffee tomorrow. We'll all need it."

Robby followed them down the hallway toward his room. But when his mom and Felicity entered the guest room, he snuck down to his parents' room to check on Megan. Like his mom said, she seemed to be sleeping soundly. She didn't move. Her face looked serene even. And she was beautiful.

Chapter 20

When 6:30 rolled around, Felicity had already showered and dressed in the same clothes she'd worn the night before. She helped with the coffee, but Susan Hightower wasn't in a talkative mood as she prepared breakfast. *Why?* Felicity detected fear. *Probably for Robby. But maybe it's something else.*

She decided to probe, gently. "Susan," she said softly. "Do you know if there's bad blood between Ben and anyone? Have there been other shootings of the local Natives?"

"Oh god, no." Susan stopped whipping up the eggs to be scrambled. "A shooting is rare around here." She rubbed her hand over her eyes. "There's a lot of anger about the proposed Bears Ears Monument. But I never thought it would come to murder."

"It's not murder yet, Susan."

"I know. I know. But just the other day Robert said he worried the monument controversy could boil over into violence. Which surprised me." She put down the bowl and looked at Felicity. "He said he sensed people getting really riled up."

"And you're worried about Robby now, I'm guessing."

"Oh lord, yes! He's just a kid but he thinks he's got manhood all figured out. I'm sure he wants to avenge Ben's shooting. Wants to play cop. Like you."

Felicity smiled, her voice calm. "Not sure I'm much of a role model. I was kind of hoping to get away from shootings down here."

A slight smile rose from Susan's lips. "Yeah. I'll bet. Some vacation, right?"

"Listen, Susan. Joe and I won't let Robby get in any danger. He'll be home with you and Megan."

"Do you think Joe will shut down the dig for the summer?"

"Yeah. It will be hard, but he'll realize it's the right thing to do under the circumstances."

On this last point, Felicity was wrong.

Joe and Felicity left the Hightower home around 7:30 and stopped by the hospital in Blanding to check on Ben's status. It was touch-and-go, they were told, but his vital signs were better. The hospital refused to reveal more details because neither was family. The sheriff had given explicit instructions that everything needed to go through him first.

Felicity looked over at Joe as they headed south toward Bluff and Comb Ridge in his pickup. His forehead was deeply creased, his eyes narrowed. They'd ridden in silence for ten minutes.

"Want to talk about it?" she asked.

"No...Yes. I just have a lot to think about. But.." His voice trailed off. He shook his head.

"But?"

"I can't think straight."

"Maybe you should slow down your thoughts a bit."

"Sure," he snarled. "How do I do that?" He turned to Felicity, his eyes bloodshot.

A car in the oncoming lane blew its horn loudly. He had drifted over the yellow line and jerked the steering wheel to course-correct his truck.

"Whoa, Joe! Take it easy!" She didn't want to end her Utah stay in a grave. "I'm your partner here. I know what it's like to feel frustrated and pissed in a situation like this. But it does shit for good most of the time."

"I don't need a lecture, detective," Joe said. His lips pursed even more.

There was silence for a few breaths. She looked down the road. Up ahead, it curved and disappeared behind a rust-red bluff that rose a thousand feet up, a scattering of sagebrush and stunted junipers on its slopes. They were still many miles from Comb Ridge and the excavation site.

"Okay, no lecture," she said. "What's on your mind?"

She watched Joe nod a few times, his eyes narrowing.

"I want to find Ben's shooter..." He paused. "And continue the dig."

Silence. Felicity considered her response.

"Okay, Joe. I promise no lecture. So I'll just make a statement."

He glanced her way, then quickly looked back to the road.

"Don't count on the dig continuing," she said softly but firmly. "It's a crime scene. A big one. The sheriff is going to shut it down."

"That's bullshit!"

"Maybe so. But that's what I'd do."

***

As Joe drove up to their excavation site, he spotted Sheriff Cooper sitting at one of their tables. Two deputies were stringing crime scene tape around the team's campsite. He pulled alongside Doug's pickup. He slammed the driver-side door as he exited. He hated to think his dig site was now just a crime scene. *It's wrong!*

"Good day, Professor," Cooper said as they approached. His wide smile was fixed across his face, its authenticity questionable.

"Not so much," Joe said.

"Good day, detective." The sheriff nodded in Felicity's direction, and she nodded back.

"Good morning, sheriff."

"Looks like you've been busy already," Joe said.

"Yep. Couldn't sleep. How was your night? Restful, I hope."

Yeah, restful. Cooper seemed like he wanted to jerk Joe's chain. He considered his reply. "Fine, thank you. We stayed at the Hightower's home." He knew Robert's paper hadn't endorsed Cooper for the last election.

"Good family," Cooper said. "Especially Robert's dad. Rest his soul."

An hour passed as Joe, Felicity, and Doug accompanied the sheriff and his deputies on a slow tour of the campsite, then the spot where the water tanks had been emptied out—although the footprints left two days earlier had mostly been obscured by blown sand—and finally the location where the shooting occurred near the large boulders at the foot of Comb Ridge.

Dried blood where Ben had fallen had soaked into the sand, becoming a deeper shade of purplish-red. Unlike dark red discoloration in sandstone caused by minerals and lichens, the splatter pattern could only be blood. A trail of bloody spots at irregular intervals went down toward the location where Doug's pickup had been parked.

"You can see my footprints where I bent down to pick Ben up," Doug said. They were standing about five feet from the location where Doug found the body.

"Yes, Doug. We see them footprints." The sheriff sounded as if he was humoring an eight-year-old. The deputies quietly grinned. "We'll get some samples of those boot prints and your boot prints. Like they do in the big city police departments. I suspect they'll match just fine."

Felicity nodded. "They do."

Sheriff Cooper turned to Felicity. "You sound damn sure of yourself."

"I am." She held her cell phone out. "They match this photo of Doug's boot print I took yesterday."

Joe noticed Doug's eyebrows rise. Doug hadn't known Felicity recorded the footprints of everyone on the team. The sheriff just smiled.

"Good detective work, detective," he said. He added his signature smile. "Maybe you should consider a job down here in our dusty little slice of Eden."

Felicity nodded and offered a small smile. "I just might."

Over the course of the next hour, Felicity, Joe, and Doug answered a few questions but mostly observed as the sheriff's team took a slew of photographs, placed blood samples in evidence bags, and looked for other clues that might reveal what happened the previous night. To everyone's chagrin—especially Doug's—no other discernable footprints were found within twenty yards of where Ben's body had lain. And no shell casing was located. It could still be lost in the sand, as it seemed improbable the perpetrator found it in the pitch dark before fleeing the scene, or, if a single-shot bolt-action rifle was fired, the cartridge would have stayed in the chamber.

Joe could feel his frustration rising. He scanned the ground in all directions. He looked up the Comb. He searched the horizon for...what? He saw nothing. No useful clues anywhere. *Why had someone been willing to shoot Ben? Why had someone sabotaged their water and food?*

Sheriff Cooper requested that everyone return to the main camp. He put one foot up on the bench of the camp table, noisily unwrapped a piece of gum, and placed it in his mouth. He smiled.

"Juicy Fruit don't even come close to a good chaw," he said, "but the ladies in San Juan County don't care for a tobacco-chewing sheriff like the good ole days." He spit for effect.

"Sadly, you might live longer too," Doug said.

Cooper chuckled. "That I might, that I might." He paused. "Listen, folks. My guys are going to be out here a few more hours checking things out. I'm headed back to the office. Professor, I'd like to see you and Doug there this afternoon for your official statements." He paused. "I'm sure you'd like to get those done."

"Mind if I stay out here with your guys?" Felicity asked.

"Yep. Sure do mind." The sheriff smiled again. "You're out of your jurisdiction here, detective..."

"Daniels," Felicity said.

"Detective Daniels. But I'll try to keep you informed." He turned to Joe. "In the meantime, professor, you may want to send your team home. I think your dig is done for the summer. I'm shutting it down."

"What?!" Joe said. "You can't do that."

"Actually, I not only can. I just did."

Joe turned to Felicity, looking for help. She offered a weak smile, her palms opened at her side.

"Of course, he can, Joe," she said calmly. "He's the law."

Joe turned and stomped away. Nothing was going right.

Chapter 21

Romance was clearly not in the air when Joe opened the door to his room at the Red Rock Inn. He thrust out his arm indicating Felicity should enter first. He watched the back of her head as he followed her into the room. He flicked on the light.

The drive back from Comb Ridge had been a silent one, the grumbling of the Ford's old engine not loud enough to drown out Joe's fierce talking inside his head.

Whose side is she on? The sheriff's? Helen would never have taken sides against me. Never deserted me like that.

But he knew that was bullshit. She likely would have said the same thing. Just not as bluntly.

That damn cop directness!

He looked over at Felicity standing in the motel room, facing him. She was calm, but not smiling. She expected him to speak first. He gathered the loose strands of his thoughts, slowed his breath, and tried to unwind the knot in his chest.

"How long do you think the excavation will be closed?" he asked.

"That depends, Joe," Felicity said in an even tone. "Maybe only a few days while they gather evidence. But it could be longer. Even weeks."

"That asshole Cooper seemed to take a lot of pleasure in shutting it down." Joe's brow creased, his heart rate notched up again. "I wanted to punch his face and knock his juicy fruit and a few teeth to the next county."

"If you had, you wouldn't be worrying about the dig. Just jail and bail."

Joe shook his head but didn't say anything. Felicity took three steps and closed the distance between them. She smiled gently.

"What you need more than you realize is a hug," she said. "I'm off duty. Hugs are allowed. Want one?"

Joe's anger simmered but he still smiled. He opened his arms and Felicity stepped inside them. He closed his arms around her and held her tight, as she put her head on his chest. Neither spoke as they breathed in each other's presence.

Felicity pulled away gently. "You need to tell the team."

"Yeah, I know. I think Megan should stay with the Hightowers until we know what's going to happen. She'll want to stay close to Ben in case he gets better. Or if he doesn't."

His anger had subsided. He invited Felicity to sit next to him on the bed. The bed squeaked slightly as both sat, the whirr of the air conditioner the only other sound. He looked down at his feet and shook his head back and forth as if trying to loosen a rock lodged under a boulder.

"What's going on, Felicity?"

"I don't know. But I don't think someone was out to kill Ben. I think Ben interrupted the saboteur from the night before. And it turned ugly."

"Why do you say that?"

"The shooting was some distance away from camp and steps away from large boulders where the shooter was probably hiding. I think Ben had seen something and went to investigate."

Joe frowned. "I should have stayed out there myself after the incident with the water tank."

"What would you have done differently?"

Joe frowned. "I don't know. But I feel responsible." What he mostly felt was *guilt*.

"Joe, beat yourself up if you want," Felicity said. "But you being there instead wouldn't have made any difference. That's not how criminal violence goes down. Shootings don't get stopped by people playing hero."

Joe knew she was right. And hated the truth.

"But who would want to sabotage the excavation enough to shoot someone?"

"That's what I was going to ask you."

Joe called each team member to announce he was shutting down the excavation and didn't know if he could restart it. He called Russell first, who took the news with classic Navajo calm. Joe knew the lack of income would hurt and suggested Russell start looking for work elsewhere. Russell agreed but said he'd be around if the dig restarted. Joe tried to reach Doug, but just got voicemail. *He's probably out of cell range.* He tried to reach Angie and was surprised when the call went to voicemail instantly. He thought she'd still be in Bluff. *Maybe she's gone to stay with her aunt and uncle in Monticello.* He called Ruth Ann. She wasn't surprised by the news and told Joe she had reached out to friends up in Moab. They'd offered to put her up for a while to go rock climbing. *She's not one to be stopped easily.*

When Joe called the Hightower home, Robby answered. Joe told him there was no timeline for how long the site would be closed, and he couldn't keep paying everyone to wait.

"Sure, Professor," Robby said.

"Just Joe, remember."

"Yes sir," Robby said, but Joe could detect a smile in his voice.

But then Robby's tone changed, became serious.

"Joe, I saw something out at the site our last day I haven't told you about. Something I've been thinking about since. I don't know, it could be relevant."

"What was it?"

"A truck."

Joe could tell Robby was troubled by this information. "Hold on, let me put you on speaker so Felicity can hear."

He placed the phone on the edge of the dresser.

"Go ahead, Robby. We're listening."

"The day we discovered our water tank had been sabotaged, I hiked higher up the Comb's rock face to look around. I spotted a white pickup and a small blue tent maybe a quarter mile to the north."

"Did you see anyone?"

"No. Nobody."

"Anything unusual about the truck?" Felicity asked.

"No," Robby said. Joe could detect disappointment in his voice. "It was just a plain white pickup like a thousand around here. It was too far for me to even see what make it was."

"Sure, I understand," Felicity said. "Hold on a minute, okay?"

She picked up the phone, switched it off the speaker setting, and placed her hand over the mike. She looked at Joe. Her eyes narrowed.

"I want to go check out this campsite. I don't give a crap what the sheriff said about this being his investigation. Besides, we won't be at the crime scene."

Joe nodded.

Felicity switched back to the speaker setting. "Listen, Robby. Can you come back to Bluff, then take us out to where you saw this campsite?"

"Sure!" Robby clearly wanted to help. "I can be there in a half hour."

"Good," Felicity said. "Meet us at the café."

Joe interrupted. "I'm supposed to drive up to Monticello and give an official statement at the sheriff's office."

Felicity put her hand over the phone's speaker. "You had a flat."

Joe smiled and took the phone from Felicity. "Robby, please put Megan on the phone. I need to tell her what's up."

Chapter 22

Hot, dry air had settled in like heat rising from a cast iron skillet left on the burner, and Joe and Felicity stood outside the café waiting for Robby in the shade of an old cottonwood on the edge of the dusty parking lot. It was 2 p.m., past the lunch hour peak, and only a few vehicles remained. They'd grabbed a sandwich at the café, not knowing when they'd get another chance to eat.

A vaguely familiar jangling sound approached from the dirt trail that wove through the scrubby shrubs down by the dry creek bed. Before Joe could recall where they'd heard it, the Navajo medicine woman named Johona approached as if expecting to find them there. She wore the same tan dress they'd seen her in earlier that week, but instead of beads around her neck, a large silver bear, embedded with turquoise stones, dangled to the middle of her chest. A crack of a smile showed on her lips, but her brow was deeply furrowed. Maybe it's always like that, Joe thought.

"Ha'át'íí biniyé ta'hdii kóó naniná?" she asked.

Joe didn't respond. He had no clue what she'd said. The old woman nodded.

"Why are you still here?" she said in English. "You haven't followed the wisdom of the Coyote."

"Please don't bother us," Joe said. He did not plan to engage in a conversation with a woman who likely wanted to negotiate another exchange of cash for some mysterious powder.

"Do you have no fear?" she asked.

"Of what?" Felicity intervened. The old woman turned her gaze upon her.

"Of the spirits you disturb where you dig."

Joe was not in the mood for her spirit world digressions, and it was difficult to keep from being rude. "Right now, you're disturbing us." He looked directly into her eyes. "Please move along."

The old woman didn't react, her face imperturbable. "Where is Ben?"

"In the hospital," Joe answered.

Her eyes widened. "The hospital?"

"Yes." Joe felt she should know the truth. "He's been shot. He's in a coma."

The old woman, shocked, took a half step back, the shells around her waist jangling as if they, too, were upset.

"You are lying."

"No," Felicity said. "Ben was shot by someone at our campsite last night."

"Will he...live?"

Joe sensed her genuine concern. He softened his voice. "It's too soon to know."

The old woman lowered her head and nodded slowly, her lips moving as if praying. She reached into her leather bag that hung from her side and removed a small pouch, no larger than a coin purse.

"Take this to Ben. Place it under his back behind his heart." She handed the pouch to Felicity. "I will go to my village, and I will speak to our wisest medicine men, and we will pray for him in the sweat lodge."

Joe expected her to want money, but instead, Johona turned and started to walk away, slowly but deliberately. She seemed to mutter to herself. Joe thought he heard the old woman say, "Ben should not have been shot."

Chapter 23

"That's the spot," Robby said, pointing to a cluster of large boulders at the base of Comb Ridge about a hundred feet off the road, the largest rock the size of a dump truck.

Joe pulled his pickup over to the side of the red dirt road. He, Felicity, and Robby had driven only a short distance past their excavation, where two sheriff's department vehicles remained. But the road had curved and dipped, and from their location, the deputies who were still at the crime scene had not likely seen them.

We don't need them, Felicity thought. And Sheriff Cooper thinks he doesn't need us.

"The pickup and the tent were maybe twenty feet from those two large boulders," Robby said.

Felicity spoke up as the three of them exited Joe's truck. "Okay guys, I know you're itching to go check out where this camper was, but, well, I'm taking over from here on."

Joe smiled. Robby raised his eyebrows.

"We approach the site very slowly, side by side. Watch the ground. If you see footprints, stop immediately and say something. We'll take photos of any footprints, but we don't want to disturb them. This could be an important part of the crime scene. If we screw it up, we don't get second chances."

Felicity wasn't expecting a sudden solution to the shooting, but they might stumble on evidence that mattered. Fortunately, it hadn't rained since the shooting, but the wind, as usual, had blown enough dirt and dust that any footprints might be covered over or indistinguishable.

The three of them approached the spot where Robby remembered seeing the campsite. As they neared it, they stopped when they came upon tire tracks. Felicity took a few photos with her phone, and they kept walking. After a short distance, the tracks overlapped in a mishmash of directions.

"I think this is where he backed up, moving the truck around," Robby suggested. He didn't want to sound overconfident.

"You're probably right," Felicity said. "But why do you think it was a 'he'? Did you see a man?"

"Well, no...but, you know."

Felicity smiled. "I get it. You're probably right. But don't make hasty conclusions."

They went farther, avoiding stepping in the tire tracks.

"This is where the tent was...I think," Robby said.

"I don't see any sign of a firepit," Joe said.

"Or footprints," Robby said.

The absence of footprints intrigued Felicity. She instructed the men to look even more closely at the dirt in front of their steps. "Look for signs someone may have tried to cover their tracks. And let's spread out now to cover more ground."

Covering one's tracks completely would be difficult, she figured, but she wished Ben was there to help, suspecting his long experience in the wilderness would come in handy.

After twenty minutes, they'd found no footprints.

"Over here!" Robby shouted. He was standing near the juncture of two of the larger boulders.

Felicity and Joe carefully made their way over, watching their steps as they went. What Robby had found wasn't going to be much help. The ground had been trampled multiple times, suggesting someone had stood there for a period of time, likely moving around slightly, but the jumble of prints, which appeared to be from boots, made it impossible to see any print distinctly. Felicity took pictures anyway. When she stood back up, she noticed the gap between the two boulders was just wide enough it offered a view toward their camp, although the main camp itself was obscured. *Not a bad reconnaissance location.*

"Let's go look over there," Joe said. He pointed to a spot thirty yards away where a cluster of wild sagebrush and rabbitbrush tucked up against a good-sized boulder. It was over a flat, slickrock rise that would have naturally camouflaged footprints.

"Why there?" Felicity asked.

"It's a natural spot for taking a dump."

Felicity laughed. But she got serious fast when she spotted boot prints after they crossed the flat rock and entered a sandy area.

"You're right." She bent down for a close look. The location was better protected from the wind, and the footprints were sharply defined. "I'm no expert, but I'd guess it's a man's boot, maybe a size eleven or so." She took multiple pictures of both left and right boot prints.

"You two stay here, so we don't add unneeded prints. I'll follow them some more."

She followed the footsteps, walking alongside them a few feet to the side. She noticed a slight difference in the left and right prints, and in the distance between steps. Both indicated the person favored his left leg. Maybe an old injury or a bad hip or knee.

She arrived at the shrubbery enclave. "Holy shit!" she exclaimed.

"What is it?" Joe called out.

"It's shit!" Felicity shook her head. "You were right. This was the latrine." A pile of crap, clearly human crap, lay on the ground tucked in a gap between the shrubs. *He didn't even bury it!*

Felicity had long ago learned that most criminals, even smart ones, make fundamental mistakes. Details missed. The obvious overlooked. Like taking a crap. Human feces offered an opportunity for DNA matching if other evidence pointed to a suspect, or if the criminal had previously been sampled.

They snapped pictures of the location and the feces, then stored a portion of the feces in a plastic sandwich bag in the absence of the kind of paper bag normally used for evidence from which DNA would be extracted. Eventually, the sheriff would want a sample,

Felicity knew, and would want to, or at least *should* want to, gather his own evidence from the site.

They continued to carefully scan the ground in a widening arc, looking for shell casings, scraps of paper, food remains, basically anything. But they failed to find any other evidence. Whoever had camped there had made a concerted effort at "leave no trace" camping. With one additional exception. Near the tire tracks, they found a single bold boot print as if it was the final step the person had taken as he got into a truck and drove away. Lacking the material needed to make a mold of the shoeprint, Felicity took pictures.

They never found evidence of a second person's presence.

Chapter 24

Megan was mad at everyone.

She was mad at the sheriff for stopping the dig. She was mad at her dad for not stopping the sheriff. And she was mad she'd been left at the Hightower home while Robby went back to the dig site to play detective along with her dad and that other detective in his life, Felicity.

But underneath it all, she was sad and scared. Ben's condition was stable, but he wasn't out of danger. He could die. He could die for no good reason, she thought. *Like mom.* She resisted thinking Ben might die, tried to will him well, but it wasn't working. Ben might die. And she'd had enough death in her life.

She didn't want the dig to end. Didn't want to go back to Hyde Park. Not yet. She was enjoying her flirtations with Robby. He was so different. *He likes me for just me.* It was nice to feel wanted like that, to be with someone who wants me to be happy. Someone who wasn't full of himself. Who knew stuff. Who could do stuff. Who is comfortable even in the wilderness!

But her dad...He seemed so much harder to love these days. He wasn't mean exactly, but he didn't understand her. Her needs. Sure, he was the boss on the dig, and he had to set rules, but still... *Why did he have to bring Felicity on the trip? It could have been just the two of us. Almost like the past.*

But she also knew the intruder might have shot her dad if he'd been the one who stayed in the camp.

Everything is just so complicated.

Megan brooded as she sipped her coffee in the Hightower's great room. It was after four in the afternoon. Susan Hightower was out grocery shopping because she had more mouths to feed, she'd said. Robby's dad was expected back from his wilderness outing soon. She had no idea when her dad, Felicity, and Robby would return;

they were out of cell phone range. Her phone definitely didn't feel like a companion, and she certainly didn't feel like texting some Hyde Park "friend." Nobody there would understand.

Her restlessness found a solution—go to the hospital and check on Ben.

Her phone was good for one thing. A map to the hospital. According to her phone, the hospital was over a mile away, about a thirty-minute walk. The route would take her through a few back streets, then through the main shopping area, across the highway that cut through town, and out to the hospital on the other side. Compared to how she got around Hyde Park's dizzying urban streets, it would be simple. No problem.

Chapter 25

Megan's walk to the hospital initially took her through the kind of mixed housing common among rural towns in the West. Some homes were of recent construction, with brick or stucco facades and shingle roofs, attached two-car garages, and prefab windows tightly closed up that hinted at central air-conditioning—houses the homeowners believed reflected a degree of success. But on the same block stood older homes, likely built before 1950, with wood exteriors or refitted with aluminum siding, an expansive front porch, and more sharply pitched roofs. Most of them were air-conditioned too, with one or two window units purring loudly in the afternoon heat.

With her phone as a guide, Megan zigzagged through several blocks of homes that abruptly gave way to commercial and industrial buildings. She passed Lou's Body Shop, then Blanding Muffler, and Blue Mountain Used Cars. As she went by Marvin's Auto Repair, two men looked up from the bay where they were replacing a tire on an old Buick. The thumping and hiss of their air compressor continued, but they stopped working and watched her as she passed. Megan waved. One of them waved back and grinned. But it was a grin that made her uncomfortable.

She unconsciously hastened her steps. And got lost.

She stopped to study her phone in the shade of a tall cottonwood just outside the perimeter fence of Blanding Self-Storage. She was off course, but she could still see where she needed to go to reach the hospital. She was about to get started when the security gate to the self-storage facility clanked open, and a dirty white pickup entered slowly, two men inside. There was writing on the side of the truck.

I recognize that truck.

It was the truck driven by the rednecks they'd confronted outside the Rainbow Bridge Café the first day!

She slipped behind the tree and watched cautiously. The truck backed up to a full-sized storage unit, the kind with a roll-up door, and two men got out.

Yes, it's them! That's the one Doug called Rider or Riley or something like that.

He seemed to be the ringleader then, and here he was, at the storage facility.

Why?

She watched and tried to hear them.

"Okay, Frankie, let's move fast," the ringleader said.

The one named Frankie yanked off the truck bed tie-downs and pulled the blue plastic tarp up toward the cab. Because she was looking at the side of the truck, Megan couldn't see what was in it. Frankie jumped into the truck bed, retrieved a plain cardboard box, and carried it to the back of the truck.

"Hey Riley." He lifted an old basket out of the box to admire it. "This here basket is gonna fetch a pretty penny."

"Yeah, you idiot. Why don't you just show it off to the whole world. Put it back in the damn box!"

Frankie did so, and Riley took the box into the storage shed, returning to the truck as Frankie brought another box back to where he waited.

"These ain't the best pots we've ever found," Frankie said. "Hell, only one little one is still in one piece."

"Yeah, but there's buyers for all this shit. Never fails."

The two men stayed busy, focused on squirreling away their loot and neither looked in Megan's direction. From her hiding place, she couldn't really see into the storage unit. And she really wanted to.

If I can sneak over to that next tree while they're not looking, I can see right into it.

She was, she briefly acknowledged, spying on criminals who might not want to be seen, who, in fact, clearly would not want to be seen, and who could get in trouble if seen.

When the Riley guy carried another box into the dark of the storage unit and the Frankie dude bent over to retrieve another box, she made a dash for the next tree and quickly ducked behind it. She stood sideways to the tree to maximize her coverage, but she needed to pivot to the side to peek around the edge of the tree. She did so slowly.

Holy shit! It's loaded with shelving and boxes of stuff!

Megan could see a few large pots on shelves, but mostly she saw boxes, their contents tucked out of sight.

I know they contain artifacts!

She stood on her tiptoes, straining to see better, and kept looking. That was her mistake.

"Hey kid!" It was the one called Riley. He had returned from the dark of the unit. "What are you doing over there?"

Megan ducked behind the tree and remained quiet.

"I said what are you doing over there?"

Frankie spoke up. "Do you think she saw anything?"

"Shut up, Frankie." He lowered his voice. "I'm going to walk over to the fence and get a closer look."

But his words had carried well enough for Megan to hear them.

What now?

The answer was obvious: Run!

Megan burst from behind the tree and started running back in the direction from which she'd come.

"Stop kid! I said stop!" The Riley guy was running toward the fence, but there was no way he was going to get over it. He stopped. "Damn!"

The last words Megan heard as she ran away jolted her heart and sped up her legs.

"Frankie! Shut the storage unit door now! We're going after her in the truck." She could have sworn the one called Riley said, "I think I recognize her."

Megan was a fast runner—had even won a few ribbons—and her legs carried her quickly through the commercial area she'd walked through only minutes earlier. As she ran past Marvin's Auto Shop, she glanced over to the open bay hoping the men wouldn't see her again. But a sprinting teenage girl—the same one who had waved earlier—naturally caught their eyes, and they stood and watched, tools in their hands, as she raced by. This time she didn't wave.

Oh god! I hope they don't tell the guys in the truck they saw me run by!

She decided to alter her course, find someplace to duck into and hide. But where?

She looked over her shoulder. No truck yet. At the next corner, she looked down the adjoining street and spotted a possible solution. A coin-op laundry. From inside she could see the corner and watch and wait to see if the white pickup passed by. It would have a bathroom to hide in if needed.

She slowed her pace as she approached the building so she didn't draw attention. She didn't have laundry with her and decided, if anyone asked, she was waiting on her mother.

Mother, she thought, with no special meaning, just an intense longing.

Megan stood back from the window and waited. Ten minutes went by. Nothing. But a few minutes later, a white truck—*the* white truck—proceeded slowly down the street. She moved further back into the far corner of the laundry, near the bathroom entrance. *I'll be trapped if they come in!*

The truck, although it slowed, kept moving along.

Twenty long minutes later, she exited the laundromat and, using her phone for a guide, cautiously made her way back to the Hightower home, alert for places to hide or escape routes to run. As she came to the corner of the street on which the Hightower home stood on the edge of town, she spotted a dirty white pickup parked in the driveway.

Oh shit! Is that the truck?

She couldn't tell from where she stood, so she decided to cut over into the open field that ran behind the last row of houses. She made her way along the edge of the homes, partially hidden by sagebrush, until she came to the small barn at the bottom of the Hightower's property. She slipped through the fence and waited. When the Hightower's horse snorted, she jumped, startled, but avoided making any noise. She made her way along the edge of their property to get a look at the truck in the driveway.

It's not theirs! It must mean Robert is back home.

She stepped onto the back deck, quietly opened the door, and silently stepped into the Hightower's great room. Back home in Hyde Park, she'd always been good at moving through their house, or leaving it, without her dad noticing. So she didn't call out, wanting to compose herself first and decide if she was going to tell Robert what she'd seen or wait for her dad. Wait, she decided.

She sat down on the large leather sofa and took in a deep breath, feeling safe for the first time in...like, what, an hour? That's when she heard Robert's voice—but only his—and realized he was on his phone in his office. And he sounded angry. Certainly tense.

She wasn't trying to listen, but she could swear she heard him say, "Okay commissioner, I get it. But I don't think the professor is going to present any trouble." There was a pause. "I just don't, that's why!"

Is he talking about dad?

It didn't make sense—*nothing does!*—but it seemed like a good idea to *not* be sitting on the sofa when Robert's call ended. Without a sound, she rose from the sofa, made her way stealthily out to the deck, and waited. She counted to sixty and opened the door as noisily as she could.

"Hello!" she called out. "It's me, Megan. Anyone home?"

A few moments later, Robert Hightower exited his study, his smile bathed in a look of deep concern.

"Megan!" he said. "I'm so sorry for everything that happened while I was gone." He took a step toward her. "Let me give you a hug."

Chapter 26

They were just entering Bluff on the return trip from Butler Wash when Joe's cell phone buzzed. He didn't recognize the number, a local one. Better answer it.

"This is Joe Cutler."

He listened intently, then turned his head briefly toward Felicity sitting next to him. He covered the phone's speaker. "It's about Ben."

Felicity's eyes widened and her lips tightened. "Is he dead?" she asked softly.

Joe shook his head. "No."

He listened intently, nodding as the caller spoke. After a few moments, Joe asked, "When?" Another pause followed as he absorbed the news. "Okay...okay. We'll be there in about thirty minutes."

The call ended and Joe stared ahead, gathering his thoughts.

"They're going to airlift Ben to a Level 1 trauma center in Salt Lake City. The local docs admit they're out of their league. Said Ben needs the best specialists in the state if he's going to have a chance."

"When?" Robby asked from the back seat.

"In about an hour. We're heading to the hospital now." Joe took a slow, deep breath. "I need to see my friend...you know, just in case..."

Felicity spoke up. "You've got to stop and pick up Megan first."

"You're right," Joe said.

The moment Joe and Felicity pulled into the driveway of the Hightower home, with Robby following in his truck, Megan flung open the front door and sprinted toward them. Robert Hightower was close behind, striding up to the driver's side window of Joe's truck. With a quick tilt of his head, he signaled for Joe to step out.

"She's really distraught," Robert said when Joe stepped out. "Even before Megan got your call, she was fidgeting constantly. Couldn't sit for more than a few minutes."

Joe glanced at Megan over by Robby's truck. She was holding Robby's hand.

"This is really hard on her," Joe said. "I don't know if she should even go to the hospital."

"Well, it's clear she has strong feelings for Ben." Robert put a hand on Joe's shoulder. "But I'd hate for her to again go through what happened after her mom died."

Joe frowned, remembering his daughter's challenging behaviors back then. Her depression. Her anxiety. And running away. *There aren't easy answers.*

"Are you coming to the hospital?" Joe asked.

"No. I'd just be in the way. We'll have dinner ready when you return."

***

Felicity had seen more than her share of intensive care patients in Chicago, where a bullet far too often left someone hanging on by a thread or, more realistically, by a maze of tubes and wires. Too often, she was there to see if the patient could or even wanted to tell her who had pulled the trigger. And too often, the patient never regained the ability to speak, eventually leaving the room without a heartbeat. She didn't know what to expect for Ben. *He's certainly not young; that never helps.*

"How's he doing?" Joe asked the attending physician, as he, Felicity, and Megan stood outside Ben's intensive care room. They'd gotten permission to see him briefly before his ambulance ride to the airport.

"Not good. His vital signs have been going in the wrong direction today. He needs surgery as soon as possible. They'll operate in Salt Lake as soon as he arrives."

Megan reflexively put her hand to her mouth, her eyes wide. "He's going to make it, right?"

"He'll get the best care in the whole state," the doctor replied.

Joe put his arm around Megan's shoulder. "He'll make it, sweetheart."

"Talk to him if you want," the doctor said. He nodded, smiled gently. "Maybe he'll hear you. About an hour ago, the nurses said the nurse station monitor showed his heart rate bumped up a bit. They swear they heard him say something in Navajo as they walked toward his room. But when they got there, he was unconscious."

"Really?" Felicity asked. She'd heard of similar incidents in Chicago. Sometimes they were a kind of last gasp before the patient died.

"We've been keeping him in a coma," the doctor said. "I think they heard someone else." He looked at his watch. "You've got five minutes."

Felicity looked at Megan. She knew Megan was tougher than most girls her age, but she knew seeing Ben would be hard. She softened her voice.

"Megan, I know how strong you are. You're actually pretty amazing." Megan looked down. "But seeing Ben is going to be hard. Really hard. They've put him in a coma, you know, and, well, he's going to look like he's barely alive." She paused, took a breath. "You going to be okay?"

Megan nodded, a weak smile on her lips. "I don't know." She nodded again. "But I need to tell him something."

"Let's go in," Joe said.

Like intensive care rooms everywhere, the furnishings were sparse, the walls bare, and the window closed. A roller coaster of wires and tubes wound their way around the sterile, stainless-steel bed, and monitors blipped noiselessly. The side rails of the bed were raised, but Ben's motionless body clearly didn't pose a risk of tumbling out.

Joe noticed Felicity studying the monitors closely, then glanced over at his daughter who was standing back but intently watching Ben. Felicity was right. *No tears. She is strong.*

"May I get closer and tell him something?" Megan asked.

"Of course, sweetheart."

Megan approached the bed from the far side, looked down at her Navajo friend, bent low to within inches of his ear, and, with a slight mischievousness in her smile, whispered. She finished quickly and, without considering whether it was okay or not, kissed his serene-looking brow.

Joe smiled, tears welling in his eyes. He studied Ben's calm visage, wanting to tell him so much. That he was sorry his friend had been given the first night watch. That he would never forgive himself. That he would avenge his shooting. That he had never realized how much his Navajo friend meant to him...and...is it too late?

"Your time hasn't come, friend," Joe said aloud. Loud enough to startle everyone in the room, including himself. It appeared to startle Ben too.

Ben's head swayed slightly from side to side, his right hand twitching. His eyes fluttered open, mere slits but clearly awake. His pupils drifted to the side, landing on Megan, and for a brief moment, a faint smile touched his chapped lips. He turned his eyes slowly toward Joe on the other side of the bed, shifted his head a half-inch, and motioned slowly but deliberately with one finger. His lips moved but he was too weak to speak above a whisper.

Joe approached closely and bent his ear to Ben's lips. He listened closely, nodded, then reflexively frowned. Ben continued to speak softly.

Joe nodded again and his chest swelled with a deep breath.

"Who shot you?"

Ben shook his head as best he could. He didn't know or wasn't going to answer. He closed his eyes. He was done talking. His face lapsed back into serenity. He was still breathing, but unconscious again.

***

Felicity had to step aside when the attending physician, two nurses, and a med tech entered. It was time to move the patient to the waiting ambulance that would take him to the air transport. At the nurse station, they'd noticed a slight increase in Ben's heart rate, but they were incredulous—and appeared to doubt—the veracity of Joe's claim Ben had awakened briefly.

"Did he say anything?" the physician asked.

"Not really," Joe replied.

The obvious lie puzzled Felicity, but she didn't speak up.

Megan spoke to the doctor. "You were right. I talked to him and he heard me."

"That's nice," he said. But he was busy preparing Ben for the risky medical flight. Felicity had been around enough ER docs to know the doctor wanted Ben to make it to the next hospital alive, that he'd done all he could.

"You need to leave now," one of the nurses said.

"I'd like to say a brief goodbye first," Felicity said.

Quickly, when all eyes were focused on Ben's needs, Felicity smoothly reached into the back pocket of her field pants and removed the small pouch the medicine woman Johona had given her. As she bent over Ben and mouthed "good bye," she slipped the pouch under Ben's back. No one saw her.

A few minutes later, they stood in the entryway as Ben was wheeled out. Megan stepped into the parking lot to watch the ambulance depart.

Felicity couldn't wait any longer. "What did Ben whisper?"

Joe frowned, took a deep breath. "He told me to go home. To forget the excavation. He said it will cost me more than I can imagine to keep digging."

"What could that mean?"

Joe took a deep breath, then shook his head. "I have no idea."

Megan walked back inside, and Joe held out his arms. She let him hug her hard, and she hugged back.

"What did you tell Ben?" he asked her.

She looked up into his face. "I told him I was still waiting to learn about Coyote."

Chapter 27

An SUV plastered with "Sheriff" in large letters pulled up just outside the entrance as Joe, Felicity, and Megan exited the hospital into the hot summer air. Sheriff Bull Cooper stepped out of the vehicle. Not good, Joe figured.

"Again?" Joe said to Felicity but not loud enough for the sheriff to hear.

"Don't irritate him. You didn't show up for your deposition, remember?"

The sheriff approached. His smile didn't hide his distaste for Joe.

"Robert Hightower said I'd find you here. He said your Navajo friend was being airlifted to Salt Lake."

"Yeah, they just left." Joe wasn't going to offer more details voluntarily. The sheriff made him wary.

"Well, I hope he recovers. Did he ever regain consciousness and say anything about the shooting?"

"No," Joe spoke with directness, and Felicity knew not to contradict him. Megan's eyebrows went up, but she stayed silent.

"That's too bad, isn't it?" The sheriff looked Joe in the eye. "Anything else to report?"

"Not..." Joe started to say. But he was interrupted by Felicity.

"Sheriff Cooper. I'm sure it's, well, irregular, but we had a chance to check out a campsite just north of our dig site today, and..."

"And you decided to do it yourself rather than contact us," the sheriff interrupted. "Yeah, I know all about your little excursion. My guys saw you arrive and leave about an hour later. They reported it, and I told them to check it out too." He shook his head, pursed his lips. He looked directly at Felicity. "I feel like pressing charges for disturbing a crime scene. But that isn't going to stick, will it, detective? Because nobody knew it was a crime scene."

"I couldn't say," Felicity replied calmly. She had no interest in getting further on Cooper's bad side.

"We found a whole shitload of footprints, which I suspect are mostly from my guest detectives." Cooper's eyes narrowed. "Made our work a lot damn more difficult."

"Yes sir," Felicity said. But she wasn't gushing with guilt. "We were careful where we stepped. We documented what we found."

"Which was?"

"The same boot print we'd seen in our campsite the day before."

"Yeah, my guys said the same thing."

"Did they make a plaster cast?"

"Is this an interrogation, detective?"

"No, sheriff." Felicity stayed calm. "Let's just call it a suggestion."

The sheriff turned his head slightly to the side, winked partially. "That's a good one. Just a suggestion. Ain't nobody likes an interrogation, do they? They make folks uneasy." He smiled a bit more broadly. "Anything else?"

"We found feces," Felicity said.

The sheriff didn't say anything immediately. It was clear his men hadn't found feces. "I'll send someone out to gather a sample," he said, his voice flat.

"We can give them some idea where to look," Joe said. He wanted to provide relief for Felicity, but she gave him a look that clearly said, *I've got this.*

"We also took a sample," she said. "In case bad weather or something destroyed the evidence."

"But you chose not to stop and tell my guys what you found when you were at the campsite." The sheriff was determined to establish his authority.

"Our mistake," Felicity said quickly. "We wanted to get back to say our goodbyes to Mr. Hatathli."

"I see," the sheriff said.

Felicity suspected he did, that he could see through her paper-thin argument.

"Anything else my men missed?"

Felicity looked him directly in the eye. "Nothing else, sheriff." She was determined to answer him exactly the way she answered her boss. Which sometimes included holding back any assumptions or guesses she had until they could first be explored.

"Good," the sheriff said. He took a deep breath that seemed to refill him with the power of his elected position. "Which brings me to the second reason I came to see our esteemed archaeologist."

He turned his focus on Joe, his mouth ticking up into a slight, wry smile. "Any idea where Angie Young is?"

"No," Joe said. "I tried to call her this morning but didn't reach her."

"Well, her uncle, my good friend Harris Young, called me personally to report she's missing. He said she was expected last night but never showed up. They haven't been able to reach her all day."

"That's not good," Joe said.

"No, professor, it's not. His wife wanted to file a missing person report. I asked if her parents back in Illinois wanted to file the report, but she hadn't spoken to them yet. I promised I'd alert my guys to be on the lookout for her." He chuckled. "When they saw her picture, they were happy to comply. A few of them knew her when she lived here."

He looked down briefly, and when he looked up, his smile stretched a little farther. "The Youngs blame you, professor."

"Me?"

"Can't say I blame them, professor." He wanted to make sure his words hit home. "A man shot. A beautiful woman missing. Harris Young said he was going to call the county commission and the BLM and, I quote, make damn sure that idiot's permit to dig is pulled. Professor, if I have anything to do about it, you're never going to dig even a hole to shit in in this county ever again."

Joe didn't have a reply.

***

Megan couldn't stay quieter any longer. "I know where looters have hidden stolen artifacts!" she blurted out. She had been holding it in, growing more restless during her dad's and Felicity's exchange with the sheriff. But as he turned to leave, she couldn't keep it in any longer. It was now or, what, never?

All eyes turned to stare. A deep furrow crossed her dad's forehead. *Does he doubt me?*

"What are you talking about?" her dad asked.

She raced through her description, not wanting to hear more questions until she was done.

"I was walking to the hospital earlier today to see Ben, and I went by one of those storage places. And that's where I saw two men loading artifacts out of a truck into a storage unit. And it was already full of other boxes that I know had even more artifacts. And they were bragging about what they had they could sell, describing a basket they'd just stolen as 'really great shit.' I was hiding behind a tree, but when I got closer to see inside the storage unit, they saw me and..."

"They saw you?" Joe interrupted.

"Yeah, they saw me. And the one called Riley started walking over to the fence, and..."

"Riley Smith?" the sheriff interrupted.

"I don't know his last name, but he was the same guy who got in our faces at the café our first day here, and..."

"The one that grabbed Ruth Ann's arm?" Felicity asked.

"Yeah, that idiot, but..."

"Whoa, little lady, who is this Ruth Ann person? And you're saying Riley Smith grabbed her arm last week?"

And that's when Megan wrapper her arms around her body and hugged herself. And started to sob. *It's just all too much!*

Joe took three steps toward her, and she looked into his eyes. *They were...what? Concerned?* He put his arms around her shoulder, bent down, and kissed the top of her head.

"It's going to be all right," he said. "We're all just stunned." He looked into her eyes. "Just slow down and tell us the whole story."

She finished describing how she ran away, how she hid at the laundromat, and how she snuck back into the Hightower home through the back because she saw a white truck parked on their street. When she finished, Sheriff Cooper radioed one of his deputies to meet them at the storage facility so Megan could identify which unit she'd seen being used.

Ten minutes later, they converged on Blanding Self-Storage, and were admitted inside the fenced area by Jim, the manager.

"I think it's that one," Megan said, pointing out the one she was almost certain had to be it.

"Get me your lock cutters," the sheriff told the manager.

"You'll need a warrant," Felicity said bluntly. "Or the evidence won't be admissible in court."

The sheriff turned toward Felicity. "I thought we had a nice little agreement that you were out of your jurisdiction down here?"

"I am," Felicity answered. "But you're about to ruin your chances of winning a case." She paused, narrowed her eyes. "But I suspect you know that."

Sheriff Cooper didn't immediately respond.

"You know, sheriff," Jim, the manager said. "That's what Howard Finley, he's the owner, told me back when I started. He said, and I quote, 'our tenants got a right to privacy. Don't go opening their units without a warrant.'"

For a moment no one spoke.

Finally, the sheriff smiled. "Maybe you're right, detective." He nodded. "What's the hurry? I'll get a warrant to search it and get the records on who rented it. Probably can't get a warrant today. But we'll be back tomorrow and see if this unit is loaded with old artifacts like this little lady says." His eyes narrowed. "That good enough for you, detective?"

Felicity just nodded as Joe and Megan looked on, keeping their thoughts to themselves.

***

When Sheriff Cooper and his deputy departed, Joe turned to Felicity, shook his head, and smiled.

"I thought you said not to irritate him?"

"I changed my mind," Felicity said. "I don't trust him."

"I don't either," Megan said. "You do believe me, don't you, dad?"

Joe squeezed his daughter around the shoulders again. "Of course."

"You're damn right we do!" Felicity said. "What do you say we help put the looters in prison?"

"Yes!" Megan said. She wanted to give Felicity a high five but settled on a big smile.

Joe was not expecting Felicity's next comment.

"Where can I buy a gun?"

Chapter 28

The mood was somber at the Hightower home as dinner approached. Joe was on the back porch staring toward the distant Bears Ears peaks, Robert was down at his small barn tinkering, and Robby and Megan were off who knows where. Felicity cooked alongside Susan Hightower in the kitchen, helping prepare a large bowl of mashed potatoes, smashing chunks of butter and warmed milk into the steaming potatoes, as Susan pulled an aromatic pot roast out of the oven. Soon everything would be ready for what should be a delightful meal, but no one was in a delighted mood. Even Susan. She had been mostly silent as they cooked together, her movements jerky, deep breaths exiting her lips instead of words.

"You, okay?" Felicity asked.

"Yes, yes." She took another deep breath. "It's just so much. So..." Her words drifted off.

Felicity waited, didn't reply.

"So confusing," Susan said, the last air in her lungs escaping. She seemed to fight back tears.

"You mean what happened to Ben?"

"Yes, yes, and everything else. I just don't understand."

"What is it? Can I help?"

"No." Susan looked down at the floor. "It's just so confusing."

"What is?"

Susan didn't answer. She just shook her head, her brow furrowed. She tried to sound cheerful.

"Tell you what. Just let me finish up dinner, okay? I love your company in the kitchen, but I need some time to myself." She lifted the lid of the heavy pot holding the roast. Steam and amazing aromas flooded out. "You go outside with Joe, and I'll call everybody in in a few minutes."

"Sure," Felicity said. "But holler if you need a hand, okay?"

Felicity walked through the Hightowers' great room toward the exit to the porch. The ancient artifacts throughout the room seemed merely decorative now and somehow less appealing than when she first saw them. Yes, they were fascinating and beautiful, but they'd lost some of the aura she'd felt then. She'd spent a sun-scorching week digging in red clay for other ancient artifacts. There, anything they found would have been lost to time if it weren't for their team's nosey digging. In the desert, even a small potsherd gave off an aura of authenticity, of meaning, whereas the ones displayed here were like polished silver, removed and refined from the earth that had held them. And a gentle soul of a man had been shot—for some reason—because of their digging. Susan was right. *Confusing. A puzzle to solve.*

Robert approached the porch from the small barn as Felicity stepped outside. Joe stood to greet her.

"Dinner in a few minutes," she said. "It'll be good."

"Susan's a great cook," Robert said. "Thanks for helping."

"My pleasure," Felicity looked at Joe, then turned back to Robert. "I need a favor."

"Sure," Robert said. "What is it?"

"I want you to sell me a gun."

Robert's eyes widened. "A gun?"

"Yes. A handgun. I'm not picky. You have one, right?"

Robert looked at Joe, who remained quiet, his lips tight.

"Sure. I have a couple." He put on a weak smile. "Why don't I just lend one to you?"

"No thanks," Felicity said. "I'd rather take ownership. Bill of sale and everything."

Felicity and Joe had argued about her plan to purchase a gun when they returned from the hospital. He'd lost the argument. Joe wanted the sheriff's department to handle both investigations—Ben's shooting and Megan's close call with the looters. When Felicity asked, "do you really think the sheriff's team is more competent than me?" he didn't have a good answer. She reminded him he would likely be dead if she and her partner hadn't been armed back in Chicago. She didn't need to remind him that she'd taken a bullet to her chest, saved by her Kevlar vest, during his rescue. But she knew that hadn't convinced him she needed a gun. It didn't matter, she needed one now.

"Dinner's ready!" Susan said as she opened the porch door. "Where's Megan and Robby?"

"They were down at the barn a while ago," Robert said. He turned to Felicity and smiled. "Let's talk after dinner."

"Thanks," Felicity said. She looked over at Susan, who was frowning, her lips tight, her eyes tired.

"I'm going to try calling Angie again," Joe said. "I'll be right in."

Felicity and Robert headed inside, and Megan and Robby came up from the barn. At first, the two had been holding hands, but Megan, seeing the adults, let Robby's hand go as they walked up. She made eye contact with Joe, added a perfunctory smile, but didn't say anything as she entered the house.

Joe looked to the West. The sun was still high and wouldn't drop behind the Bears Ears buttes for another two hours, but the shadows were lengthening, the day ending.

Not a good day either.

Joe dialed Angie's number for the fifth time. It rang then rolled over to voice mail. "The mailbox you are calling is full and cannot accept your message." Joe wasn't surprised. Lots of people were trying to find her. He'd already left three messages.

He tried calling Doug again. Same result. But when voice mail clicked over, he left a simple, direct message. "Doug, it's Joe. Call me when you get this message regardless of the time. It's important." He wondered if Doug and Angie had gotten together and tried to bury the hatchet—maybe in each other's skull.

The mood at the dinner table hovered between forced good cheer and an ill-defined dread like a dark cloud that might deliver needed rain or deadly lightning bolts. Megan appeared tense and hardly touched her food. "I'm fine," she'd snapped back when Joe asked if she felt okay, but she clearly was not okay. The ordeal with the artifact thieves had undoubtedly rattled her. Felicity praised Susan's cooking repeatedly, but Susan's "thank-yous" lacked enthusiasm. Robert tried to play the good host, asking questions about the excavation results, trying to cheer up his old friend. But even when Joe reported the successes of their first week, his mind shifted to the blunt message from the sheriff—he would never dig in the county again. His potential groundbreaking discovery would remain buried. And Felicity had seemed to support the sheriff.

Why did Cooper take such personal pleasure in shutting me down?

Chapter 29

Trained by his dad to move quietly while hunting, Robby instinctively moved silently through their darkened home in his moccasins. Restless, unable to sleep, he'd pulled on sweats over his briefs and slipped his arms into a chamois shirt that hung behind his bedroom door. He wanted to sit on the back porch and think about the events of the past two days, especially their discovery at the campsite near the dig. *Who had been there? Why had they left, and why had they seemed to cover their tracks?*

Despite his stealth, as he walked onto the porch, he was surprised when a voice softly said, "Hi, Robby."

It was Megan. She was seated on the outdoor settee that faced West. Stars filled the sky. It was almost midnight.

"You couldn't sleep, either?"

"Something like that," Megan said.

He could barely make out Megan's face in the weak light. Her hair was pulled back in a ponytail, and her eyes were mere shadows under her brow. She appeared to be wearing a flannel shirt for pajamas. He couldn't see what was below her waist because she was wrapped in a wool blanket.

"Are you going to just stand there?" Megan said.

Robby smiled. "Is that an invitation?"

"Something like that."

The settee on the covered porch had a padded seat. His parents often sat there during sunsets enjoying a glass of beer or wine. Sometimes they sat silently, sometimes they held hands, sometimes they conversed intensely. Robby often sprawled across the settee while reading or doing homework. But he'd never sat there with a girl before.

Megan smiled when he sat down. She didn't move closer to him, but she shifted her body so that she faced him. She was just as pretty in the dark as when he first saw her in the airport. Prettier, maybe.

"You've had a rough day," Robby said. He was thinking about her close encounter with the artifact thieves. *I wish I'd been there to help.*

"I don't want to talk about it."

"Are you sure?"

"Yes." Megan's tone didn't allow for disagreement.

"Everything's going to be okay." He wanted to exude confidence.

"Are you sure?"

"Yes," he said boldly. He wanted to reach over and put his arm around her. But he stopped himself.

Megan smiled. Her eyes softened. She took a deep breath.

"I hope you're right," she said.

Without thinking, Robby put his hand on hers. She didn't move. In fact, she smiled more.

"You know," she said. "I didn't really want to come on this dig. I didn't want to leave Chicago."

Robby laughed. "Really? When you landed at the airport, you seemed really excited to be here in the desert."

Megan chuckled. "Okay, smart guy. Don't make fun of me. I was spitting mad and you know it."

"And how do you feel now?" Robby looked into Megan's eyes.

"Truthfully?"

"Yeah."

"I'm scared, Robby. And worried about Ben. And...and my dad." She took a deep breath and grabbed Robby's hand with both of hers. "But I...I'm glad to be here with you." She lowered her eyes.

"I'm glad you're here." Robby reached over with his other hand and placed it on her shoulder, worried she would pull away. Instead, she looked up and smiled sweetly.

They looked at each other for a few very long seconds. Then Robby leaned in and Megan closed her eyes. He kissed her softly but didn't immediately withdraw. Megan kissed him back. They pulled apart for a moment and looked into each other's eyes, wide and dilated. They stopped holding hands, and Robby pulled Megan toward him. She leaned in willingly, her arms entwining themselves around his neck. He kissed her again, harder. She kissed back, matching him.

"Oh, Robby," Megan said, but nothing more. They kissed again. She pulled her head back briefly, looked him in the eyes, then nestled her head against his chest. He held her tighter and felt her breasts moving against his chest. A moment later, she lifted her head, looked him in the eyes hungrily, and kissed him deeply.

Her passion surprised him. But he kissed her back, his breath getting shorter, his heart racing, his body tensing, his self-control slipping. *What does she want?*

He got his answer when Megan leaned back and pulled Robby toward her as she lowered her body on the settee. She kept kissing him as his body pressed against hers fully. He stopped to look down at her. Her ponytail tumbled off the side of the settee. The blanket fell partially away, and her breasts rose against her soft flannel top. Her slender neck invited kissing. He didn't want to stop.

Her eyes never left his as she ran her hand through his hair at the back of his neck, causing a reflexive shiver. He kissed her again, and without thinking, his hand slid up the side of her taut body. He could feel her body respond to being touched. *But what did it mean?* Moments later, Megan placed her free hand on his, squeezed it, and slowly guided it to her breast. Robby's mind raced but without any formed thoughts. He squeezed gently.

"I like that," she whispered in his ear.

Robby didn't answer. He looked down at her hungrily, his hand still on her breast. He didn't want to stop. *She is so beautiful!*

And then another thought broke through. *She's fifteen.*

He took a deep breath and lifted his hand away from her chest. He saw her frown.

"What's the matter?" she said.

"Nothing." He tried to smile.

Megan didn't smile back. "Don't you like me?"

"Yes, of course. I think about you all day long. But..."

"But what?" She pulled her hand away from behind his head and straightened her shirt.

"You're fifteen," he said through a tight smile.

He saw fire blaze in her eyes, watched her nostrils flare.

"You think I'm just a kid, right?"

"No. But..." Robby started to sit up.

"So you're the big grown up. And I'm just some punk kid who has a crush on you, right?" Megan sat up and shifted toward her side of the settee.

"No. I didn't say that!"

"You don't have to. I get the message." Her tone was cold and biting.

"Megan..."

"What?" she said curtly.

"I'm sorry."

"No kidding!" Megan practically leaped out of the settee and snugged her top down. "Good night!" She turned and walked quickly toward the back door of the house. She didn't look back.

Robby watched her go but didn't call out. Nothing he could say would help. He wished she would come back but knew she wouldn't.

Everything happened so fast.

As Megan entered the house, shutting the door noisily behind her, he put his hand on the settee where she'd lain. It was still warm. The heat she'd left behind radiated up his arm, and he could recall the feeling of her slender body underneath her pajamas and his delight in her kiss.

She really is beautiful.

***

Joe heard the backdoor of the Hightower home shut and glanced at the clock on the bedside table. It was 12:32. He figured someone was struggling to sleep, like he was, and had gone outside. It might be Megan, he realized, and he frowned.

He thought Megan was safe from the artifact thieves, but he wouldn't be comfortable until they were behind bars. He believed his daughter's story, but they couldn't corroborate it until the storage unit was opened after Sheriff Cooper got a warrant.

He shifted his weight in the bed, nudged his pillow reflexively, and tried to resettle his head.

"You awake?" a female voice asked.

It was Felicity, lying perfectly still beside him.

"Do you ever sleep?" Joe asked.

"About as much as you, I figure."

Joe had decided not to continue the pretense of Felicity sleeping in the guest room while he slept on the sofa. He wanted her next to him. And he knew Megan wasn't naïve. Fortunately, she hadn't made any snarky comments when she became aware of their sleeping arrangement.

"Still thinking about Ben's shooting?" Felicity asked.

"Yes." Joe turned toward Felicity. "And Cooper shutting down my excavation."

"He didn't have much choice, Joe." Felicity's voice was calm, matter-of-fact.

"He didn't have to take such glee in it."

Felicity took a deep breath and sat up in bed.

"Joe, just let it go. At least for now."

"That's easier for you to say."

"Yeah, it is. But the site's a crime scene. A major crime scene."

"They already have all the evidence from the scene. Why shut it down?"

"Because they don't have a suspect yet. They may need to go out again searching for clues."

"Like the clues we gave them that they missed."

"Yeah, like those." Felicity looked directly into Joe's eyes. "Cooper doesn't like you, but you need to stay on his good side. Maybe we can continue to explore the case on our own, but Cooper is driving the real deal."

"Jeezus, Felicity. Whose side are you on?"

"Whichever one solves the crime."

"What about the dig?"

"Joe, the dig will be fine. Eventually. That stuff has been buried for ten thousand years. It isn't going anywhere if you can't excavate it this season. You can come back next year."

Joe's brow furrowed. "Now I see how much you really value it." He breathed hard, his nostrils flaring. "It's nothing more than a pastime to you. A hobby."

"I didn't say that, Joe. I know it's important to you."

"Yeah, to *me*. What about you?"

"Listen, Joe. *You're* important to me." Felicity's eyes opened wider. "But don't confuse the importance of the living, which for now includes Ben—I hope—with a long-buried ancient civilization."

"That's not fair," Joe said.

"Are you sure?"

"Don't patronize me, Felicity. I'm not in the mood for that shit."

"I'm not patronizing you," Felicity said, her tone confident, unintimidated. "Just trying to stay clear headed."

Joe knew she was right, but that didn't quell his feeling she was unsupportive, like a betrayal.

"Helen would be in my corner," he said and instantly regretted it.

"Really, Joe?" Felicity nodded her head repeatedly, her lips pursed. "You think she would have tolerated your bullshit about the importance of the excavation while your old friend is fighting for his life? Is that what you expect from a life partner?"

Joe had never heard her say "life partner" before—he'd never said it either—and the words' impact were immediate.

He gritted his teeth, then spoke. "I'm sorry, Felicity. I am." He took another breath. "Will you forgive me?"

Felicity looked at him but didn't reach out to comfort him.

"Sure," she said. "Now I'm going to try to get back to sleep. You should too. Tomorrow may bring something positive." She offered a faint smile. "Good night."

Felicity turned her back to Joe, punched her pillow, and tried to settle her head. She wasn't going to offer more comforting.

She's mad. And I'm mad. Just great.

Joe lowered his head to his pillow, hoping to find a way back to sleep.

Chapter 30

Megan figured it was the Hightower's air conditioner clicking on that awakened her. The alarm on the side table read 5:04. Early. But Megan was fully awake.

In the year before her mother's death, Megan had become a fitful sleeper, awakening easily and listening for sounds of discomfort from the extra bedroom her mom stayed in. Mom's recovery room, Megan had insisted on calling it more stubbornness than optimism. She learned to slip quietly from her room to go and sit outside her mother's door, listening, just being there, wishing. In the end, her wishes and her prayers proved fruitless, but she didn't regret a minute of lost sleep.

Fully awake, getting back to sleep would be difficult. As usual. Megan thought about her midnight rendezvous with Robby. The memory both thrilled her and angered her. She'd never felt so connected to a boy before, and he'd abruptly ended it, *Why? Because he thought I was a kid? Like everyone else. Just great.*

She slipped out of bed, put on her jeans underneath the plaid shirt she'd worn to bed, and slid into her walking shoes without tying them. Quietly, she stepped into the hallway and moved silently toward the great room. The room was mostly dark, a hint of light creeping in from a streetlight out front. Soon, the sun would begin to brighten the sky, but to the West where Megan looked a deep blackness filled the windows.

She moved softly toward the kitchen, intent on making coffee without disturbing anyone else, and turned on the small light over the stove. Having helped make coffee previously, she knew where everything was located and quietly made a pot, filled a large mug, turned the light off, wrapped herself in an Afghan off the couch, and retreated to the back porch. She sat in the dark, her mind racing yet somehow stuck in place.

She'd only been there ten minutes, when a light flickered on inside the house. A bright glow momentarily lit up Robert Hightower's office but was reduced to a mere slit of light under the door as it closed. She hadn't seen who entered the room.

Did they see me?

She tucked down in the porch chair, peering cautiously around the cushion to get a glimpse of anyone leaving the room. Fifteen minutes passed. Finally, the door of the office opened, but just as quickly, whoever was there turned off the light. Megan saw only a hint of a silhouette.

That was a man, right?

Her confidence in what to do was low, but her curiosity was high. She waited another ten minutes, silently opened the porch door, listened for any noise coming from down the hall, entered the house, and moved quietly toward the office. When she entered, using her cell phone light as a flashlight, she edged over to Robert's large desk.

What am I looking for? Why am I even in here?

She knew the answer. Ever since she'd overheard Robert Hightower's mysterious call the day before —with whom?—she'd become unnerved in his presence. And, despite every emotion screaming for her to talk with Robby about what she'd overheard, she resisted bringing it up. Robby thought her scare with the artifact thieves had rattled her. That was part of it, for sure, but the other stuff about his dad she couldn't mention. To anyone. Because she didn't know what it meant, Robby would think she was crazy for suspecting his dad of something unpleasant. And she doubted her dad would believe a word she said.

Nothing on the desk looked interesting. No surprise. Robert wouldn't have left something incriminating lying around. She sat in his chair, the leather seat hissing a pulse of air, which sounded frightfully loud to Megan. *Almost as loud as my beating heart!* She opened the top desk drawer. Again, nothing of interest. She slowly slid open the large file drawer and was greeted by dozens of file folders. She scanned them quickly. Most were related to the newspaper business—files labeled news operations, articles, budgets, printing press repairs, mortgage. The one labeled "defamation lawsuit" caught her eye, but she passed over it, as well as the one labeled "commissioner." She thumbed further into the files.

In the far back she spotted one labeled "Bears Ears Mining Opportunity." While the file might be about a potential news story, its presence in the back of the drawer made her suspicious. And curious. She pulled the bulging folder out and thumbed through it, unclear about much of what she found, which included multiple charts and data on spreadsheets. But she knew she was seeing something Robert Hightower didn't want her, or anyone, to see.

She slipped the folder back in its place and quietly closed the desk drawer. As she sat up, the overhead light came on suddenly.

"Oh!" she blurted. Her startled reaction didn't startle the person who had turned on the light.

"I'm sorry, Megan." Robert Hightower sounded concerned. "I didn't mean to scare you."

"No, no...It's..."

"I saw flickers of light and thought there might be a prowler or thief in the house. Are you looking for something?"

"No...I mean, yes." Megan needed an answer. "I was looking for a pen and a notepad. I couldn't sleep. I wanted to write down exactly what happened at the storage business earlier today. I mean, yesterday. To give to the sheriff tomorrow. I mean, later today."

"That's smart." Robert smiled. "You'd make a good reporter."

Megan attempted to smile, glad Robert couldn't hear her heart pounding.

"Here," Robert said. He opened a drawer in the file cabinet in the corner of the room and retrieved a yellow pad, which he gave to Megan. He lifted the pen cup off his desktop. "Pick any one you want." He smiled. "Some reporters use pencils to write faster, but you probably want to take your time."

Megan took a plain Bic ballpoint. "Thanks."

"Are you going to write it down now?" Robert asked.

"Maybe. I can't sleep."

"Okay. Well, I'm going to head back to sleep for a while. Turn on some lights if you want. It's almost daylight. I don't think you will disturb any of the other sleepy heads." He turned and walked back down the hall.

Megan didn't move until she heard the door to his bedroom close with a soft click. She reentered the great room, notepad in hand, turned on a table lamp, and sat in one of the comfortable leather chairs. But she wasn't comfortable. She stared at the yellow pad in her lap, wanting to write—wanting to write so much!—but was afraid to pick up the pen and start. *Who will believe me?*

She could feel tears coming on but didn't want to cry. She hated crying. She thought she would explode—too much happening, too fast, and too confusing. If only she could talk to her dad about everything. *If only he would really listen!*

She hated *if onlys* more than she hated tears. They never worked out. She had to tell him what she knew.

Unable to write, she carried her coffee, now barely warm, out onto the back porch. To the East a hint of morning light glowed. To the West everything remained dark. The Bears Ears buttes would catch the sun soon, but for now they were still invisible.

So, too, was the person who snuck up behind her, unheard. The person who listened to her exhale a weary, wary breath. The person who, when she inhaled, grabbed her from behind and placed a cloth over her mouth and nose.

She struggled but her assailant just held her tighter, a hand squeezing her left arm, the assailant's other arm wrapped around her body as it held the cloth tight against her face. She could detect a chemical smell on the cloth, and she held her breath, knowing without thinking she shouldn't breathe. The grip on her arm was intense, painful. She could hear the attacker's hard breathing inches from her ear and knew it was a man's breath. She elbowed him in the stomach and heard a grunt. But his grip on her arm tightened and she let out a cloth-muffled scream. Which is when, her lungs exploding, she took in a deep breath. Within moments, the fight went out of her.

Megan—unconscious and dreamless—was little more than a loose heap of bones and flesh as her body was deposited onto the front seat floor of a white pickup.

Chapter 31

Joe could smell coffee brewing as he stirred. *I wonder if that's Megan?* She was the barista at home, and the pleasant thought helped him awaken. He looked at his watch. 7:30. He'd slept better than he expected. Exhaustion helped. The day before had taken a toll. Their visit to the camp near the excavation had generated questions. The visit with Ben in the hospital and his insistence Joe stop the excavation—was it a warning?—raised more questions. The run-in, again, with the sheriff put him in a foul mood. And Megan's close call with artifact looters, the same rednecks they'd encountered at the café their first day, was she making it up? No, he concluded. She'd been scared.

Women's voices sounded from the kitchen. Susan's and Felicity's. And then Robert's. Joe pulled on his jeans and a denim shirt and entered the warm kitchen where the unmistakable smell of bacon instantly caused a pleasant rumble in his stomach.

"Hello, sleepyhead." Felicity stood next to the stove, an apron on. She put down the spatula in her hand and moved toward Joe. She gave him a quick kiss.

Joe returned the smile. Felicity didn't seem to hold a grudge after their disagreement the night before. "Seems like my timing is pretty good. All the work is done."

"You can help set the table," Robert said. "Take these plates."

Robby entered the room wearing clean jeans and a plaid shirt, the shirttail tucked in neatly. His hair was neatly combed. "Is Megan awake yet?"

"I don't think so," his mom said.

"She was up real early," Robert said. He was holding a fistful of knives and forks. "I heard a noise around 5:00 and came to investigate. She'd made herself coffee and was planning to write her notes from her run-in with the looters yesterday." He turned to Robby. "Go knock on her door and tell her breakfast is ready."

"Sure." He headed down the hall.

The others started to set the table for breakfast and dish up the food. They heard Robby knocking on Megan's door. No answer. He knocked again. Still no answer.

"I'll go check on her," Joe said.

Always cautious about intruding on Megan's "space," Joe silently turned the doorknob. The lights were out, but sunshine crept into the room from around the edges of the still-closed curtains. The bed was empty.

That's odd.

He looked around the room. Nothing particular stood out. There was no sign of a problem. No sign of any activity.

He walked down to his room to retrieve his phone to see if she'd left him a text. Moments later, he returned to the kitchen, puzzlement in his expression.

"She left me a text." He read. "Up early. Got hungry. Walked to the diner on Main Street to get coffee and breakfast. Need time to think about what happened yesterday. Back by 8 or so."

"Oh my," Susan said. She blinked. "I mean, that seems so brave and all after her scare yesterday."

"Or just dumb," Joe said. He shook his head, worry and anger mingling like water and dirt, muddying his thoughts.

"I'll take the Beast and go get her," Robby said.

"Right after you eat," his mom said. "She seems to want some alone time."

"But..."

"I can check in on her," Robert interrupted. "I'm running late as is. I've got to head to Monticello for a meeting. I'll stop in and make sure she's okay, see if she wants a ride back." He turned to Robby. "I'll call you and you can come pick her up."

"Okay." Robby wasn't going to argue with his dad.

"I better get going," Robert said. He gulped down a few bites of eggs, took a swig of coffee, and grabbed a strip of bacon. He struggled to get up, a hint that aches hanging around from his Marine days or work stress were part of his life.

Before he left the table, he leaned over to Joe and whispered. "Do you think she ran away again?"

Joe shook his head. "No," he said aloud.

Robert never called Robby. He called Joe instead.

"She's not here."

"She's probably walking home," Joe said.

"Maybe." A pause. "But I asked at the café, and no one remembers seeing her."

Joe didn't respond. *Megan's missing. Again.* It was a thought he wanted to dispel but couldn't.

Robert tried to fill the silence. "Listen, Joe. I've got to go to Monticello and then up to Moab. Call Sheriff Cooper and report Megan missing."

"That asshole despises me. I don't think he'll lift a finger."

"It's his job, Joe. Call him."

Chapter 32

The call to Sheriff Bull Cooper went better than Joe expected. He'd anticipated the sheriff would suggest Megan was just out for a walk and would turn up soon, that he would want to make Joe feel like some whiny city-slicker dad.

"What's up, Professor Cutler?" the sheriff said, answering his cell phone. "Your daughter change her mind about what she saw?"

Was he implying Megan had made up her story the day before? Joe's brow tightened, and he took a calming breath before answering.

"No, sheriff. I don't think she's changed her mind." He paused. "But I need your help."

"How's that?"

"She left a text early this morning before anyone else got up that she was going to the diner for breakfast. She was planning to write her notes about what happened."

"And…?"

"She never made it there." Joe took another deep breath before saying the words he never wanted to say again. "She's missing."

"Are you sure?"

"No, I'm not sure." Joe was growing frustrated and hated the uncertainty of it. "Robert Hightower stopped by the café just a few minutes ago, and no one there saw her."

"Is that right?" the sheriff asked. Joe didn't reply. "Robert reported it, did he?"

"Yes."

"All right, professor, I believe you. I sincerely hope she's just out for a walk and went somewhere else." He paused. "What do you want me to do?"

Felicity had advised him what to say. "I want to officially report her missing. Put a report out to all law enforcement in the county and add her information into the FBI's NCIC database."

Cooper chuckled mildly. "Sounds like you've had a little coaching."

"You could say that."

"Okay," Cooper said. "Here's what we'll do. You call it in to the department in ten minutes. I'll call ahead and tell them to expect your call. They'll want a picture of her and some other details and...damn it!" A few seconds passed. "Some jackass just ran a red light and almost clipped my vehicle! I'd go after him myself if I could!"

Joe could hear Cooper take a deep breath, as if he was counting to three—or ten.

"Where were we?" Cooper said.

"The missing person report," Joe said. "And there's one more thing." He looked over at Felicity, who nodded. "I want you to check on Riley Smith's whereabouts. Because he..."

"Yeah," Cooper interrupted. "Already thought about that. I'm on my way to the Blanding Self-Storage now with a warrant to search his storage unit. I'll be there in about thirty minutes if you want to join me."

Joe covered the phone and whispered to Felicity. "He wants to know if we want to meet him at the storage unit."

Felicity nodded emphatically.

"We'll be there."

"I'm guessing the 'we' includes your detective friend." Cooper's voice tightened slightly.

"That's right."

"Well, that's just fine." Sheriff Cooper's voice brightened, but not convincingly. "Always good to have a real detective on the case."

"She'll be honored, I'm sure," Joe said.

"Okay, see you in about thirty...Christ almighty! What's with these damn drivers today! Can't they see 'sheriff' written in giant letters on this vehicle? No damn respect for the law, that's for damn sure."

The call ended.

***

Felicity helped Joe call in the missing person report. The photo of Megan that Joe found on his phone to send to the sheriff's department had been taken when she found the Clovis point, her hair pulled back in a practical ponytail under a Chicago Cubs ballcap. Red dirt smudged her face and arms. Her smile beamed. The dirt didn't hide her beauty, Felicity thought.

Joe started pacing as soon as he'd made the report. They still had twenty minutes before their scheduled meeting with Cooper at Blanding Self-Storage.

"Go look for her, Joe," Susan Hightower said. She'd been listening from the kitchen as Joe made his report. "It's a small town. You'll find her before the sheriffs do."

Felicity detected deep worry in Susan's voice. Was it fear of the artifact looters? Or something else? Did she think Megan had run away?

"I'm going to look for her too," Robby said. "I'll take the Beast down some of the dirt roads that lead out of town."

"The beast?" Felicity asked.

"That's my truck."

"Good name." She'd seen the truck.

"Call my cell right away if you find her," Joe said.

They all made preparations immediately. Robby headed to his room, Joe excused himself to use the bathroom first, and Felicity used the opportunity to walk down to Megan's room and take a look.

The curtains were still drawn, so she turned on the overhead light. Megan's favorite flannel shirt was hanging over the chair, her blue jeans on the seat. Wouldn't she have worn those? Maybe she was wearing the khaki pants she wore at the dig? What did she wear to bed normally? PJs? No, she slept in one of her flannel shirts. Felicity rifled through Megan's duffel, her cop instincts outstripping respect for privacy. She spotted Megan's boots on the closet floor and her puffer coat. Wouldn't she have worn them? Early mornings were chilly. Was she planning to go somewhere other than the diner? Was the text just a diversion?

"Are you ready?" Joe called from the great room, his voice anxious.

"Be right there!" Felicity called. She hoped they'd find Megan in a matter of minutes. If they didn't, she would talk to Joe about her observations in Megan's room.

As she was about to leave, she spotted Megan's backpack behind the door. Wouldn't she have taken it too?

***

Before meeting with the sheriff at Blanding Self-Storage, they drove slowly along the route Megan would likely have taken to the diner, peering into alleys, backyards, and parking lots. They stopped by the diner—just in case—and Joe showed the staff his picture of Megan. No one recalled seeing her, as Robert had reported earlier. "She's a lovely girl," the woman at the cash register said.

Joe's phone buzzed. It was Robby. His heart skipped a beat. He put his cell phone on speaker.

"Did you find her?" he asked before Robby could say a word.

"No." Robby's voice was somber. "I was hoping you had."

"No. No one has seen her that we've asked."

"Yeah. Same for me." Silence filled the moment. "Would she run away, Joe?"

"No!" Joe's emphatic answer hid his own confusion. Megan had been in deep emotional pain when she ran away three years earlier. But he believed—wanted to believe with every cell in his body—that she was different now. She was headstrong and unhappy about Felicity and hard to talk to at times, but she wasn't stupid. Just the opposite. And she would never leave until she knew about Ben.

"After we meet the sheriff at the storage facility, we're going to keep looking," Joe said.

"Do you think she hitchhiked on the highway?" Robby asked.

It was a possibility that hadn't occurred to Joe.

Felicity interrupted. "She didn't."

"What makes you so sure?" Joe said.

"I'll tell you in a moment." She whispered, not wanting Robby to hear.

Joe, puzzlement on his face, got the message. "Keep looking for her, Robby. We'll be back at the house in about an hour. Meet you there."

"What was that about?" Joe continued to drive slowly, scanning left and right, glancing down side streets and alleys and into backyards. He'd done the same twice before in Hyde Park when Megan had gone missing—once, her own decision to run away, once, when she had been abducted. He took no solace in having experience looking for a missing daughter.

"Megan didn't flee on some long-distance adventure," Felicity said. "I'm sure of it."

Joe pulled over to the side of the road. "Go on."

"I checked her room. She didn't take her backpack or her puffer jacket. She isn't wearing her boots, either. She wouldn't take off on a long journey without those. She's too smart."

Joe frowned. "Why didn't you tell me back at the house?"

"I hoped we'd find her right away."

He didn't respond, knowing it wouldn't help in the moment, but Felicity keeping something like that secret, even for only a few minutes, felt like a betrayal. He was about to pull back into the street when his phone buzzed again. It was Cooper; he was waiting for them.

When Joe and Felicity drove up to Blanding Self-Storage, three men had gathered next to the unit rented by Riley Smith. The sheriff and a deputy stood next to Jim, the manager of the storage unit they'd met previously, and another older man dressed noticeably better. The owner, Joe figured, correctly, when they were introduced. The owner, not wanting to get sued, wasn't going to okay breaking into the unit without seeing the search warrant himself.

"Here you go, Owen," the sheriff said to the owner. "Judge Smith was happy to sign it. He's Riley's uncle once removed but not so fond of his relative. Said Riley t-boned him one evening running a red light, totaling his Lexus and giving him neck issues ever since."

"Small town," Felicity said.

"It happened up in Moab," Cooper said. "I'd of heard of it if it happened down here."

"Sounds like Riley gets around," Joe said.

"Trouble spreads, like dirty water after a rainstorm," Cooper said.

Jim, the manager, hefted a huge pair of bolt cutters used to whack the locks off other units when renters failed to pay their rent. The lock Riley Smith had used was substantial, the cutter more so. With the deputy holding one handle of the cutter and Jim the other, the lock shackle snapped, and the lock fell to the ground. The deputy grabbed the handle, yanked hard, and the reticulated roll-up door zipped up and out of the way.

The sight that greeted them wasn't what Joe expected, although, he wondered, maybe one of the others standing there wasn't surprised at all.

Empty shelving.

Chapter 33

With everyone out looking for Megan, Susan Hightower was startled when the home phone rang in the quiet house. Normally, family or friends would call her cell.

She looked at caller-ID before answering and had a vague sense she'd seen the number before.

"Hightower residence," she answered.

"Mrs. Hightower, this is commissioner Samuel Begay. I'm sorry to bother you at home, but I tried to reach Robert on his cell and it rolled to voice mail. Is he home?"

She remembered now; she'd seen the number a few times before. "No, commissioner. He left this morning for Monticello and then Moab."

"Do you know when he will return?"

"He didn't say. Can I give him a message?"

The commissioner hesitated before answering.

"I'll try him later on his cell." He cleared his throat. "Tell me, Mrs. Hightower..."

"Just Susan, please."

"Susan, is Joe Cutler still staying with you, or...or has he left town?"

"Yes, he's still staying here." She was surprised he knew Joe was staying at their home.

"I see," the commissioner said. "May I ask you one more question, Mrs. Hightower, I mean, Susan?"

"Certainly."

"Do you know the status of Ben Hatathli? He's a member of my clan, and I was devastated to learn he'd been shot."

Susan didn't know who'd told him about Ben, but she wasn't surprised word had spread.

"He was flown to Salt Lake yesterday. He was going to be operated on yesterday, but they delayed it until this morning to try to stabilize his heart rate first."

"I hope all goes well." His voice was more somber. "I will have my assistant check up on his progress."

"We're all praying for him."

"Yes, we must pray," the commission said. "I will try Robert's cell again. I want to thank him for his editorial in the paper today. They are wise words we can all get behind."

"I haven't read it yet." In the confusion of the morning, she'd forgotten it was Tuesday, the day the print version came out. "I'll tell him you liked it."

"Ahéhee'," the commissioner said.

"You're welcome," Susan replied. The call ended.

Commissioner Begay and her husband had grudging respect for each other, but this was the first time she'd heard Begay praise one of Robert's editorials. Strange. And curious.

Robert had been restless and distracted for weeks. She attributed his behavior to the constant struggles to produce revenue, especially to cover the upcoming costs of sending Robby to college. He would get out of bed in the middle of the night and pace or head to his office. At first, she asked if he wanted to talk or snuggle. But he'd just say no, his *semper fi* Marine toughness his way of proving his worth. After several offers, she stopped asking. Instead, she went back to sleep when he rose, wandered into his office, and fretted.

It was her turn to fret. Had Robert's opinion of Begay changed? Or maybe the commissioner was acting nice because he knew Robert was working on a story, perhaps a scandal, that would create trouble for him. She needed to read the editorial Begay mentioned. Robert would have left a copy of today's paper in his office. She headed there immediately.

She sat in Robert's desk chair and read the editorial. Then read it again. And shook her head. She didn't know what to make of it.

Robert hadn't even hinted he was working on something like it. Why? Was it because he knew it would start an argument between them? She imagined it was already starting arguments all over the county. She leaned back in the desk chair, thinking. Worrying.

The editorial dramatically shifted the newspaper's position on the Bears Ears Monument. For many months, years, in fact, Robert's editorials had boldly sided with the tribes and conservationists who pushed for a large-scale national monument. Now, Robert's editorial recommended a "go slow approach" and a "right-sizing" of the proposed monument boundaries. The editorial stopped short of opposing the monument designation like many of the local Anglos wanted, but it argued for a more "balanced approach to resource use." Those were the exact words opponents had been using for five years.

Why now? Why would Robert have a change of heart now—if it really was a change of heart? Or were the commissioners and business leaders who opposed the monument holding something over Robert's head?

They would have to talk. Not having told her was not okay. Not at all.

And what would Joe think? What did it mean for Joe's excavation? Getting the dig restarted was already going to be challenging. Robert had left that morning without even mentioning the editorial to Joe.

Susan was curious. Robert kept files of his current projects in his desk file drawer. It was also where he kept their financial records, and last week, when she went to retrieve some receipts related to a homeowner's insurance claim, she'd seen a file labeled "Commissioner." At the time she didn't give it a second thought; she figured it was related to some story. That was then. She felt some guilt rummaging through Robert's files, but not enough to stop her.

She found the "Commissioner" file in the back of the file drawer. And just behind it, a fat folder labeled "Bears Ears Mining

Opportunity." She took out both files and, for the next thirty minutes, pored over memos, letters of understanding, financial projections, a heavily marked-up map of the county, and a wire-bound report stamped "DRAFT" titled "Proposed Master Land Use Plan for San Juan County." The author was Connor Smith, San Juan County Director for Land Use, the county official whose body had been discovered at the base of Overlook Bluff in Recapture Canyon under suspicious circumstances. Susan was certain the report had never been made public; supposedly, it had never been finished.

Susan didn't hear the birds singing in the blue spruce out back, or the twinkling of the wind chimes as a soft breeze blew, or her washing machine buzzing as the load finished. She heard only her own fast-paced breathing as her heart pounded.

Chapter 34

Joe drove slowly back to the Hightower home, pausing to glance down every street and alley they passed. Nothing. Felicity wasn't surprised. She suspected Megan was far away, for one reason or another. She focused on why. And whom.

Joe tried to reach Angie again with no luck. He called Angie's uncle, hoping she was with him. She wasn't. Instead, he got reamed out by her uncle who blamed Joe for her disappearance.

He tried Doug. Nothing.

"Do you think they're together?" he asked.

"No," Felicity said. "But it's possible." She thought Joe was worrying where he didn't need to. "Put Angie out of your mind for now."

"But I feel responsible for her."

"Listen to me, Joe." Felicity's voice was steady, clear, and direct.

"What?"

"That's bullshit. She's an adult. You're not her keeper."

"Well, her uncle sure thinks I am. And he plans to make my life miserable."

They pulled in front of the Hightower home, leaving the driveway open for Robert's truck when he returned. Joe cut the engine. He leaned his head against the steering wheel and didn't move. Felicity remained silent.

"What's going on, Felicity?" Joe spoke in a low, rasping voice.

"I don't know, Joe. But we'll figure it out."

"Figure what out? Where she is? Who she's with? Is she safe?"

"Yeah, all of those questions." She reached across and rested her hand on his arm.

"How?"

"I don't know yet. But we will." Optimism and determination always drove her. She always started a case believing she could solve it, even if she was sometimes proven wrong.

"Let's go inside," she said.

It's going to be up to me, Felicity realized. And she relished the role. But before she'd taken twenty steps, she was in store for a surprise. She came to a sudden stop when she glanced down at the dirt and gravel driveway.

"What is it?" Joe said.

Felicity bent down for a closer look. "This tire track, it looks like the one we saw in Butler Wash at that camp near ours."

"Are you sure?"

"No, of course not. But I know it's similar."

"Maybe it's from Robert's truck."

Felicity considered her next words carefully. "That's what I'm thinking."

"Could it be someone who pulled into the driveway during the night? Someone who took Megan?"

"We shouldn't rule it out."

She took out her camera. As she bent down to take pictures, she noticed bootprints. Familiar-looking bootprints. They were similar to the ones they'd seen at the suspicious campsite in Butler Wash.

"Bootprints?" Joe asked.

"Yeah." Felicity took pictures of them too. She would later compare them to the pictures she'd taken in Butler Wash. Joe gave her a hand as she stood back up, but he didn't let go. He looked her in the eyes, beseeching.

"I'm scared, Felicity," he said softly.

She took his other hand and squeezed them both. "I'm sure you are."

She let go and gave him a hug—to reassure him, if only a little. Words only went so far.

"Let's go inside and make some tea," she said, a gentle smile on her face. But she kept studying the ground as they walked to the door. *I need to come back out here, alone, to take a closer look.*

The Hightower home was quiet when they entered, Susan nowhere to be seen.

"Susan," Joe called out. "We're back."

"I'm back here!" Susan's voice called from her bedroom. "I'll be there in a moment." A pause. "Any sign of Megan?"

"No," Joe said.

"I'm so sorry," she called.

Felicity spoke up. "We're going to make some tea. Want any?"

"No thanks."

Susan joined them in the kitchen as the kettle of water began to boil. Her hair was pulled back in a bun. She had changed into a denim shirt, tan hiking pants, and hiking boots.

"I think I may go looking for Megan myself."

"In the wilderness?" Joe asked.

"Something like that." She didn't offer more details.

Felicity finished pouring hot water into the waiting mugs. She looked up and saw Susan's face clearer now. *She's been crying.* Felicity decided not to ask. Not yet.

With tea in hand, Felicity slipped back out the front door as Joe headed down the hallway to the bedroom to make a few calls. He was going to try reaching Angie and Doug again and check on Ben's status at the hospital in Salt Lake City.

As Felicity walked to the front door, she stopped again to look at the foyer photo of Robert, twenty-plus years younger, proudly wearing his Marine uniform. Which was when Felicity recalled something she'd noticed about Robert on their first meeting. His limp. The first night they stayed there, she'd asked about the photo, about his service in the Marines. Robert told her he'd served in the first Iraq War and taken a load of shrapnel in his right leg and hip. A dishonorable discharge had ended what he thought might be a military career. Instead, he'd returned home to recuperate, married Susan, started working at an Arizona newspaper before returning to Blanding when his dad died. "And that," he'd said, trying to spin his words for laughs, "is the rest of my puny story."

Felicity studied the driveway more closely. The tire tracks weren't definitive; lots of trucks in the area might have similar tracks, Robert's truck among them. She studied the bootprints carefully. Other footprints had disturbed the dirt, so it was hard to track the ones that matched the bootprints from Butler Gulch, but she was sure she spotted a few, and took pictures. None clearly indicated the wearer had a limp.

As she went over to the passenger side of the driveway, she spotted more of the same bootprints. And something else. Something she'd seen at crime scenes in Chicago—evidence of something being dragged. Like a body. The path of the marks along the ground indicated that something, or someone, had been dragged around the side of the house. She took more photos.

She was about to carefully explore around the side of the house when a truck pulled up. It wasn't white but a dull green. Robby's truck, the Beast.

"Park in front, not in the driveway!" Felicity called out.

"What's up?" Robby asked, as he stepped out of his truck. "Find something?"

"Maybe." She knew it wouldn't be wise to explain all her thinking, all her worries. But he needed to see the bootprints.

Chapter 35

Robby's head started to ache, pain slicing through his skull from one temple to another, the kind of pain that makes tears seem a waste of time. He shut his eyes but couldn't shut out the thoughts that were hurtling around inside his head from what Felicity had shown him.

Robby had never studied bootprints before, but now it was all he could think about. The bootprints and tire tracks in his driveway were the same ones they'd seen in Butler Wash. *What does that mean?*

Maybe Megan had been abducted by the artifact thieves she saw at the storage unit. But something didn't make sense.

He entered the house and went into the kitchen. His mom was polishing the silver flatware they hadn't used in years. She seemed as distraught as he felt.

"You okay, Mom?"

She smiled briefly. "Yes, sweetheart. But how about a hug?"

He walked over and she hugged him so hard he could feel her ribs poking into his.

"You sure you're okay?" he asked.

"Just stressed."

"Yeah. Me too." He opened the refrigerator. "I'm going to grab a Coke and head down to the barn."

"What for?"

"Just to think, I guess."

"Are you hungry?"

"Not really." But his stomach growled in disagreement.

"I'll fix you a sandwich and call you when it's ready."

"Thanks, Mom. You're special." He headed for the door.

"Hey kiddo. You think you're going to just say something nice and walk away? Come back here and let me give you a kiss."

He walked back, his lips opening into a smile. He bent his knees slightly and bowed his head, and she pecked his forehead. It was a gesture she'd done every day as far back as he could remember, back when she was the one who'd bent down to give the kiss.

Felicity and Joe were still standing when Robby walked through the great room. They were talking quietly, and, it appeared, would be happy if he didn't interrupt. Joe's brow was furrowed, his eyes tight, and he didn't seem pleased with what Felicity was saying.

Robby raised his can of Coke, nodded their way, and Felicity nodded back.

As he walked up to the fence at the bottom of their property, as usual he looked out on the Bears Ears buttes in the distance. They seemed farther away than normal. Distant, Robby thought. Like a lot of things.

The last time he'd stood there looking at the Bears Ears buttes, Megan had been by his side. He'd told her all about their history, about the Navajo and Ute myths surrounding them, and about his own experiences hiking to the top of each one. Now all he could think about was Megan. She meant a lot to him. Which still surprised him.

And she was missing. Robby knew the saying that absence makes the heart grow fonder, but fear, he realized, is stronger. It held his heart in a death grip. His head continued to pound.

He heard a door shut, turned around, and looked up at his home. Joe and Felicity had come out on the deck. His father had practically built the house with his own hands, and Robby loved everything about it. He also loved everything about the stark, unforgiving land that stretched out beyond his home in every direction. Yet it all felt puny compared to Megan missing. Its beauty was invisible for now.

He closed his eyes and lowered his head. When he opened them, he was looking just beyond his feet. He saw something he wasn't expecting. He turned slightly and kept scanning the ground. He kept seeing more of the same.

His heart ached. He knew what he had to do, but he didn't want to.

"Felicity! Joe! Come here! There's something you need to see."

***

The three of them sat in the great room, but no one said anything. Robby had shown them the bootprints that were down by the fence in the dried mud, and similar ones in the barn. There was little room for debate, and yet...

"Maybe the bootprints came from someone else." Joe wanted to sound defiant, but his own voice revealed his doubt.

"They're from Dad," Robby said softly. "Nothing else makes sense."

"It's just evidence at this point, Robby," Felicity said. "Not proof of anything."

Robby burst out. "Don't patronize me! What has my dad done?"

His mom came in from the kitchen quickly. "Robby? Why are you yelling at our guests?" She wiped her hands rapidly up and down her apron. "Don't be rude." She wiped her hands rapidly again.

"It was nothing," Felicity said.

"Nothing?" Robby stood. He shook his head. "This is not about *nothing*." He looked at his mother. "Mom, do you know where Dad was Thursday and Friday night?"

"He was fishing up in the Henry Mountains with someone."

"Who?"

"I don't know. He didn't say."

"When did he get home?"

"Early Saturday morning. He slipped in while I was still asleep."

"Was his truck dirty with red dust?"

"I don't know, Robby. It's always dirty."

"Did Dad bring home fish?"

"He said they weren't biting."

"And you believed him, even though he almost always catches something?"

"Yes, I believed him." She dropped her eyes. "I always believed him," her words just above a whisper.

Robby toned down his voice. "I'm sorry, Mom." He took a deep breath. "It's just...it's just that Dad may have done something to Megan."

His mom took a deep breath. "I know."

The other three watched, speechless, as Susan, in what seemed like slow motion, sank into one of the large leather chairs.

"You...you know?" Felicity asked. "What do you mean?"

"I mean...well, I don't know if Robert has Megan. I don't know that. I don't. But I know something is wrong. I know he's not himself. I mean he's hiding something, at least he's been hiding something from me, and I just found out today, and I'm so terribly confused. I don't know what to think. I don't know what he might do."

Joe stood and went over to her. He bent down in front of the chair where she sat. "Relax, Susan." He put his hand on her arm. "Tell us what you know."

"Yeah, Mom." Robby's headache swelled to fill the entire room. "Tell us what you know."

***

Susan rose slowly from her chair. "Follow me."

She led them into Robert's office and handed Joe the editorial about the Bears Ears Monument that Robert had written. He read it aloud so the others could hear. When he was finished, he shook his head.

"That doesn't sound like something Dad would write," Robby said.

"No, sweetheart, it doesn't."

"It also not evidence of anything," Felicity said.

"Oh, it's evidence all right," Joe said. "Robert wouldn't have written this without a reason. He's been saying the opposite for, like, five years." He shook his head. "Do you think someone pressured him somehow?"

"That's what I wondered too," Susan said. "Commissioner Begay called this morning asking for Robert.

"The commissioner called?" Joe asked. He knew the commissioner and Robert had been the opposite of bosom buddies for years.

"Yes. It was very unusual. I told him Robert was headed to Monticello. Begay said he just wanted to thank Robert for the editorial. I hadn't read it yet, which is why I came in Robert's office to get his copy and read it. Then..." She took another deep breath and looked at her son.

"Then what?" Robby said.

"I found something else," she said.

Susan sat in the desk chair, opened the file drawer, and retrieved the draft copy of the Proposed Master Land Use Plan for San Juan County. She handed it to Joe. He looked at the table of contents, then scanned the executive summary, not saying anything. He sighed and handed it to Felicity.

Susan tried to maintain a calm voice. "When Robert wrote the story about the death of the Land Use Director, he wrote that the land use plan hadn't been finished."

"Robert could have come by this *after* that story was written," Felicity noted. "There may be no connection."

"I considered that," Susan said. "But why was he silent about the report when he had a copy? And why did he write today's editorial?" Her face tightened. "I think I know why."

She stopped. She looked over at Robby, whose face was knotted in confusion and worry. "Hey kiddo, why don't you go eat that sandwich I made for you? You don't need to hear all this blather about reports."

"I'm tracking," Robby said. "I'll stay."

"There's more," his mom said.

Susan handed Joe the file labeled "Bears Ears Mining Opportunity." He quickly studied the map in the file. He couldn't make sense of the various markings, but an area of Butler Wash that included the excavation site was marked "L3," whatever that meant. He reviewed the summary of a business plan—boldly marked "confidential"—for a company called "Advanced Rare Earth Mineral Extraction LLC." The company had done studies—on both private land and government land—and the plan indicated there could be five hundred million dollars, maybe a billion dollars, worth of rare earth minerals that could be extracted over twenty years.

Joe found it hard to believe. He was under the impression nothing but uranium had been found in mineable quantities in the area, and uranium mining had mostly stopped. He didn't pay much attention to the constant searching in southern Utah by the extractive industries, but he knew rare earth minerals were a booming market worldwide.

He picked up the Memorandum of Understanding from the file, also boldly marked "confidential," dated April 30, two weeks before the Director of Land Use's death. It appeared to be a term sheet with covenants and restrictions for the limited partners. He thumbed through its dense text, but when he got to the signature page of the document, he came across the names of all the limited partners. He didn't recognize most of the twenty or so names, but he knew a few. One in particular.

He glanced at the picture of Robert, Susan, and a younger Robby that had a place of prominence on the wall next to the bookshelves. They were standing on the back porch of the house, and all three of them looked wildly happy.

"Holy shit," Joe said. "Holy. Shit." He dropped his head.

"My thought too," Susan said. She turned away to look out the window and began to sob.

Chapter 36

"We still don't know if Robert has Megan," Joe said. "It could be the jerks who stole the artifacts. They might have grabbed her when she walked to the diner. We know they tried to find her when she ran from the storage place."

"It's also a pretty good cover story for Robert," Felicity said. "He even called from the diner to report she never got there."

"Do you think he had her in his truck the whole time?"

"If she was bound and gagged, he could have."

"Did he grab her when she was walking to the diner?"

"I don't think so," Felicity said. "The drag marks I saw on the driveway suggest a body..."

"For god sake, Felicity! Don't refer to Megan as a body."

"I'm sorry, Joe. But I don't know who or what was being dragged."

"Okay, I get it." He took a deep breath. "I can't imagine Robert hurting Megan."

"I don't think he hurt her." Felicity decided *not* to mention the absence of blood could mean Megan may have been unconscious but not badly hurt when her body was dragged.

"Megan's text." Joe took out his phone to read the text again. "We don't even know she wrote it."

"That's right." Felicity had already realized Robert could have written the text himself if he had Megan and her cell phone. He would know it was a story Joe would believe, that Megan took off to the diner by herself. The thugs who'd stolen the artifacts likely wouldn't concoct that story.

Joe's phone rang. He looked down, hoping against hope it was Megan. It was Cooper. He put it on speaker.

"Hello sheriff," he answered flatly.

"Hello professor." Cooper sounded all business. "The office said you called in the missing person report. That's good. And tell your lady detective friend thanks for helping. I mean that, I do."

"She heard you," Joe said.

"I thought so. Listen, I want to tell you what I can about our visit to Riley Smith's house a while ago. I can't tell you a lot because he's been arrested, and I don't want to screw up our case." He chuckled. "Does that work for you, detective?"

"All good," Felicity said.

"Well," the sheriff continued. "We arrived, search warrant in hand, and Riley opened the door after the third ring, bleary-eyed like he'd been awake all night. He said he was home sick from work. That boy's got some balls. He was blocking the door sort of and said we shouldn't come in cause he didn't want to give us the flu. He said that would be bad for his *reputation*. I told him his reputation wasn't what he should be worried about. I patted my holster and assured him we were pretty well inoculated from whatever he had. That boy just smiled and stood there. But he didn't put up any resistance when I pushed past him."

"Did he say anything about Megan?" Joe interrupted.

"I'm getting to that." The sheriff paused briefly. "One of the deputies Mirandized him while I went through his house. I saw a few artifacts on shelves and tables. Hell, that didn't prove squat; we all got some of that stuff around our houses. But then I went through his kitchen and opened the door to his garage. Bingo! You could fill a railcar with all the pottery and baskets and other artifact shit he had in there. A lot of it was spread across the floor in piles like it had been recently unloaded. Sure enough, the bed of his pickup was still dirty with red clay and broken pottery pieces. When I asked him about it, he said it belonged to his buddy Frankie. Jeezus, the first thing out of his mouth is trying to put the blame on someone else."

Felicity could tell Joe was about to explode, which would not be good. She spoke up. "That's excellent police work, sheriff. Congratulations." She paused. "Did you ask him about Megan?"

"Of course I did, detective." His voice became serious. "We might nail him for artifact theft, but I know that missing girl is a helluva lot more important right now. I looked Riley straight in the eye and asked him about her. I didn't use her name, of course. He shook his head, grinned just a little, and said, 'I plead the fifth when it comes to that sniveling little bitch who ratted me out.'"

Felicity looked over at Joe and saw his fear that Riley Smith had done something to Megan.

Sheriff Cooper continued. "I wanted to punch out his lights when he said that. But those days of policing are long gone. I figured I would, you know, negotiate a little. I told him things would go easier on him if he told me all he knew about your daughter. When I asked him if he'd chased after her, he said yes, they just wanted to scare her, but they gave up looking for her. They didn't know where to find her."

"And you believed him?" Joe's voice indicated skepticism.

"Yeah, I believe him," the sheriff said. "Because when I told him 'you better damn well be telling the truth because she's missing,' his eyebrows shot up in surprise, and he grinned a little. That's when I wanted to pistol whip him."

"I would have probably gone for his throat," Joe said.

"Glad you weren't there. You might have witnessed how that shitbag ended up with a broken nose when he slipped and fell."

"Where is he now?"

"In jail. We picked up his buddy, Frankie too. He wasn't as full of himself. But he said the same thing about your daughter." He paused. "Honestly, professor, I don't think those dirtballs had anything to do with your missing daughter."

"Okay, sheriff," Joe said. "Thanks for calling. And thanks for your help."

"You bet. Listen, I called dispatch to make sure all the units are on the lookout for her. But I only got a handful of deputies and it's a very big county."

"It is," Joe said.

Chapter 37

Joe sat on the couch and looked out the window of the Hightower's home toward the Bears Ears buttes. On the porch, Robby was staring in the same direction. He's probably thinking the same thing I am, Joe thought. The area is vast. If someone, someone like Robert, who knows the terrain, has taken Megan into the wilderness to kill her, her body may never be found—like a burial at sea, the body lost in an ocean of barren rocks and dirt. Waiting for Robert to return, thinking he has an alibi, could be too late.

His stomach knotted but he needed to focus on what to do next. He turned to Felicity.

"I'm lost," he said, his voice subdued. "What do we do?"

He looked over at Susan, seated across from them. She looked up when he spoke, her eyes red from crying. For the past fifteen minutes, she had repeatedly called Robert's cell phone. She left impassioned "call me" messages on the first two attempts, but after those, she simply dialed and dialed again. Nothing.

"We have choices," Felicity said. She rested her hand on his knee.

"What?" Joe asked.

"We can wait and see if the sheriff's department finds her."

"I don't want to wait."

"We can look for her ourselves."

"But where?" Joe said. "It would be easier to find a needle in a goddam haystack. If she's been abducted by..." he glanced over at Susan, "by someone, they could be a hundred miles from here in the middle of fucking nowhere!"

"I know that, Joe," Felicity said. "When my flight flew over the desert, I imagined what it would be like to be lost among its canyons and ravines with no one around."

"So what else can we do?"

"We can tell the sheriff about our suspicion of Robert and..."

"No," Susan blurted. "Not yet." She picked up the Hoop Dancer kachina that was on the table beside her. It was one Robert had shown Felicity the first day. "This is a small town. If the sheriff gets involved and Robert isn't...isn't guilty, he'll still be branded forever. It will ruin him. He would never forgive me."

Felicity could feel Susan's anguish, but she knew getting around counterproductive emotions in this kind of situation was imperative. Time was the enemy.

"Susan, this isn't about what we believe or want to believe. It's about finding Megan before something happens to her." She paused. "Do you agree?" She watched Susan stiffen, her brow furrowing, and Felicity could feel her fear and protectiveness, both borne of love, colliding.

Susan bowed her head a moment, then raised her head. "Yes, call the sheriff if you think it's the right thing to do."

The door from the porch opened suddenly.

"I know where they are!" Robby's eyes jumped from one person to the next but settled on his mom.

"Mom, do you remember the time Dad took us to that undisturbed ruin up Harper Canyon, the one that was down that small hidden slot canyon?"

"Yes."

Robby turned to Joe. "You can't see the slot canyon from the main canyon because a massive boulder fell in front of the entrance, but Dad found it one day because a stream of water poured around the boulder after a storm. Normally, it would be dry. We squeezed around the boulder to get into the narrow canyon. About a quarter mile up there's an elevated flat area with an old ruin."

Susan spoke up. "The ancient dwelling was in pristine shape, protected overhead by a higher ledge. The adobe walls looked untouched, and we found several undisturbed pots and two old baskets. They looked like they were from the Basketmaker era, Joe."

"Dad said it looked like the site hadn't been disturbed in a thousand years."

Susan walked over to the fireplace mantel and returned with a small pottery bowl. She handed it to Joe. There was nothing spectacular about it. "We left all the good stuff. Robert insisted. But I wanted a memento." She seemed embarrassed to admit her own removal of an artifact, something that was against federal laws.

"Dad said there were probably bodies buried nearby," Robby said. "He said the local Natives like the Navajo avoided ancient sites if they were burial grounds. I thought I was cool and said, 'yeah, if you got hurt in this hidden canyon, nobody would ever find you.'"

He looked up, as if recalling that day. "Dad said, 'You're right son, you would be lost to time.'"

"I wonder why he never mentioned it to me," Joe said.

"Maybe he wanted it to be his secret," Felicity said.

They had been driving for almost an hour, Robby leading the way in the Beast, his mom beside him, while Joe and Felicity followed in his truck. The turnoff to the road that led to Harper Canyon was west of Blanding, thirty-something miles from the Hightower home. The final eleven-mile stretch would be rough, rocky road requiring high clearance and, unfortunately, slowing down. Harper Canyon was infrequently hiked, lacking any spectacular scenic features, and the Bureau of Land Management seldom graded the red clay road that led to the canyon trailhead.

When they turned off the paved road onto the dirt road, Felicity told Joe to stop and pull over. She got out, walked ahead ten yards, and bent down to study the tire marks in the dirt. Robby had stopped as well and walked over.

In the dirt, a half a dozen tire tracks overlapped with each other, and it was hard to tell which were recent.

"Has it rained recently?" Felicity asked Robby.

"I don't think so," Robby said. "But a rainstorm could have come through here, and we wouldn't have known about it."

That meant they couldn't be sure the tracks were from today. During their week at the dig site, the horrific thunderstorms that Joe warned about never materialized, but large, black thunderclouds could now be seen to the west. A sudden downpour would quickly obliterate the tire tracks they were studying.

Felicity had her cell phone out and was looking at the photos of the tire tracks near the excavation and the ones she'd spotted at the Hightower home. "I wish Ben was here right now. He would be better matching treads than me."

Robby pointed to a tire track. "This track looks like the ones in your picture. It looks fresh too."

Felicity nodded. Another truck, not Robert's, could have made the track, but it matched the tracks Felicity had seen at the Hightower home. It wasn't proof of anything. But it was evidence.

"Let's get going," Felicity said. "Lead the way."

The dirt road was as challenging as the one in Butler Wash. Sizeable rocks imbedded in the road forced them to slow and swerve to avoid busting the truck's suspension or ripping a hole in the oil pan. Loose sand in washes necessitated speeding up to avoid getting stuck. Felicity was glad Joe was driving. He was focusing on the road and didn't seem like he wanted to talk. She was at least partially wrong.

"Something feels terribly wrong," Joe said. "What the hell are we doing out here?"

"Looking for your daughter."

"Which means we're looking for Robert. It's so damn unbelievable. Can I really be so wrong about a friend?"

"Yes." Felicity had witnessed more than her share of the *unbelievable.*

They rode on in silence.

They dodged deep ruts left behind by rainstorm runoff and crested a small ridge. A white pickup was parked a hundred yards ahead at the pullover for the Harper Canyon trailhead.

"Shit," Joe said, his voice leaden. "Robert's truck."

Chapter 38

When they pulled alongside Robert's truck at the trailhead, Felicity and Joe quickly exited his truck, but Robby and Susan stayed inside the cab of the Beast. They were talking. Susan's hand was to her mouth, and she shook her head as she stared at Robert's truck. Robby reached over and touched his mom's shoulder, but she flung his hand off. Joe could tell she was crying. *She doesn't want consoling. She's angry.*

After what seemed an interminable minute, Susan took a deep breath and stilled her crying. Joe went to the passenger window of Robby's truck.

"Stay here, Susan," he said.

"No. I'm coming."

"I need you to stay here. This is between Robert and me."

"That's macho bullshit, Joe. He's my husband. He'll listen to me."

"Maybe. Who knows. But if we miss him and he sneaks past us, you'll be here to stop him."

"Mom," Robby said. "Please stay. For me."

Susan looked at her son. "Don't you start playing the macho card too!"

"I won't. But I think he'll listen to me. And..." Robby didn't say more.

He wants to protect Megan, Joe thought.

Thunder in the distance announced itself as a low growl, but the sun still shined at the trailhead.

"Okay, I'll stay," Susan said. "But if you're not back soon enough, I'm following. I know the way."

Thunder rumbled again, and Joe looked west.

"We better get going."

Robby exited his truck quickly, carrying his backpack. Felicity pointed to the ground as they stepped beyond Robert's truck.

"Two sets of tracks." Her voice was calm, matter-of-fact.

Robby pointed to the smaller footprints. "Those are Megan's, aren't they?"

"Yes." Felicity had studied everyone's footprints at the dig. They were Megan's.

"Let's go," Robby said. He led the way.

"How much farther to the hidden canyon entrance?" Joe asked. They'd been walking quickly for twenty minutes.

"Not too far ahead, I think." Robby stopped to study the canyon wall to his right. "But I've only been there once. That was, like, three years ago."

The heavy clouds had drifted closer, and the canyon fell into shadows. Robby started to walk faster. The others followed close behind. The trail, primitive and seldom used, ran mostly along the loose red sand of the wash where water coursed after a hard rain. Today, the sand was bone dry and made it difficult to walk fast.

"There." Robby pointed to a huge boulder about fifty yards ahead off to the right. It was at least fifteen feet tall.

They broke from the main trail and scrambled toward it across the soft sand, stepping around rocks and sagebrush. A large cottonwood and two large junipers stood beside the boulder. If there was an opening of a small slot canyon behind the boulder, Joe thought, it was hidden well. As they got closer, the sand became soft and deep, a sign that water rushed around the rock in heavy rains and spilled into the larger canyon.

"Here!" Robby called. On the left side of the boulder beyond the juniper, they found a gap, a little over a foot wide, between the boulder and the canyon wall. One by one, they stepped over a large dead tree branch wedged into the entrance. They were now in the smaller slot canyon.

"I don't remember that tree branch," Robby said. "It must have washed down the canyon after I was last here."

The huge boulder, scoured by thousands of years of periods of rushing water, was smoother on the back side. A change in coloration and roughness about ten feet up indicated the historical high-water mark.

Felicity bent down to examine the sand. "More tracks."

"Yes. More tracks." Joe had seen them too.

No one needed confirmation of whose footprints they were.

"How far to the ancestral site?" Felicity asked.

"A quarter mile, maybe fifteen minutes…I think," Robby said.

"Let's go as quietly as possible."

The canyon was only ten feet across in places, the walls carved smooth by wind and water. In the narrow canyon the sky could only be seen by looking up. It had turned a dull, deep gray.

The wind picked up. Hard gusts blew at times, and the sand scoured the rocky walls, making a sizzling sound, like something electrified.

Joe wanted to look ahead but had to lower his head and shield his eyes from the blowing sand.

When they'd walked about ten minutes, Robby stopped and, silently, pointed to petroglyphs about ten feet up the rock face.

Joe nodded. One of the symbols carved into the wall was a spiral, the symbol some archaeologists and Natives believed meant the inhabitants had moved on, abandoning the site, perhaps never to return.

"We're getting close," Robby whispered.

They went another thirty yards. Robby pointed again. Up ahead an ancient structure of rocks and adobe mud nestled on a ledge ten feet up. Rough steps had been notched into the stone to make it accessible. It was an ancient granary for storing maize. But it was too small to hide a body.

They proceeded slowly. A flash of lightning was quickly followed by a loud crashing boom. The storm was getting near. Rain started to fall, large water drops that pockmarked the red dirt at their feet. A raven raced only feet above their heads, the wind at its back, as it hurried down the narrow canyon away from the storm. Twenty steps later, as the canyon veered to the left, they got their first look at the ancient settlement. It was on the right about thirty yards ahead.

Joe was impressed. The structure wasn't large, most likely the home of only one family, but it was in excellent shape. Its adobe mud walls still covered most of the underlying stone blocks. Protected by overhanging red sandstone, it had been effectively sheltered on a deep ledge several feet above the canyon floor. Like the granary, it, too, had escaped the ravages of flash floods for hundreds of years.

Joe was about to take another step when a slice of sandstone rock to the left of his head suddenly sheared off. A split second later, the loud report of a bullet echoed through the canyon.

Instinctively, all three of them ducked behind the rock face to their left and crouched down. They could no longer see the ancient habitation. They hoped that meant whoever had fired at them could no longer see them either.

"That was just a warning shot," a male voice called out.

"Is that you, Robert?" Joe called back.

"It's nobody you know," came the reply.

"Dad?" Robby called out.

There was no reply. Thunder rumbled. A few raindrops fell.

Joe turned to Robby. "Where does this canyon go? Is there another exit?"

"I don't think so. It widens a bit farther up. But I think it deadends into one of the bluffs a few miles up. I guess it could be climbed, but it would be a scramble." He paused. "I really don't know, Joe."

Joe looked over at Felicity. She drew the pistol she'd purchased from Robert. Joe knew she wouldn't hesitate to use it. She didn't have a relationship with Robert. He did.

"I'm coming to talk to you, Robert," Joe called out. There was no answer.

"Joe," Felicity said, almost a hiss. "Don't be a target. Just talk."

Je shook his head. "You don't understand." He took a deep breath, stood, and walked to the edge of the rock face. He could see the ancient site again, but he didn't see anyone—not Robert or Megan. Suddenly, the rock wall next to his head exploded, and shards of stone sliced into the side of his face and neck. A small piece hit his eyelid just as he closed it. He ducked back around the rock. He could feel blood beginning to drip down his cheek. His vision was blurry in his left eye.

"How many warnings do you need?" the voice called out.

Joe didn't answer as Felicity grabbed his face to examine his wounds.

"He could have put that bullet in your head if he wanted."

He wiped his face with his sleeves.

"I guess he didn't want to."

"He won't shoot me," Robby said. He stood quickly and stepped to the edge of the rock face. He searched for signs of his father and Megan, but the rain was falling harder and his vision was limited. Another shot rang out and another section of the sandstone exploded close to Robby's head. Instinctively, he ducked back down, total shock on his face.

"Isn't anyone listening?" the voice called out over the noise of the rain.

"That's...that's not my dad," Robby said.

Joe put his hand on Robby's arm, knowing Robby's understanding of his world had been shattered.

"I think you're right," Joe said gently. He didn't say more.

Felicity whispered. "He's probably seen all three of us. But he doesn't know we're armed." She aimed her pistol straight up to avoid ricochets and fired off a shot. For a moment there was no reaction.

"Someone might get hurt shooting like that," the voice called out.

The rain was falling harder, and rivulets dripped down the sides of the canyon walls.

"Are you talking about Megan?" Joe yelled.

There was no reply. The absence of a reply hovered like an evil spirit as the thunder rumbled again. They waited. A full minute. A very long minute.

The voice finally called out again. "It's time for me to leave."

"What do you mean?" Joe called back.

"Leave," the voice said. "Just leave, Joe." The tone was calm but loud enough to be heard over the rain.

"No," Joe said. "Come out. With Megan."

Another rifle shot echoed down the canyon. The three of them stayed crouched behind the stone wall. Robby began to weep quietly. He'd tried to hold back tears but failed. The rain was falling hard, and an inch of moving water filled the narrow slot canyon.

"Where are you?" Joe called out. Nothing.

"Give him a moment to think," Felicity said.

Another long minute passed.

Joe had to yell to be heard above the rain, the water now cascading in a hundred small streams down the canyon walls, and cymbals-smashing cracks of thunder. The water racing through the slot canyon was getting deeper.

"In thirty seconds, I'm coming out in the open. And I'm going to get Megan! Do you hear me?"

Nothing. He waited only seconds. He yelled out each number.

"29!...28!...27!...26!...25!...24!...23!...22!...21!...20!...19!...18!...17!...16!..."

"Dad! Dad!" Megan's voice rose above the noise. "He's gone! Come get me!"

Felicity put a hand on Joe's sleeve to stop him. Then she let go and nodded. Joe raced around the corner rock, Robby right behind him. Felicity held back a moment at the edge. When no rifle shot followed, she quickly caught up. The water on the floor of the canyon was up to midcalf.

"Here!" Megan shouted. She was sitting on the ledge in front of the ancient abode, mostly out of the rain. She tugged at tape that bound her feet.

Joe raced ahead against the swirling current. He spotted the hand-and-toe holds notched in the sandstone that ascended the rock face. The first two were almost worn away. They'd been carved a thousand years earlier and were worn down by innumerable flash floods but gave Joe just enough of a toehold to climb. Adrenaline did the rest. He turned to Megan when he reached the ledge.

"Don't move! I've got to get Felicity and Robby up here first. Where's Robert?"

"He went up the canyon. He said he would take off the gag if I agreed to stay quiet until you finished counting. He said everything would be okay. He grabbed his rifle and backpack and raced up the canyon." Megan shivered. "I didn't wait. You were counting too slow."

Joe smiled. "I'll count faster next time."

Felicity and Robby stood below in the rising water.

"Give Felicity a boost," Joe told Robby.

Robby got under Felicity and helped her climb the slippery, worn-shallow notches. After the first few, Joe reached down and pulled her up.

"Okay, Robby. Climb the first few notches, and I'll give you a hand the rest of the way."

Robby put one foot on the first notch but didn't move. An uprooted sagebrush and a small tree branch tumbled past in the rushing water that had turned an ugly, muddy red. He looked up the canyon.

"I'm going to get Dad."

Robby, your mother is waiting back at the trailhead. She needs you."

"I'll be okay."

"Robby! I need you!" Megan clawed at the tape that still bound her feet.

"I'll be back," he said.

"Listen to me, Robby." Joe tried to look him in the eyes, but the rain made him squint. "Don't do something stupid."

"I'm not the one who did something stupid."

"If you don't find him within a minute, get back here fast. You know what could happen."

Robby looked at Joe. "I'll come back. He'll be with me." He turned and strode into the rushing water that swirled around each step. He didn't look back.

"Robby!" Megan screamed. She writhed. "Cut these tapes off me!"

"Do you think I will let you follow him?"

Megan's eyes widened, her nostrils flared. She grabbed at the tape. Then stopped. Her shoulders fell, followed by falling tears. "No. I won't follow him."

"Hold still." Joe moved up closer, took out a pocketknife, and sliced the tape.

Megan flexed her legs when they were free, but she didn't move. Joe inched up on the rock next to her and wrapped his arm around her shoulders. She leaned into him.

They waited. Father and daughter holding each other. Felicity crouched a few yards off, peering—at least trying to peer—up the canyon.

The air was chilly, the wind sharp. Lightning flashed and cracked at the same instant. The storm was right on top of them.

The hair on their arms and back of the neck stood on end from the electric charge in the air. But lightning wasn't their big worry. Water was.

The muddy water rushing through the canyon was over a foot deep and rising fast. Debris tumbled downstream. Joe realized it would be hard to withstand the current —hell, hard to stand at all— if it got worse.

Suddenly, it got worse. A rumbling, like the low, deep roar of an animal—a bear's roar, a lion's roar, some angry beast's roar—reached their ears.

"What is that sound?" Felicity asked.

"It's bad news." Joe looked at her, his eyes set hard but filled with fear. "Up the canyon, I don't know how far, the water has built up." He held Megan tighter. "Like a wave."

"Oh lord," Felicity said. She glanced down at the striations on the narrow canyon walls that had been scoured by prior flash floods over eons.

"We'll be safe up here." Joe didn't say anything about Robby...or his dad.

Seconds passed. The water rose another foot quickly. A few moments later they watched as a crushing wave of water roared down the canyon pushing debris in its turbulence.

A backpack floated among the debris. Robert's, no doubt. But no body, Joe thought. At least, he didn't see one. He glanced over at Felicity, who shook her head, a signal she hadn't seen a body in the water either. Megan sobbed.

Another thirty seconds passed. The water turbulence lessened after the wave passed, but the water was waist high, running fast, and rising. A slip would be deadly.

"Hello!" a voice called out. "Are you there, Joe?" It was Robert's voice.

Joe called out loudly. "Yes. We're at the ledge."

"Robby's hurt."

Joe could feel Megan's body tighten in his arms. Seconds later, Robert came into view, his shoulder under Robby's arm, guiding him. His rifle hung across his other shoulder. Robby appeared to be conscious, but his head was drooping, and Joe could see blood streaming from his temple. The water rushed from behind, pushing them, and Robert had to move slowly to keep them both from tumbling in.

No one spoke as Robert reached the carved steps that led up to the safety of the ledge. The lowest one was already underwater. He shifted his body to get leverage.

"Robby. Son." Robby didn't answer. "Put your foot in that old step like you did the first time we were here. I'll push you up to Joe."

Robby slowly raised his leg without speaking, and his dad guided his foot into the first notch. Joe lay down on the ledge and reached down, extending his hand. Felicity and Megan each held one of Joe's legs. Robert got his body under Robby's and started to lift him up.

"Grab my wrist," Joe said loudly, and Robby did.

His grip is weak, Joe realized. Joe clenched his fingers around Robby's wrist, knowing Robby couldn't provide much help. "Look at me," Joe said, and Robby did. "Can you put a foot into the next step when we pull?" Robby nodded.

"Ready! Now!" Joe called out. Robert pushed as hard as he could, and Robby's body rose from the murky water. Robby put his other foot in the next notch, and Joe pulled again. Robby's body was now out of Robert's reach, and he could no longer help. Joe pulled again and Robby landed on the ledge. A moment later, he passed out.

Joe turned back to the churning water. To Robert. He swayed as the crush of water, chest high, buffeted his body. White knuckled, one of his hands gripped the notch in the rock visible above the water to keep himself in place. His rifle was still slung over one shoulder. He looked upstream, then downstream, but he didn't look at Joe.

Joe reached out as far as he could, but his reach was a long way from Robert's hand.

"Robert!" Joe yelled. "Take off your rifle, grab the butt, and hand up the barrel to me."

Robert looked up. His eyes softened. "Robby's going to be alright, won't he?"

"Yes, but he's out cold."

"I mean he's going to grow up to be alright?"

"Yes, of course he is."

"No matter what?"

Joe looked into his old friend's eyes. "Yes, no matter what. Now hand me up the rifle."

Robert nodded, said nothing. With his free hand, he slid the rifle off his shoulder, but he didn't hand it to Joe. With a flip of his arm, he tossed it into the rushing water.

He smiled at Joe. "What rifle?"

Joe's brow furrowed in anger, his only thought—*that fucking semper fi!* He started to slither farther down the rock to extend his reach. A large tree branch was tossing in the rapid water headed their way. He turned his head back toward the ledge.

"Felicity!" he yelled. "Hold me tighter!"

But when he turned back a moment later, Robert was gone. His friend was gone.

Chapter 39

With Megan's help, Felicity pulled Joe up on the ledge, and he collapsed backwards. He craned his head to look down the slot canyon, but he didn't see any sign of Robert.

What am I going to tell Robby when he awakens? The truth?

Joe wasn't sure he understood what that meant.

The rain slackened. The storm, fierce but short, raged on farther east like a locomotive that has passed. Robby stirred, and Megan moved back to check on him.

Felicity leaned over Joe.

"Don't talk," she said softly. "Don't think. Just breathe."

Joe closed his eyes, but he couldn't stop thinking about Robert.

"Why didn't he let me save him?" he whispered.

Felicity planted a soft kiss on his forehead. "Maybe it was his way of saving himself."

Joe took a deep breath. "How's Robby?"

"He looks like he's going to be fine. But he needs to recover a bit before we take him out."

Joe pursed his lips. "Susan will be worried. We need her to know Robby is okay...and what happened to Robert."

"We'll go as soon as we can. What are you going to tell her?"

"I don't know."

As the four of them trudged back down the trail, the water still flowed ankle-deep in the slot canyon. Trickles of water dripped down the rocky walls like a hundred miniature waterfalls, irresistibly beautiful. The sun reappeared, and the red walls, darkened by the rain, glistened as the sun peeked under the clouds. Soon, it would all dry out, the desert swallowing the water like a thirsty beast.

Robby was wobbly on his feet but able to walk, and he held Megan's hand. His head injury had stopped bleeding. His breath was slow. His teeth were clenched and he said nothing. Instead, he looked ahead for his father's body and tried to hold back a sense of confusion and despair.

"Where's dad?" he had asked as soon as he recovered enough to talk. Still on the ledge, he'd lifted his head and saw only Joe, Megan, and Felicity.

Joe responded truthfully. "The current took him. I couldn't help him."

The dreaded answer to Robby's question came as they approached the place where the hidden slot canyon emerged into the larger canyon. There, where the large boulder hid the slot canyon entrance, Susan sat against the dead tree branch they'd stepped over on the way in. In her arms, she held the body of her husband of twenty-five years. She was stroking his hair but not crying. Her clothes, like his, were drenched and the color of mud, and her hair dangled in wet rivulets around her face. Blood spread on her khaki pants.

"When the water subsided, I found Robert's body pinned against the branch like a rag," she said. "He wasn't breathing." She looked down at Robert's lifeless face. "He had a gash on his forehead, but I stopped the bleeding. I don't like blood."

Her voice was steady but flat. She needed to tell the story.

"When I saw the storm was approaching fast, I headed up the canyon. It was easy to find the entrance to the slot because water gushed around the boulder. It was scary but it was...it was also beautiful." She shook her head. "Do you know what I mean?"

Robby went over to her. He wrapped his arms around his mom as she cradled his dad's body.

"He saved Robby," Joe said. "But he lost his footing before he could get up on the ledge, and he..."

"He got swept away," Robby said. He kissed the top of her head.

"Yes," his mom said. "Swept away."

They headed toward Blanding, intent on taking Robert's body to his home, not immediately to the hospital or mortuary. Susan drove Joe's truck, with Robby next to her, his head now bandaged, and Robert's body nestled in the back seat. Joe, Felicity, and Megan took Robby's truck, the Beast, seated tightly three-across on the bench seat. They would return for Robert's truck later. As they got into cell phone range, Joe called Sheriff Cooper and told him they'd found Megan; he could call off the missing person alert.

"Where was she?" he asked.

"I'd rather not say right now," Joe said.

"You'd *rather* not?"

"That's right. She's with me in the car. I'm taking her to the Hightowers' home. She's pretty shaken up. Then we can talk. Okay?"

"Well, okay. But I want details."

Joe had been expecting as much. "And there's been an accident."

"An accident?" The Sheriff's voice rose a half octave.

"Yes. But I can't talk about it right now. I'll give you the details later."

"You will, will you? That's mighty damn nice of you, professor."

"I'm sorry, but I can't talk about it now," Joe said as casually as he could.

"How about I send someone to meet you at the Hightowers? Maybe you can find time to file a report while you're having tea and crumpets."

Joe didn't react. "Actually, Sheriff, I was hoping you might meet me at the Blanding police station in an hour. I think you'll want to hear the details directly."

Joe could hear Cooper take a deep breath. "Okay, professor. I'll head down that way as soon as I can. This better be good."

"It's not good, sheriff," Joe said, his thoughts on the Hightower family. "It's definitely not good."

Chapter 40

Dirty vehicles were common in San Juan County. Consequently, no one paid any notice to Joe's mud-splattered pickup followed by The Beast as they slowly entered Blanding on Highway 191. Certainly, no one imagined the twisted emotions of those inside. And no one could have guessed one of the vehicles carried the body of a man who would never again open his eyes on the town where he'd been born—a decorated Marine, newspaper publisher, respected community leader, husband, father, and criminal.

Both vehicles stopped in the driveway of the Hightower home, but for a long moment, no one exited. In the pickup, Susan, in the passenger seat, turned and looked into the back seat at her husband's body. Robby, in the passenger's seat, stared straight ahead. Then he reached over, squeezed his mom's arm, and exited. He walked over to the Beast where Joe, Felicity, and Megan still sat. He held the door as Megan got out.

"I'm sorry," he said.

"You don't have to be. It wasn't you," she said.

He grimaced. "I'm still sorry."

Megan didn't reply but took his hand, and the two headed into the house.

Joe leaned his head against the steering wheel. He took a deep breath.

"What now?"

"What do you want to do?" Felicity asked.

Joe pounded the steering wheel. "I want to undo it all. To never have come down here. To still have my friend alive."

"Okay," Felicity said quietly. "But what do you want to do *now*?"

"I don't know."

"What are you going to tell the sheriff?" she asked.

"The truth, I guess."

"What's that?"

Joe turned and looked at Felicity quizzically.

"That Robert kidnapped my daughter. That he shot at us. That he probably sabotaged our water supply. That he likely shot Ben." His voice was agitated. "Isn't that enough?"

"Maybe too much," Felicity said calmly.

The door of the pickup opened, Susan exited, opened the backseat door, and slipped inside to be next to her husband's body.

"Joe," Felicity said, "we don't *know* he sabotaged our water or shot Ben. There were no witnesses, and we don't have a weapon."

"A search could probably find his rifle in the canyon. And his boot prints will match, won't they?"

"Yes, almost certainly."

"And we know from the documents in his office that he had a motive."

"That's true," Felicity said.

"And he kidnapped my daughter."

"Yes."

"Then, what the hell are you getting at?" Joe didn't want to be toyed with.

"I want to know what you want, Joe." Her eyes were intense, focused. "Is it justice? Because Robert's dead. The death penalty is the most severe penalty the law ever enforces. Is it vengeance? He's dead, Joe."

"What about the truth?"

"You know the truth already, Joe. Susan and Robby are devastated by the truth. Megan has been scarred by the truth and will need your love and support. But she's strong. Of course, you can ruin Robert's reputation if you want."

"He ruined it himself," Joe snapped.

"Yes, but do you want Susan and Robby to be the new victims?"

Joe took a deep breath. He knew Felicity was right. Robby's and Susan's lives would get much worse. The newspaper wouldn't survive. Any life insurance policy would be nullified. Robby's chance to go to college could be snuffed out. It was going to be hard on them no matter what, but the truth would make everything much worse—their own reputations, their financial situation, their options.

"What about Ben?" Joe hadn't considered his old Navajo friend for the past several hours. He didn't know how the surgery had gone. He didn't even know if *he* was alive or dead. He had promised to avenge Ben's shooting.

"What would Ben want?" Felicity asked.

Joe thought back to the words Ben had whispered in the hospital before he was taken to the airport for the medical flight. Ben had told Joe to quit the dig, that the cost would be too high. Ben knew it was Robert who had shot him, Joe realized. But he didn't tell. He knew what Ben would say.

"He would tell me to take care of my friends first. He would want me to protect Robby and Susan."

Felicity put her hand behind Joe's head and rubbed his neck. "I agree."

"Won't Cooper want to know the truth?"

"Yes. But he won't arrest you or subpoena you for what you never tell him. He'll be glad Megan isn't an issue anymore. And he'll want to know about Robert's drowning. But he doesn't need to know about Robert taking Megan or any connection to Ben's shooting."

"What about Robert's boot prints? They'll match those near the dig."

"That's easily solved."

Joe looked over at Felicity. He was trying but failing to process the back-and-forth he was having with this Chicago police detective he cared so much about. *Is she the person I think she is?*

"Won't we be covering up a crime?" he asked.

"Call it whatever you want."

Joe wasn't sure he wanted to ask the question that was in his head, but he needed to know.

"Have you ever done something like this before?"

Felicity didn't hesitate to answer. "No. Never."

Joe looked into her eyes. He needed to believe her.

Susan exited the back seat of the pickup and leaned against the car door. She stared at her home, the one she and Robert had built twenty-five years earlier. She headed inside.

"Let's go talk to Susan and Robby," Joe said. "They have to agree."

"Megan too."

Chapter 41

"What do you think, Robby?" Susan looked directly at her son.

When Joe calmly explained to Susan, Robby, and Megan why he didn't plan to tell Sheriff Cooper about Robert's abduction of Megan or the evidence he had shot Ben, Susan was stunned. Robby and Megan hadn't spoken yet.

"I don't know," Robby said quietly. "What do you think, Megan? You're the one he abducted."

Susan looked over at Megan. She could tell Megan was badly shaken. She wanted to hold Megan's hand and stroke her head and apologize to her again and again. Her revelations about Robert's mining deal had helped persuade the others that Robert had abducted Megan, which led to her rescue, but that revelation had led to the death of her husband. Her own thoughts were a muddled mess. Megan's must be worse.

"I'm going to support what my dad thinks is best," Megan said finally. She looked at Robby and Susan. "I don't want to hurt you. And...he was my dad's friend."

"Megan, sweetheart," Joe said, his voice measured but warm. "Are you sure? Because this is a secret you must hold inside for a long time. Maybe forever."

Megan smiled weakly. "No problem, Dad. You have no idea how many of those I already have."

"Should I worry?" He smiled back softly.

Susan looked at Joe. "What about the others behind the secret excavation company? Justice needs to be served."

"Let's talk," Joe said. "I have a plan."

Susan nodded. "Robby, please take Megan out on the porch. We're going to talk some more."

***

Sheriff Cooper was waiting for Joe and Felicity in a meeting room the Blanding Police Department made available for his use. Six metal chairs with Naugahyde cushions surrounded a slate grey table that showed a smattering of cigarette burns from a bygone era when smoking was permitted. A long, narrow clerestory window, too high to see out of, let in natural light, and an old white board, marked only with the day's date, hung from the far wall.

Felicity figured the room, ugly and boring, had been used for more than meetings, like interrogations. No doubt Cooper would rather be in his own building in Monticello where the meeting could take place in his own imposing office. He sat upright as they entered. He wanted to get the meeting over with quickly.

"Sorry we're late," Joe said. "We had to drop off something."

"I'm glad to hear your daughter's okay," the sheriff said. "Where was she?"

"Up Harper Canyon, down a narrow side canyon," Joe said calmly.

"Really? That's a far piece." He stared directly at Joe. "How'd you find her?"

"Robert Hightower found her. He was out looking for her and got a tip from someone in the area who had given her a ride hitchhiking."

"Really? Not afraid of hitchhiking? Kinda unusual these days."

"That's Megan."

Felicity detected a sliver of pride in Joe's words.

The sheriff tapped his pen on the pad in front of him. "Hmm. Mind if I talk to Robert about it?"

"You can't," Joe said.

Cooper's eyebrows rose. "Oh, really? Why not?"

"He's dead."

Cooper's eyes widened as he looked at Joe, then at Felicity. He nodded his head repeatedly, quickly, as if deciding how to process it. "That's a shocker, professor."

"I know," Robert said. "That's why we wanted to tell you in person."

"Okay. I'm listening." Cooper's brow furrowed slightly. "What happened?"

Felicity remained silent, observing, as Joe explained that Robert had called them, that he'd talked to the people who'd given her a ride, that Megan wanted to go to Harper Canyon to see a slot canyon Robby had told her about.

"We headed out there in my truck, but by the time we got on Route 95, he was out of cell range. We never talked to him again. We found Robert's truck at the trailhead. By the time we got there, a storm was coming up fast."

"Yeah, it was a big one. It dropped buckets of rain in Monticello."

Joe continued. "Megan said Robert found her as the water was rising, that he helped her get up on a ledge but then got hit by a log coming down the slot and was carried away by the raging waters."

"Let me guess," Cooper said. "You found the body downstream."

"That's correct. We headed up the main canyon in the rain and found his body. I don't think the log killed him. I think he drowned."

Cooper frowned. "That'll be for the coroner to decide."

"Yes, I know," Joe said.

"Where's the body now?"

"At the morgue." Joe paused. "That's what we dropped off on the way here."

Sheriff Cooper took in the news calmly. His head nodded slightly, repeatedly. His eyes moved rapidly left to right and back again. His lips pursed slightly. Felicity knew he was in the process of making a decision, wondering—*How much more do I need to know? How much do I want to know?*

"Robert is...was...an important citizen of this county. His death will be a shock around here. A real news event." Cooper's voice was calm, measured. "How is Susan taking it?"

"She's devastated," Joe said. "She was waiting at the trailhead when we brought out the body."

"Shit," Cooper said. "That must've been hard."

"They were married twenty-five years."

Cooper nodded. "What's gonna happen to the newspaper?"

"Don't know. I think Susan wants to keep it going. She said there will be at least one more issue for sure."

"With the obit, right?"

"And one other important story." Joe paused and looked at the sheriff. "I don't think the death of your County Land Use Director was an accident."

"Tell me more," Cooper said.

Chapter 42

Commissioner Begay was seated at his desk when his assistant showed Joe into his office. He smiled the smile of a politician for whom a warmth-free smile is as easy and reflexive as a yawn.

"Professor, it's good to see you." He motioned for Joe to take a seat.

"Thank you for seeing me." Joe put a smile on his face even if he'd preferred not to. He slipped off the small backpack he was carrying but held it in his lap.

"I'm sorry to hear about Robert Hightower," Begay said. "We didn't always agree, but I respected him. His death is a loss to our community. He was a good man."

"Yes, he was."

"I'm guessing his wife...Susan, right?...will be selling the paper. We'd hate to lose it. I may even know a potential buyer."

"She plans to keep it going herself."

"Really?" Begay's eyebrows rose in genuine surprise.

"She's working on the next issue now. I'm helping, in fact. She has some stories she wants to tell."

"That's...that's good news."

Joe smiled perfunctorily. "Yes. But I don't think the news stories planned are exactly *good*."

"Oh?"

"As a matter of fact, I'm here because of one of the stories we're working on."

"What might that be?"

"This, for starters." Joe opened the backpack and took out two documents. "This is the prospectus and initial corporate papers for Advanced Rare Earth Mineral Extraction Limited Liability Corporation. It appears you're one of the owners."

Begay tensed. "That's true." His words were measured, each carefully chosen.

"What did you pay for your shares, commissioner?"

Begay glowered. "That's none of your business, professor." His voice was curt, low.

"Is it the public's business, then?"

A moment of cold silence followed.

Begay smiled. "I don't think it needs to be." His face tightened. "I assume you're aware Robert Hightower was an owner too."

"Yes, I know. Susan knows too."

"Is that information for public consumption?"

"It may be," Joe said calmly. "Susan is deciding."

"What did he pay for his shares?" Begay asked.

"I assume it was the same as you. Nothing. Or rather, both of you paid with influence. For your zero-cost shares, you're expected to throw your weight around, speed up permitting, and gin up the support of local business, maybe the support of the Native tribes too. Robert was expected to back the effort in the *Register*, the only news source in the county. In the end, his buy-in was much more costly. It cost him his integrity. Maybe his life. He believed in the Bears Ears Monument, but the newspaper was struggling, and he was worried he couldn't afford to pay for his son, Robbie, to go to college."

Begay was blunt. "Don't give me any holier-than-thou shit, professor. You can't prove any of that."

"I think you're underestimating the power of the press, commissioner. And the public's appetite for scandal. I suspect the citizens of San Juan County and the members of the five Native nations will find the corrupt, self-dealing of their commissioner, let's just say, unappealing. Maybe even the word 'graft' will come up. That won't help sell cars at your Monticello dealerships I suspect."

"Are you threatening me?" Begay's voice rose. The veins in his neck bulged. "I'll crush that paper! Susan Hightower will be looking for work at the Dollar Store."

Joe paused to let his own temper cool. "I'm not threatening anything, except maybe the truth."

Begay responded coldly. "The story will die on the vine, professor. It will be old news in a week."

"There are other names in the document, too," Joe said. "How will they feel when it goes public?"

"Screw them!" Begay shouted. "The whole fucking Bears Ears Monument is one giant screwup. It's a waste of good land supported by a bunch of tree huggers and hikers who don't even live in this area. The tribes have been conned into supporting it. You can drag my name in the mud along with Robert's and half a dozen other leading citizens, and it still won't matter. The proposed Bears Ears monument is too damn big. It's a bloated idea that needs to be stopped. It will suck up land resources that should be used to create real jobs, not lame ones like escorting hikers from New York who want to see 'authentic Native American' cultures. Dead cultures, professor. Like the one your precious dig was supposed to study. What a waste."

Joe nodded. "You mean a waste of land that might just be better for mining rare minerals."

"I wouldn't know that."

"I believe you do." The corners of his mouth turned up, but he fought the urge to grin. He reached into his backpack and pulled out another document, the Master Land Use Plan for San Juan County. He turned the cover toward Commissioner Begay, who reached for it. Joe didn't hand it over.

"Where'd you get that?" Begay's voice was flat, but a hint of apprehension slipped out.

"Sorry. I don't reveal sources."

"I see where it says 'draft.' on the cover," Begay said. "That must be what Connor Smith was working on when he had his tragic accident." He paused. "The county commission never got to see it."

Joe opened it to the first page. "Then why does it have your initials and a date on this routing note, although none for the other commissioners?"

Silence filled the moment, except for Begay's hard breathing. Joe could feel his own heart rate beating faster, and he turned to look out the window to calm himself. The sky was a pale blue, a touch of haze hinting at the heat that would come.

"You know, Joe." The commissioner's voice was calm, every syllable enunciated clearly. "Advanced Rare Earth Mineral Extraction is probably never going to get off the ground. When it comes to digging holes in the desert, sometimes that's all you get. Holes."

Joe nodded. "I know something about digging holes where you don't find what you're looking for. It's really hard when someone tries to stop you, isn't it?"

Begay chuckled. "Yeah, it can be real hard." He paused. "I suppose you'd like to restart your dig in Butler Wash. Find some arrowhead from 10,000 years ago that maybe twenty people in the world give a shit about." He looked out the window, then turned to Joe. "How about we make a deal? How about I talk to Sheriff Cooper and see if he won't let you start that dig back up?"

"And the mining company?"

"They're just a bunch of speculators, Joe. Hitting it rich digging a hole is a crap shoot a whole lot less certain than selling Fords. I think, maybe I should extricate myself from that partnership. Too speculative for my blood. Hell, they may never even get a permit to dig their first hole, if you get my meaning."

"And the land report?"

"That's a different matter, Joe." Begay tilted his chair forward briefly, then leaned back. "I don't think it reflects the best interests of the county. I think it shows the prejudices of one man, the deceased Director..."

"You mean, the one who was the expert." It was more of a statement than a question.

"He believed what he believed, Joe. I believe he was wrong. And lots of local folks would agree with me if that report came out as is. It needs *revising.*"

"Maybe we will find out how the public feels when the Register publishes it."

Begay leaned forward more, his elbows on his desk, his eyes staring. "You do that and our deal is off. I'll crush that paper."

"Commissioner, we never had a deal. I don't want one. I've already spoken to Sheriff Cooper."

"Really?" Begay was taken aback momentarily but regained his composure. "It'll be your word against mine. You're an outsider, Joe. Who's gonna believe you?"

The door to the office opened. "I will." Cooper entered, followed by Felicity.

Begay sat back in his chair. He tried to smile.

"Nice to see you, Bull. Who is my other guest with you?"

"This is Detective Daniels. Chicago PD. And part of Joe's dig team."

"Really?" Begay stood, extended his hand. "Nice to meet you."

Felicity didn't take his hand.

"Were you listening through the door, Bull? That seems a little beneath you."

"One better," Cooper said. "Joe?"

Joe opened the small compartment on his backpack and removed a small microphone. "You made some nice speeches, commissioner."

"A wiretap? That'll never be admissible."

"Oh, it is, Sam," Cooper said. "As long as one party agrees to it, which evidently Joe did, everything you said can be played in front of judge and jury." He turned to Felicity. "I'm sure the detective here from Chicago would completely agree."

Felicity just smiled.

Cooper played the winning card. "The investigation into Connor Smith's death is still open, you know."

No one spoke. Commissioner Begay, still standing, walked over to the window and looked out. The sky was still hazy, the day getting hotter. He took a deep breath, his shoulders rising and then falling. He turned back to his office guests.

"Maybe we can still make a deal."

Chapter 43

The large, dark blue pickup, covered in rust-colored dust and splattered in red mud, pulled into the Blanding police parking lot as Joe and Felicity exited the building. Joe recognized the truck and its two occupants immediately but was more than a little surprised they were together. The truck pulled into a nearby parking spot, and the two occupants emerged.

"Hi Doug...Hi Angie." Joe was pleased to see them but didn't smile.

Doug spoke up. "We just got back into town. We went by the Hightower home. Susan said you'd be here."

"What else did she tell you?"

"Nothing," Doug said. "But she didn't look good. What's up?"

"Robert Hightower is dead."

"Oh my god!" Angie exclaimed.

"What happened?" Doug asked.

Joe thought for a moment about what had really happened. Instead, he needed to embrace the lie. Again.

"He drowned during a flash flood in Harper Canyon earlier today. But first, he rescued Megan."

"I don't understand," Doug said. "Why were Megan and Robert in Harper Canyon?"

Joe explained that Megan had become stressed and disappeared, choosing not to use the words "ran away." They got a lead she was in the area from a stranger who'd seen her. Robert got there first and found her up a narrow slot canyon just as a thunderstorm delivered a ferocious flash flood. Robert had been hit by debris and knocked off his feet in the rushing water.

"Where have you been?" Joe asked. "I tried calling both of you a dozen times."

Doug didn't answer immediately. Angie spoke up.

"I heard about Ben getting shot and reached out to Doug because I knew his experience handling Ben's body would have been hard." She smiled sheepishly. "Back in the day, we leaned on each other a lot and helped each other through some tough stuff. I...I figured he needed me." She gave Doug's hand a squeeze.

"We decided to get away together," Doug said. "Someplace quiet. We camped up in the mountains, near Abajo Peak. No cell coverage."

"It was a special place we'd camped at long ago." Angie smiled as she talked.

"How's Ben?" Doug asked.

"The doctors delayed his surgery a day to stabilize his condition after the flight," Joe said. "He's in surgery in Salt Lake City as we speak. The bullet is near his spine. We expect a report later today." He paused. "Say a prayer."

Joe thought about his Navajo friend whose life was now in the hands of surgeons hundreds of miles away. He glanced over at Felicity who remained quiet. There was one other topic that troubled him, one more thing he needed to ask Angie, and he looked to Felicity for quiet guidance. She nodded.

Joe's brow furrowed slightly involuntarily. "Angie, there's something I need to ask you about. Is now a good time?"

Her eyebrows rose. "Sure," she said, mild hesitation in her voice.

"Do you know anything about Advanced Rare Earth Mineral Extraction LLC?"

"No. Why?"

"It's a new mining company. Your uncle Harris is an investor. They plan to mine for rare earth minerals in the area planned for Bears Ears Monument. Did he say anything about it to you?"

Angie blushed. "When we went to dinner the night we arrived, he said something about a new mining company he was investing in. I don't know why he wanted to tell me. I figured he was just bragging or something."

Joe nodded but didn't immediately reply. He looked Angie in the eyes. "What else did you discuss?"

Angie looked down, then looked at Doug. "He asked me some questions about the dig?"

"Like what?" Doug said. He released Angie's hand and turned slightly to look at her closely.

"I don't remember," she said. "Just things. Like how long we were going to be there. What did we expect to find. Was it a big deal."

"Why didn't you tell us about your conversation?" Felicity asked.

Angie took a deep breath. "Uncle Harris asked me not to."

Joe was angry but, truthfully, more sad than angry.

"Sheriff Cooper is opening an investigation. And he's reopening the investigation into the death of the land use director. There may be a connection."

"Oh my!" Angie said.

"Was there anything else your uncle asked about?" Felicity asked.

Angie looked down and shook her head. When she looked up, her eyes were teary. Her voice was soft. "He asked me what kind of security we had at the dig site."

She looked at Joe. She looked at Felicity. Finally, she looked at Doug.

"I should have said something. I'm sorry. I'm so sorry."

Doug shook his head and walked away.

Chapter 44

The weather in San Juan County didn't change much over the next ten days. Nights cooled the forbidding desert landscape, and the sun rose each morning brightly, even cheerily, before it roasted the ground and everything on it as the day progressed. On a few afternoons, massive clouds formed to the west, laden with rain; once, rain fell heavily enough to surge through desolate canyons, across dry roadbeds, and through the streets of Blanding.

But storms of a different kind did blow tempestuously, and Joe's life, and those close to him, changed dramatically with each passing day, rain or shine.

The *San Juan County Register* reported a lot of it. More accurately, it caused the storm.

Susan Hightower made the decision to continue publishing the *Register* after Robert's death. For her, it was a surprisingly easy decision. For starters, she needed the income. So did the other four members of the staff—the one other newspaper journalist, the designer, the pressman, and the ad sales manager. She was not ready to ruin their lives, she told Joe, no matter how much she felt hers had been swept away. Later she might sell the paper, but that would mean finding a buyer, and that would take time.

Joe helped her put together the special edition that featured three stories that, when published two days earlier, had rocked the three towns in the county—Monticello, Blanding, and Bluff. Joe had persuaded Susan to double the usual print run, and all the extra copies were snatched up within twenty-four hours.

The top story on the front page of the *Register* was the announcement that County Commissioner Samuel Begay had decided he was retiring from the council within the next sixty days. He cited personal reasons, including his need to focus on his family and his auto dealerships in Monticello. He thanked his constituents, "the wonderful voters of San Juan County, both Anglo and Native," for their support for the past seven years. He listed several accomplishments he was proud of and reflected on the "great efforts of his staff and county employees."

The part of the article that generated the most buzz, however, contained the commissioner's "new insights" about the Bears Ears Monument proposal. He revealed that the land use proposal developed by the recently-deceased Director of Land Use, which the county believed had never been finished had, in fact, been located. It contained, Begay said, "persuasive arguments for supporting the Bears Ears Monument as an engine of economic growth in the county." He went on to say that as a leader of the Navajos living in San Juan County, he would support the monument designation, and, he said, "help bridge the divide between those supporting and those opposing the monument."

The *Register* article did not include comments from the other county commissioners, but it speculated that numerous individuals, both Anglo and Native, would likely be jockeying to replace Begay.

The second story that created buzz, titled "Sheriff Cooper Concerned About Rising Crime," detailed Sheriff "Bull" Cooper's updates on significant crimes occurring in the county. He revealed that the shooting of Ben Hatathli remained under investigation, but that the department didn't have any suspects. "The circumstances around the shooting," he said, "will make it difficult to resolve."

Cooper also corroborated rumors that two individuals, Riley Smith and Francis Holland, had been arrested and arraigned for "theft of numerous antiquities on federal land." He noted that the federal courts would be prosecuting the two men under the Antiquities Act and the Archaeological Resource Protection Act, the latter making it a felony to traffic in Indigenous artifacts. When asked about the recovered items, he said his office would work with the archaeologists at Edge of the Cedars State Park in Blanding to properly dispose of the objects after the trial. Cooper also revealed that the untimely death of Connor Smith, the Director of Land Use, from a fall in Mule Canyon was still under investigation, although he speculated the evidence still supported an accidental fall and that evidence of another cause of death was, he said, "sketchy at best."

The Sheriff promised increased diligence by his officers, asked San Juan County citizens to "all help in our effort to stop crime of all kinds," and called for an increase in the sheriff department's budget to field additional officers. "We may see a lot of visitors once Bears Ears becomes a monument," the sheriff said. When asked if he would run for Sheriff the following year, Cooper didn't provide a direct answer, only that "he wanted to leave the County a safer place before he left." The Register speculated the answer meant "yes."

The third big story was titled "Publisher of *San County Register* Dies in Flash Flood." Written by Joe but without a byline, the story explained that Robert Hightower had died in a flash flood in a small, unnamed slot canyon off Harper Canyon. The article was brief. It explained that Robert had been in the slot canyon as part of a search for a missing minor, that a sudden storm created a flash flood in the narrow canyon, and that he had been caught by the rushing water and drowned. The story reported that "the missing minor had escaped the rushing water on a ledge after being assisted by Hightower and stayed until the water receded." To maintain the confidentiality of the minor, no names of other search party members were provided.

The story directed readers to the obituary for Robert Hightower found on the back page of the newspaper.

The story did *not* mention that the ledge held an ancient Puebloan site in pristine condition. Not relevant to the news story, Joe convinced himself.

Robby planned to delay starting college to help his mom with the paper and to earn some money for his education the following year. His mom had argued against the delay, but she lost the argument decisively.

"I'm eighteen, Mom," he made clear. "This is my call."

"He's so like his dad," she'd said, then hugged him.

Within days, he'd begun looking for a new job, a more permanent one than working on an archaeological dig. Susan confided in Joe that the life insurance settlement was enough that Robby could start college right away, but, she said, "I'm glad he'll be around, for me."

Joe made the call to stop the excavation. The site was still a crime scene. Sheriff Cooper indicated Joe could start digging again soon, but two wasted weeks cut the season too short. He let the team know. Ruth Ann said she would stay in southern Utah with her friends for a few weeks of rock climbing before going home but expressed an interest in returning the next year. Angie stayed in Monticello with her uncle and aunt for a few days, but then returned to the Chicago area without a goodbye. Given Angie's confession about her knowledge of her uncle's involvement with the proposed mining operation, Joe did *not* plan to invite her back the next year. The others on the team, Randall and Doug, would find new employment quickly, Joe knew. Both were hard workers, smart, thoughtful... each in their own way. Randall was puzzled by the news about his uncle Begay, but in Navajo style, showed little emotion. Doug was disappointed but hoped to join the dig the following summer.

"You sure make digging these holes in the ground interesting," he said. He was more upset that his hoped-for relationship with Ruth Ann hadn't flowered into something nice; she'd ended it like deadheading a wilted rose when she learned about Doug and Angie's "reunion." Doug remained optimistic. "Maybe next year," he told Joe with a wink.

Joe wouldn't need to tell Ben about his plans for the excavation.

Chapter 45

The small Beechcraft twin turboprop banked smoothly to make the landing into Blanding's small airport, and one of the passengers onboard struggled to lift his head enough to peer out the small window at the red rock landscape he knew so well. One word came to his mind.

Home.

There were only three passengers in the air ambulance: an AirMed tech, a nurse, and one patient—Ben Hatathli. He lay on a wheeled stretcher locked into place to stabilize it, hooked up to a monitor that tracked his heart rate and blood pressure. He'd been given pain medications and a mild sedative. But instead of sleeping, he smiled. He was almost home. His immediate thought was a practical one.

I hope the landing is gentle.

The past ten days had not been gentle, not even remotely, but he had pulled through well. Remarkably well, the doctors' said, given his age. Which made him smile. He knew more than surgeons had helped him. Now, he was returning home for the remainder of his recuperation. He'd already been allowed to sit up in a wheelchair for short stretches... choosing *not* to tell the nurses how painful it was.

He looked forward to the welcoming group he knew would be at the airport—family members, Diné clan members, and Joe and Megan. He needed to tell Joe certain things. And he had a question. Now that he would live.

***

Megan didn't know what to expect as the plane taxied to the tiny airport terminal where she stood with her dad and Felicity. The last time she'd talked to Ben, he was preparing to remain at the dig site along with Doug while the others returned to Bluff for the weekend. She never imagined something terrible would happen to him on sentry duty. Just the opposite. She always felt secure in his presence, in fact, *because* of his presence. He was her rock, her anchor, her friend. Then he'd been shot. And almost died. Afterwards everything went from awful to worse.

Megan, her dad, and Felicity held back as Ben, on his stretcher, was carefully lifted from the air ambulance, transferred gently to a wheelchair, and pushed slowly toward the terminal by the nurse. A handful of his clan members surrounded him, their warmth and concern and joy bubbling forth in a torrent of Diné.

That's so cool, Megan thought.

But after a short while, her patience worn thin, she started tapping her foot. She looked at her father.

"Can we go over there now?"

"Let's wait for an invitation from Ben. He knows we're here. I don't know if he even wants to speak to us, given what happened to him on my excavation."

Their wait lasted only a few moments longer. Ben asked his nurse to wheel him over to where they stood. He smiled at Megan.

"Isn't the *chi'iké'í* going to give me a hug?"

Megan beamed. She jumped forward, bent down, and wrapped her arms around him. She felt him wince from her hug and eased up.

"I was so scared you might..." She didn't finish her sentence.

"Die?"

"Yes."

"I might have *chi'iké'í*, but it wasn't my time yet. It will come soon enough. I am more ready now."

Megan, still squatting, held onto the arm of the wheelchair as her smile waned.

"I've had enough of people dying," she said.

"I am sorry for your pain, young Megan." He looked over at Joe. "It is never easy to lose someone you care about."

Megan stood up, looked at her dad, then back to Ben.

"Will you forgive my dad?"

Ben smiled. "He's my friend. He has done nothing to forgive."

***

Joe was stunned when Megan asked the question that had troubled him for days—would Ben forgive him?

The night before Ben's return, he had lain in bed pondering what he was going to say to his Diné friend. His sense of guilt was overwhelming. Ben had been shot because he was too stubborn to shut down the dig. And the only suspect for the shooting was Joe's friend Robert. Now, he was dead.

Joe had rejoiced the day after Ben's surgery when the prognosis Ben would live reached him, but the doctors wouldn't speculate whether he would walk again. The bullet had punctured his lung and lodged close to his spine. By the sixth day after surgery, Ben moved his toes a little, a positive sign, the doctors said, that exceeded their expectations. But walking was another matter. When Megan lovingly hugged Ben, the sudden pained expression on Ben's face confirmed that his friend was a long way from recovery.

"It might help," Joe said, as he tried to smile, "if you would actually say you forgive me. I feel responsible for what happened to you. I *am* responsible. I..." He shook his head.

"I forgive you, then," Ben spoke calmly. "I do so because you ask me to do so, as a friend."

"Thank you," Joe said quietly.

Ben reached into a leather beaded bag that sat by his side on the wheelchair. From it he lifted a small pouch and held it up for the others to see.

"Do you know where this came from?"

"No," Joe said.

No," Megan said.

"Yes," Felicity said. The corners of her mouth lifted in a soft smile. "It was from Johona. She told me to put it under your back near your heart. I did it before the air ambulance team flew you to Salt Lake."

Joe looked over at Felicity, his eyebrows raised high.

"I will have to thank her," Ben said. "Apparently, it stayed with me until I went into surgery." He handed it to Megan, who grasped it tightly. "May it bring you good fortune too."

The attending nurse, who'd been standing off away, came over. "It's time to get you to the hospital for some rest."

It was apparent to them all, Ben included, she was right. He motioned for Joe to come closer.

Ben took Joe's hand between his two hands and held them firmly. "One question, kemosabe. What do you think we will eventually find at the dig?"

Chapter 46

"Okay, that should do it," Joe said.

He leaned on his shovel, removed his hat, and wiped his brow. Megan, Robby, and Felicity immediately stopped shoveling. They all reached for their water bottles. Robby took a long drink of water from his, then poured some of it over the back of his neck. The sun shone intensely and the heat was oppressive. Joe didn't care what a thermometer would reveal about the temperature. "Damn hot!" was his reading.

He looked down where the hole had been. Only a few weeks earlier, his team had carefully excavated three feet down, sometimes by hand, and meticulously removed and identified every morsel of artifact they uncovered—tiny shards, bones, seeds, anything that looked interesting. Now their precious excavation was covered with dirt, intentionally reblended with the surrounding soil. They'd already filled the other two excavations. They'd started in the cool of the morning, and by noon, all three excavations showed only hints of his team's earlier meticulous digging.

Just dirt again.

But Joe didn't believe it. Dirt was never just dirt, he knew. The earth is always changing. It lives. Even in the harsh environs at the foot of Comb Ridge, the earth held the roots of massive Cottonwood trees, stubborn sagebrush, and wisps of grass. Coyotes and deer and snakes and field mice made their homes in there. Rain and floods transformed it. The earth hid stories of people who had lived there and moved on.

Now it was his time to move on.

"You three go back to the truck and get things ready for our last lunch here," Joe said.

He threw his shovel over his shoulder and walked over toward the large boulders where Ben had been shot. The sheriff's office no longer quarantined it as a crime scene, and he planned to cover over any signs of his friend's blood that remained on the surface. But nature had already done it. A thunderstorm two nights earlier had already erased all the blood stains. *Cleansed. Like nothing happened here.*

He was looking up at the steep side of the Comb thinking about all that had changed over the past few weeks when he felt someone's presence. He turned. It was Felicity, only a few feet away. He smiled.

"You're really good at the quiet stuff, you know."

"You looked deep in thought. I didn't want to disturb you."

"You give me too much credit. I wouldn't call it deep." He reached out for Felicity's hand. It was dry and warm.

"Want to tell me?" she said.

Joe looked into her eyes but didn't speak. He looked back up at the massive stone monocline.

"I was thinking about time and how things change," Joe said. "Remember when I told you how Comb Ridge was formed and then lifted up millions of years ago? And how giant mastodons roamed here once. Yet the land swallowed them as time marched on. I rambled on to the team about how we were going to make a momentous discovery about ancient Clovis people who walked this area over ten thousand years ago. Well, they were also lost to time."

"Yeah?" Felicity said.

Joe could tell she wasn't making any connection. He tried to be clearer.

"That's all so damn abstract and hardly matters to me now. At least compared to the hell we've been through the past two weeks." He took a deep breath, exhaling slowly. "I lost a good friend and..." He paused. "I could have lost Megan."

"She doesn't blame you." Felicity's voice was confident, matter of fact.

"I wouldn't blame her if she did."

"Don't be so damn hard on yourself, Joe." Felicity shook her head but didn't let go of his hand. "Don't you get it?"

Joe formed a soft smile, shook his head, but remained silent.

"Megan loves you," Felicity said. "She thinks you saved her. Which is true. And, I think, she has some idea how betrayed and sad you feel about Robert."

"You think so?"

"Of course." Felicity rolled her eyes slightly but continued smiling. "Ask her. She wants to talk to you more than you realize. Probably more than she realizes since she's as stubborn as you are."

Joe nodded as he smiled. "Okay, I will." But he had another question, the answer to which would truly help him move on. Help him heal.

"What about you?" he asked.

"What about me?"

"I guess I should say, what about us?"

Felicity closed the gap between them, took both his hands in hers, and lifted her face to his.

"Should I worry you haven't figured it out by now?" Felicity looked into his eyes. "I love you. I want to be part of your life."

"I'd like that," he said softly. Just hearing her say it loosened a tightness in his chest he hadn't even noticed. He kissed her, not worried in the least if anyone saw them. It was their first and only kiss at the excavation site.

They had come to the excavation site in two trucks, and after a quick lunch Joe sent the three of them back to Bluff in the Beast. Soon after they left, he began the long hike up Comb Ridge, stopping to rest, sip water, and take in the views to the north and south. In both directions, the massive monocline extended beyond his vision. At the top, he sat down, the red Navajo sandstone almost too hot for sitting. Sweat covered his shirt. Underneath his hat, his hair was a matted mess. It was, he knew, not the smartest time of day to climb the Comb. But he needed to do it.

He looked down on the patch of earth where they had excavated. It seemed small. From the top of the ridge, he struggled to identify the exact spots where they'd just filled in the team's excavations.

It really is just dirt again.

He knew, however, that seldom was anything only what it appeared to be. Or stayed the same. Change can happen slowly over eons that transform the landscape itself. And change can happen in the blink of an eye that transforms lives. Like Susan's and Robbie's. Like his.

He looked to the west. Red rock formations stood majestically in an area someone long ago had named Valley of the Gods. He had no clue which gods they referred to, but it didn't matter. The name was merely a human construct, a testament to someone's glorious sense of self.

His own sense of self was a bit shaky and needed attention. He had lost more than he could have imagined because of his desire to make a historic discovery. *And for what? Would he and Ben and the team really come back next year? Why?*

Megan would need lots of attention as well, and he resolved to be there for her. To help her get beyond all that happened to her…on her schedule. Nothing else held comparable value. Except maybe Felicity.

A cloud slid over the sun creating instant shade, and a cooling breeze penetrated his sweaty shirt and lifted his spirits. He thought of Helen. His wife had always been the life-sustaining force in their family. Gentle, resourceful, patient. He had missed her terribly, and he would cherish her memory forever. But it was also time to let go. To move on. Felicity was in his life now. Helen would understand.

He lifted his hat to feel the breeze in his hair. With his other hand, he blew Helen a kiss for the wind to carry to her.

EPILOGUE

As events go in Blanding, the funeral of Robert Hightower was a big deal. The minister estimated attendance of at least two hundred—family members, friends, and citizens of San Juan County—some because they mourned Robert's passing, others because it was an event where they wanted to be seen. At the request of Robert's wife, Susan, the service was held in the auditorium of the Albert R Lyman Middle School in Blanding rather than a local church or Mormon meeting house.

The attendees cut across a wide swath of the population. Filling the auditorium were hunting buddies and former classmates, business owners who'd advertised in the paper, past and current politicians, including all three county commissioners, lay LDS Bishops and Stake Presidents, Sheriff Martin "Bull" Cooper, the Blanding mayor, elders of the Navajo and Ute tribes, and even Elijah Smith, owner of the Bluff Inn. Joe and Megan Cutler and Felicity Daniels sat one row behind the family.

Two thoughtful eulogies recognized Robert's life, his many friendships, and his contributions. Tears welled in many eyes. Susan Hightower and the couple's son, Robby, remained silent, their faces drained of emotion. "They looked stricken," one family friend later observed. Susan didn't speak other than to thank all who had attended. "Robert," she said, "would be humbled to know he had so much impact on so many lives."

The obituary that appeared in the *Register* earlier that week had been succinct.

Robert J. Hightower

1967 – 2015

Robert Hightower, owner and publisher of the *San Juan Register*, passed away suddenly on June 25th. He drowned in a flash flood in a slot canyon off Route 95. He was helping another person to safety when he was swept away by rushing water.

Robert was born in Blanding on November 1, 1967, the son of Howard and Rebecca Hightower. He was educated at the University of Utah and, he liked to say, did his "finishing school" with the U.S. Marines. Following a four-year enlistment that included service in Iraq during the Gulf War, he spent six years as a journalist in Phoenix, Arizona. He was recognized twice for his investigative reporting by the Arizona Newspaper Association.

Following the death of his father, Robert returned to Blanding to assume leadership of the *Register*. It was, he would say with a smile, "a labor of love but, like childbirth, not without a lot of pain."

The canyons and mountains were Robert's escape from the challenges and pains of publishing a newspaper, and he was an accomplished outdoorsman. He knew and loved the surrounding countryside as well as anyone, and he enjoyed wilderness camping, fishing, and hunting with his family. He was a member of the local Rotary Club, a Boy Scouts leader for several years, and active with the conservation group Friends of Cedar Mesa. He was respected by business and civic leaders throughout the county and by leaders of the Navajo and Ute tribes.

Robert is survived by Susan, his wife of twenty-five years, and his son Robby, a recent graduate of San Juan High School. He was preceded in death by his parents Howard and Rebecca.

Robert was someone who believed in the potential for goodness and acted on it to save someone else.

Almost immediately, rumors circulated as to what really happened to Robert. Some said he didn't drown but was killed because of something he wrote in the paper. Others said he was engaged in a shady business deal that went sour. Suicide was rumored. Many speculated that the newspaper was going to fail. Some said it was already headed that way and would close "any day now." Only a few local women believed Susan Hightower was capable of keeping the paper's doors open.

The rumors, like all rumors, faded within weeks and all but disappeared within months as other stories, large and small, supplanted the guesswork about Robert. When a year had passed, and the *Register* was still covering the local scene each week, those who had doubted Susan had readily forgotten their earlier opinions.

Acknowledgments

The background research for this novel was extensive. I want to thank the many authors of insightful and compelling books and articles that deepened my understanding of the history and geography of southeastern Utah, Bears Ears Monument, and the Navajo (Diné) people. A special thanks goes out to four archaeologists who offered their insights or reviewed the manuscript: Vaughn Hadenfeldt, Jonathan Till, Shannon Boomgarden, and R.E. Burrillo, author of Behind the Bears Ears. I want to thank my fellow writers who critiqued parts of the book as it was developed and my wife, Lucy, who was both a great support and a thoughtful, helpful reader.

www.ingramcontent.com/pod-product-compliance
Lightning Source LLC
LaVergne TN
LVHW041759060526
838201LV00046B/1052